THE
LAST
PIRATE

Printed in the United States of America

Editing by Ariel Ryan
Copy Editing by Anthony Bolkema
First person to read the book: Heidi Wenzel.
Book design by Myriad Creative (they're awesome)

First Printing, 2017

ISBN 978-0-692-97141-3

Jonathan M. Wenzel
www.IAmJonWenzel.com
Hi@IAmJonWenzel.com

The Last Pirate
A Tale from Neverland

Jonathan M. Wenzel

For Terry & Connie.
For believing in Neverland and in me.

Neverland,
You will be remade, reforged.

You will be called 'Nightmare', for on your
shores I will bring destruction and pain.

And every sense of peace, every memory
of goodness will be snatched away and
cast into the fire of my retribution.

For I am coming.
Like a storm, I gather.

PROLOGUE

Wwhat have you gotten yourself into, Teach?" James muttered to himself. He watched the battle unfold from the
safety of his own ship, anchored well away from the
cove. Prudence suggested scrutinizing a situation before entering
into it. And a simple survey from the fringes of the island told James
everything he needed to know.

Things were not going well.

His decision to delay his own involvement in the battle had been
sound if the massacre the island's inhabitants were unleashing on the
fleet in the harbor was any indication.

Edward Teach, known to most as Blackbeard the Pirate, had en-
listed the aid of eight of the most renown pirate captains ever to sail.

He had made promises of treasure beyond any of their wildest imaginings. All they needed to do was wrest control of the island from the natives—a task proving more difficult as the battle wore on.

"What's happening out there, Capt'n?" a voice asked behind him.

"Nothing we're about to get caught up in, Mr. Smee," James said, lowering his spyglass to watch the battle with his eyes alone.

Though far from finished, the battle's outcome was obvious, and he had no intention of adding his own ship, the Jolly Roger, to the growing list of casualties.

"Are we going in, then?" Smee asked. "Shall I ready the men?"

Perhaps not obvious to everyone.

"No," James said, raising the spyglass once more to examine the sky above the ships. "Let's hold this position."

High above the ships, the stars—at least, what appeared to be stars at first glance—broke free from their constellations. They swirled around before, moving as one, they fell, streaking towards the ships, leaving tattered sails and rigging in their wake.

"We leaving then?" Smee asked, fidgeting as he spoke.

"Patience, Smee," James replied. "We will not rush in like fools just to share in our brothers' fate."

James pursed his lips, considering his next action.

"I'm not ready to leave quite yet, however," James said after a moment. "If what Teach says about this place is true, and I gather it is," he said, indicating the cove with a sweep of his hand, "then I want to take a closer look."

James slipped his spyglass into one of his coat's deep pockets. Placing both hands on the rail, he continued to watch the battle in the distance.

He watched as the shooting stars, pixies as he now assumed them to be, surged back into the sky. Large clusters of the little creatures hauled pirates into the air, only to drop them, sending them crashing onto the decks or splashing into the churning water.

Upon reaching the apex of their flight, they descended again, leaving only the true stars in the sky to preside over the battle.

"I am sorry, my old friend," James said. "The winds did not favor us this time."

A bright flash drew his eye to one of the ships along the edge. A second later, a thunderous boom ripped through the ship, sending several men instinctively ducking under the rails for cover.

"Or perhaps they did," James amended, stealing a glance at his own ship, swaying from the explosion's shockwave sound. "For another ship would not have turned this tide in your favor."

"Do you have any orders, Sir?" Smee asked.

"Hold here for the night. Enforce blackout procedures. I don't want to hear a sound," James said. "I want to see what the morning brings, and I certainly do not want to get pulled into that." He pointed to the battle that had left several ships in flames, while others drifted aimlessly.

"Aye, Sir," Smee said, turning to leave. "I'll spread the word."

"Smee?" James said, still watching the battle.

"Yes?"

"Not one sound," James added.

"Understood, Capt'n." Smee replied, nodding.

No sooner had Smee finished speaking than something heavy crashed onto the deck, followed immediately by an intense wailing.

"I said quiet," James hissed, drawing his sword as he spun.

He squinted into the darkness, searching for the offender, but stopped short. The culprit, a tall, lanky man whom James had never seen before, lay on the deck in front of him. The man was crying and striking the deck with clenched fists.

"Who the devil are you?" James demanded, approaching the man. "And how did you get on my ship?"

"Gone," the man wailed. "Gone, gone, gone."

"Shut up!" James hissed, kicking the stranger.

The man went sprawling, his cries diminishing into incoherent mumbling and sniffing.

"Where did you come from?" James asked again, his voice brittle with strained control. "Answer me or I'll kill you. I cannot afford to have you reveal our position."

The man wiped his eyes and looked up, as if noticing James for the first time.

"How did you get on my ship?" James asked a third time, his voice cold.

"I touched the moon like Peter Pan," was all the man said, then began to weep again.

"Mr. Smee?" James said slow, still staring at the man who had impossibly fallen from the sky.

"Yes, Capt'n?" Smee answered, scurrying to James' side.

James said nothing. Instead, he stared at the crying stranger who had appeared on his ship out of nowhere.

"I'll get to the bottom of this, Capt'n," Smee said, anticipating the order James was about to give.

"Good form," James said, returning his sword to its sheath. "By morning I want to know everything about this…this, fool. And I want to know where he came from."

"Lost, lost…" the man babbled. "He's lost."

"Aye, Sir," Smee said, turning towards the man.

"And find out how he got on my ship," James added.

The man, sitting up now, hugged his knees and rocked back and forth, shaking his head all the while as if vehemently answering 'no' to a series of unspoken questions.

"What's your name?" Smee asked.

Immediately, the man stopped rocking and looked up at Smee.

"My name?" the man asked, confusion creasing his face.

"Do you know your name?" Smee asked again.

"Of course," the man scoffed, looking around at everyone as if they were the crazy ones.

"Well?" Smee asked, exchanging looks with James.

"Well, what?" the man replied.

"What's your name?" Smee repeated.

The man burst into a fit of giggles, covering his mouth to stifle his laughter. He banged his feet against the deck as he laughed. After several long moments, he composed himself enough to uncover his mouth and whisper.

"Mad Rogue."

ONE

The morning sun sparkled across the clear water as gentle waves twisted the sunlight into dizzy patterns. The patterns erupted into chaos as frantic oars splashed through them, propelling the longboat towards the shore.

Armed with an array of swords, guns, whaling pikes, and a sketchy report from a man who seemed anything but sane, the landing party paddled furiously.

Normally the boat would have made straight for the beach, taking five minutes to reach the shore. But the day was turning out to be anything but normal. Furthermore, Neverland, the name provided by Mad Rogue, was already starting to live up to her name; reaching her shores was beginning to seem impossible.

Within minutes of the longboat leaving the ship, a dark, scaly arm had erupted from beneath the surface of the water. The arm had seized an oarsmen, yanking him out of the boat and into the depths before the man had taken a breath to scream.

Now, twenty minutes later, and a mere fifty yards from the Jolly Roger, the shoreline seemed no closer than when they had first embarked.

The party had been plagued by whatever unnatural creatures haunted these waters that entire time. And James had lost four men before stumbling upon a strategy that worked.

"Heave, men, head for the shallows!" James roared, pointing with his sword towards the light patch of water ahead that indicated a sand bar. In his hand, he gripped a pistol trained on the water.

Despite the heat, he wore black boots that went up to his knees and a crimson, full-length coat, lined with white trim. Large black buttons dotted the length of one side. The coat, stained and faded, swirled around him as he spun, scanning the waters for shadows of the mysterious creatures beneath the surface.

His eyes flicked towards a movement in the water. He fired at it.

"Starboard!" he yelled, thrusting the discharged weapon into his belt before drawing a second. "Pikes, starboard!"

Immediately, those armed with pikes and large fishing hooks began stabbing and slashing at the water.

The tactic worked.

For once, the creatures in the water did not surface, did not attack. And a minute later, the longboat reached the sand bar.

The water was barely deep enough for the boat to pass over the sand. The distinct sound of sand scraping the bottom of the craft was reassuring, proof they were safe from the sea creatures for the moment.

"We'll rest here for a few minutes," James said, panting. "Gunners, take watch. Pike men, catch your breath."

While his men rested, James surveyed the water. Thankfully, there were sandbanks dotting the entire distance to the shore. Their course would wind through the cove, but that would be far better than battling the creatures in open water. There were, unfortunately, large patches of open water, but with a little luck, they might just make it.

They spent the better part of the next hour making their way from sandbar to sandbar, furiously stabbing all around the boat whenever they crossed into deep water.

Eventually, and without any additional deaths, they made it to shore.

The boat nosed into the sand and James' efforts offered him the first real glimpse of the island.

"Stay with the boat," James ordered, leaping out onto the hot sand.

He looked around, scanning the shoreline.

Apart from the creatures in the water, nothing seemed out of place. It looked much like a hundred other islands he had visited.

"Neverland," James said to himself, repeating the name the crazed pirate, Mad Rogue, had provided them. "Hardly."

He turned around, examining the cove they had crossed. There were no signs of the creatures they had fought to get there.

"A few lives lost," he said, a smug smile flashing across his face. "But hardly impossible."

He turned back to the forest and walked towards the tree line, looking for anything out of place.

Then he saw it.

Not twenty yards away sat a young boy. He lay against a tree, his arms crossed behind his head. The boy's legs stretched out in front of him, one over the other. A reed of grass hung from his mouth and twitched in time with his breathing.

He appeared to be sleeping.

James adjusted his path so it would take him straight to the boy.

"The battle's over, pirate," the boy said, clearly not sleeping.

James chuckled as he approached the boy. "The battle is never over, my young friend."

"You're a determined one," the boy said and chuckled, mirroring James' own laugh. "I'll give you that."

James couldn't tell if the boy's laugh was one of amusement or mockery.

"I couldn't help myself," James replied, deciding it didn't matter. "After hearing so much about this place, I just had to see Neverland with my own eyes."

The boy looked confused for a moment, then smiled broadly and spread his arms in a welcoming gesture.

"Well then," he said. "Welcome to Neverland!"

"And you must be Peter Pan," James said.

"At your service," Peter replied, dipping his head. "And what's your name, pirate?"

"'Captain will suffice," James said, smiling down at him.

"Ooo, mysterious." Again, the boy's tone was difficult to read.

"Tell me, Peter Pan," James said, trying to figure the boy out, "what's a young lad like yourself doing all alone on an island in the middle of nowhere?"

"Oh, I'm far from alone," Peter replied, smiling without showing teeth. "And to answer your question, I keep Neverland safe."

"And a fine job you do if last night is any evidence," James said, clapping his hands.

Peter smiled, but it didn't reach his eyes.

"You and your friends have accomplished more than you realize," James explained. "Teach had summoned every pirate captain worth his salt to Neverland. But after last night, they're either dead or turned coward. In one strike, you've reduced the number of pirate captains worth following from eight, to me."

"So, what brings the last pirate to Neverland then?" Peter asked.

"Like I said before," James said. "I've heard such wild tales of this place, I couldn't resist investigating on my own."

Peter looked around.

"Well," Peter said, still smiling, "this is it. And those 'wild tales' you've heard? They're all true, especially the ones about me."

"And what would you say if I told you I wanted to see a little more of it?" James pressed.

"Mmmm." Peter wrinkled his nose and shook his head. "That's probably not a good idea."

"Why not?" James asked.

"Your ship burns at dusk," Peter replied, his cheerful demeanor at odds with his cryptic words.

"I beg your pardon?" James said, taken aback at the sudden turn the conversation had taken.

"Your ship," Peter repeated, leaning to look past James' shoulder at the Jolly Roger anchored in the bay. "I'll give you until nightfall to make sail before we burn it."

James stared at him, still not sure what to think of the child.

"Last night was a fleet," Peter explained. "Imagine what we could do with only a single ship to deal with."

James narrowed his eyes.

"Turn back, Captain," Peter said still smiling that humor-less smile.

"Well, then," James said, spreading his arms in a mock show of hopelessness, "it appears I'm left with no other choice."

"None that I can see," Peter replied, leaning back against the tree and closing his eyes again. "Oh, and you don't have to ride the sand bars on your way back. Neat trick though, but we'll let you get back to your ship."

Peter opened his eyes and leaned to one side to get a clear view of the bay.

"Let them pass!" he shouted towards the water before leaning back against the tree and closing his eyes.

"What?" called one of the pirates waiting with the boat.

James turned and scowled at the man before turning back to face Peter.

"I will take my leave. Thank you for your hospitality," James said, extending his hand to allow Peter to shake it.

Peter opened one eye and looked at James' hand then closed it again, making no move to shake it.

"'Tis bad form not to take a man's hand when offered," James admonished, clacking his tongue at the boy.

"Another time, perhaps," Peter said, his eyes still closed.

James chuckled and fixed the end of his sleeve before lowering it. "Well met, Peter Pan," he said turning to leave. "Well met, indeed."

"Enjoy your journey, Captain," Peter called, as James walked away.

"Of that, I have no doubt, my young friend." James replayed the encounter with the boy over in his mind as he walked through the heavy sand back to the longboat.

While the boy's presence on the island was indeed peculiar, the boy himself did not seem to be anything special.

"Are we leaving?" Smee asked as James climbed back into the boat.

"Quiet, these waters have ears."

James didn't say another word while his men rowed back to the ship. Despite the boy's promise of safe passage, he kept both sword and pistol trained on the water. Once they were back aboard and he and Smee were in the safety of his cabin, he finally spoke again.

"Make like we're departing, Smee," he whispered. "I want that boy, and those creatures, thinking we've left for good."

Smee nodded, offering a clumsy salute.

"We'll sail out of sight, but stay clear of the dark waters, I don't want to have to come all the way back here. What else have you learned from that fool?" James asked.

"Mad Rogue?" Smee asked.

"Aye," James replied, turning to survey the island through his window. "I don't know which is more alarming, the fact that he seems completely insane, or that everything he's told us so far has proven to be accurate."

"I agree," Smee said, nodding.

"Once we make sail, let's see if he has anything else to say about this place," James said. "I'm afraid Mad Rouge may turn out to be Neverland's best guide."

* * *

A short while later, once Neverland was no more than the faintest speck on the horizon, the pair left the cabin in search of their guest. They found the crazed pirate sitting with his back against one of the masts, muttering to himself while opening and closing his mouth and rubbing his jaw. He had stopped crying and seemed to be in better spirits than the night before.

James and Smee approached him, but Mad Rogue did not look up.

"Ehem," Smee coughed.

The man didn't respond. Instead, he opened his mouth wide to bare his teeth and then clacked them shut. He rubbed his jaw and repeated the motion.

"Mister Rogue," James said.

Still nothing.

James and Smee exchanged looks.

"Mad Rogue?" Smee asked, trying the odd full name the man had provided the night before.

Immediately, the man looked up as if noticing them for the first time.

"Yes?" he said, appearing as sane as anyone else.

"Would you be able to tell us more about the island?" Smee asked, carefully.

"Neverland?" Mad Rogue asked.

At the mention of the island, the pirate's mask of sanity flickered for a moment, exposing something dark, something ugly. But it disappeared before James could name it.

"As much as you're willing to share, of course," James added, cautiously. By no means did James fear the insane pirate, after all, he feared nothing. But neither did he want to set the man off.

Mad Rogue's gaze shot to James, almost as if he had heard James' thoughts.

"Why yes! Yes, indeed, of course!" Mad Rogue cheered, clapping his hands and rising to his feet. "What would you like to know?"

"We'd like to know about the inhabitants," James replied. "Where do they live? A map, perhaps, would be helpful, if it wouldn't be too much trouble to draw one."

"A map? Yes, yes, indeed! Do you have a quill?" Mad Rogue asked.

"My dear fellow, I have the finest collection of dip pens you will ever see," James boasted. He turned and looked around, searching for someone. He frowned, not seeing him.

"Mr. Wellings!" James yelled.

A moment later, a shirtless man wearing a bandolier stuffed with knives ran to James' side.

"Fetch me my pens," James ordered.

"Aye, Capt'n," Wellings replied.

A minute later he returned, an ornate box in his hands. The gold-trimmed red box was hinged in the back; a golden clasp kept its contents from spilling out.

James nodded at Mad Rogue, and Wellings handed the box and

a scroll of parchment to the pirate.

Mad Rogue ignored the parchment, instead yanking the box from the man's hands. Then, squatting down, he gingerly opened it.

 Inside, in a perfect line, lay five dip pens, roughly four or five inches in length, ranging in color from black to gold to silver.

Wellings placed the scroll next to the box and turned, clearly not wanting to spend any more time near Mad Rogue than was necessary.

"Hello, pretty," Mad Rogue said, selecting a golden pen.

"The inkwell is under the pens." James instructed. "The tray pulls out–"

But Mad Rogue ignored him, instead leaping onto Wellings' back, driving him to the deck. The man cried out in surprise and tried to rise, but Mad Rogue slammed the man's head into the ground.

He pulled Wellings' bandolier off his shoulder, sniffed it, then draped it over his own head. With the golden pen gripped in his fist, he cut a jagged oval in the man's back.

Wellings howled in pain, but Mad Rogue kept him pinned down, slamming him into the deck again. Then, abruptly, Mad Rogue stopped thrashing the man and twisted to stare up into the sky.

"Too much, Mother?" he asked.

He paused for a long moment, as if waiting for a response.

James found himself, along with the others who had gathered around him, looking up at the sky as well.

"This is the cove," Mad Rogue explained, turning back to his map and tapping a long finger at the bottom right corner of the island.

He cut a tiny ship just outside the cove, pausing only to count the number of masts on the Jolly Roger, then turning back to make sure his drawing matched the ship's likeness.

Wellings continued to struggle, but Mad Rogue overpowered him.

"This whole eastern side is cliffs," Mad Rogue said, raising his voice to be heard over Wellings' cries. "Mermaids live here," he said, cutting the word 'Mer' along the right side of Wellings' back as if it were paper.

"Mermaids," James said. "The creatures in the cove?"

"Yes," Mad Rogue said, nodding.

James narrowed his eyes. "Hmmm. Not how I imagined them."

Mad Rogue shook his head, his own eyes widening.

"The cliffs turn into a shore and beach midway up the eastern ridge, then turn into the north. The forest in the north is very dense, kites up there," Mad Rogue continued.

He cut the word 'kite' across Wellings' shoulder blades.

"Very tasty," he said, underlining the word he had just cut.

He tapped at the left side of the drawing, "And here, the mountains, and the western shore. "

Finally, he tapped the place on the man's back just east of the mountains.

"This is where the dense jungle changes, turning into forest. We think the pixies live in here. But down here," he said, his addition to the map eliciting another round of screams. "Here is the marsh. No one lives there. Just crocodiles. The jungle is very dense here."

"And what about Peter Pan?" James asked. "Where does he live?"

Mad Rogue shrugged. "In the sky."

James frowned and looked to Smee. His first mate only shrugged, clearly just as confused.

Deciding to ignore the comment, James bent down and tapped Wellings' lower back.

"The marshlands," James said. "No mermaids here, you say?"

Mad Rogue shook his head vigorously. "Too shallow. And crocs."

James smiled. "Then this is where we'll make landfall. We'll sneak into the jungle, set up a camp, then explore the island right under that little brat's nose. And then the treasure Teach promised us will be ours for the taking."

TWO

Night had fallen. James scanned the lagoon's dark waters—shallow and swampy, thick with seaweed and long cattails. It was just as Mad Rogue had described it. The waters were far too shallow for mermaids, but other dangers lurked all around them.

"Over there," Smee said, pointing. "Crocs."

James nodded in acknowledgement. The reptiles' eyes glinted, unblinking: tiny glowing beads that watched them from the darkness as they made their way through the silty waters.

The landing party rowed up to an old dock. Wordlessly, they climbed out of their boats, tying each one to the dock's mooring lines.

Eight boats in all, each one filled with his most experienced fighters. James nodded in approval. He had more than enough men to establish a foothold in Neverland. His pirates were as silent as the night they sneaked through.

They would use the cover of night to forage their way through the thick jungles that made up so much of the island's southern regions. Then they would set up camp deep in Neverland's heart, far beyond the prying eyes of Peter Pan, mermaids, or any other creature that claimed ownership of the island.

"Where did the dock come from?" Smee asked, speaking for the first time since landing.

"What?" James asked, turning to his first mate.

"The dock," Smee repeated. "If no one's allowed to come here, and Peter Pan is the only person here, why is there a dock? And where did it come from? Who built it?"

"It was built a long time ago, by better men than you," a voice called from the jungle.

James spun to see Peter Pan, hands on his hips, standing on the sand that separated the trees from the dock. All of the boy's good cheer from the morning had faded with the evening's light.

"Or so I've been told," the boy continued. "You've no business here," Peter said, staring at James.

"Au contraire," James replied. "You see, I enjoyed our little chat today, but I don't think I can leave just yet. I think there's much for me here still." James was surprised by the boy's sudden appearance but not intimidated. He was, after all, just a boy.

"And besides," James continued, smiling and spreading his arms wide, "I nullified the mermaid threat in the cove with an hour and this." He tapped his temple with a finger.

"What do you think I could do with a week?" He laughed. "And what more could I accomplish with a week and an army?" He snapped his fingers.

Immediately, the forty pirates in his company began lighting the lanterns they carried, bathing the dock and shore in amber light.

"We're not going anywhere, child," James spat.

"Impressive!" Peter said, whistling. The boy seemed unruffled by the sudden appearance of so many pirates. "Very impressive."

Peter held his own hand up, inspecting his fingers. He rubbed them together and held them to his ear, listening.

"And all you did was snap?" he asked. Peter extended his arm and examined the backs of his fingers from afar, waggling his fingertips as if his fingernails might hold the secret magic to James' trick.

"I wonder..." he mused, then snapped his own fingers.

At once, the forest behind him erupted in white-golden brilliance as hundreds of pixies—for they could be nothing else—flared into light. Their dazzling glow completely eclipsed the flames from the pirates' lanterns.

"Wow," Peter said, twisting his head to peer into the forest behind him, as if he hadn't known that the army of tiny, glowing creatures were lying in wait behind him.

The pirates shifted, their nervous shuffling speaking to the unease James knew they must be feeling and equally unhappy that their surprise had been thwarted.

Peter raised both hands, palms facing James, and made a shoving motion. In response, the pixies shot from the forest, straight towards the pirates.

"I warned you!" Peter roared, striding towards James, the last traces of good cheer gone from his voice. "I told you, you would burn."

"My course is my own, boy," James retorted, beating his chest with a clenched fist.

"Wrong!" Peter screamed, drawing a dagger from his belt and pointing it at James.

The weapon was distractingly exquisite. It dazzled, reflecting the pixies' light as they zipped past him. Even in the night, illuminated only by pixie-glow, the blade was impressive.

James forced his attention away from the blade and back to his surroundings. All around him the pixies were engaged with his men. A quick glance to each side told him his men were not faring well.

It was no matter. Given a few minutes, his men would overpower the strange little creatures.

How could they not? They were led by a child.

"I don't think you understand who you're dealing with," James said, returning his gaze to Peter and slowly drawing his sword. But as soon as his weapon cleared its scabbard, the boy was directly in front of him. Peter had somehow—impossibly—closed the twenty yards between them in a second.

Before James could react, Peter struck. It was a quick, surgical slice that cut deep into his hand, sending the sword spinning from his grip and clattering to the dock. Again Peter struck; this time he lashed out with a foot, sending James somersaulting backwards.

James flung the tails of his coat from his face and looked up to see Peter standing over him. No, not standing, levitating. The boy was flying several feet off the ground.

"What?" James gawked. "How?"

The boy ignored his question.

"Turn back, Captain," Peter said, glaring down at him with bright, furious eyes.

The admonition jerked James from his shock, indignation replacing the shock and confusion he had felt a moment before. He would not be ordered about by any child, flying or otherwise.

He scrambled on his hands and knees and dived for his sword, instinctively reaching out with his injured hand.

But the boy was faster.

Just as James' fingers curled around the weapon's hilt, Peter stomped on the injured hand. James roared in pain. Before he could do anything else, Peter was in his face.

"I'm tired of killing pirates," the boy spat, his face dark with rage. "It's over!"

"A miscalculation only on my part," James hissed through clenched teeth. "But we're far from finished, boy."

"Fine." Peter raised his weapon, that beautiful, terrible dagger, and brought it down on James' hand, severing it from his arm.

Blood sprayed from the wound, splattering the boy's face.

James gaped at his arm then looked back at his hand lying on the deck, still clutching his sword.

"What have you done?" James shrieked.

Peter only stared back at him. The boy looked like something born from a nightmare, covered in golden light and blood.

He was the most terrifying thing James had ever seen.

"Turn back," the boy said, his voice lower, almost pleading.

James ignored him and stumbled forward, reaching out to retrieve his hand, but Peter nudged it off the dock with his foot.

"My hand!" James screamed, scrambling to the edge of the dock.

The sword slipped from the hand's grip, disappearing into the dark water. The hand bobbed on the surface for an agonizing second before it, too, began to sink. James lunged after it, stretching out his other hand, fingertips barely brushing against the hand before it vanished in a flash of teeth and scales.

"Nooo!" James screamed, clambering away from the crocodile that had just eaten his hand.

He whipped around to face Peter again, but the boy was gone.

"Smee!" he cried, suddenly feeling weak. He looked down at his arm. Blood poured from the wound. He pressed it hard against his side to stem the flow, but the effort sent a new, fresh pain through his arm.

"Smeeeeeeee!" he bellowed as he stumbled and collapsed to the deck.

Several hands grabbed him, and he felt himself being dragged, followed by the rocking of the boat, but he couldn't remember being lowered into it. The boat pitched and rocked as his men frantically rowed back to the Jolly Roger.

The night, previously illuminated by lanterns and pixies, started to fade to moonlight, then to darkness as clouds migrated across the sky.

Either that, or he was dying.

THREE

P eter felt warmth on his face long before identifying it as sunlight. The bright sun had peeked over the treetops and had
been shining through the waterfall with such slowness Peter
couldn't tell when he had first started to squint.

He opened his eyes to beams of sunlight radiating through the
water. It was a welcomed contrast to the cold cavern floor. He rolled
to his stomach, resting his chin on his arms, the soft moss rustling
underneath him as he moved. He stared out from under the alcove
that had once belonged to his sister, Mara. He watched the water
flowing in front of him. The falls weren't violent, or even loud, just a
steady stream of unrelenting water.

He could make out the sun now, a bright, yellow orb that lit the entire interior of White Falls, making the gold and gems in the room shine even more brilliantly.

Fairies began to leave their tiny apartments built into the walls of the cave, some visiting other rooms, others flying to the back tunnels, and still others flying up to the ceiling, where the vast reservoir of golden dust was stored.

Fairies entered the reservoir and returned, some with handfuls and some with large containers of dust, working to repair the damage White Falls sustained during the conflict started by Edward Teach.

Teach, also known as Blackbeard the Pirate, had brought Neverland within a hairsbreadth of complete destruction. But after a final rally by the island's inhabitants, Neverland now enjoyed a peace unseen for many years.

Peter rolled onto his back, folded his hands behind his head, and closed his eyes, savoring the peace.

"You're still sleeping?" a small voice demanded.

Peter felt something small land on his chest. He opened one eye to see Tinker Belle, hands on her hips, lips pursed in feigned annoyance.

"Surely there's someone left on this island to kill," she said.

Peter snorted, the motion unsettling Tinker Belle's footing, causing her to stumble back. She restored her footing then glared back at him.

"The pirate," Tinker Belle said. "Last night, why'd you let him go?"

Peter considered his response.

In the final confrontation with Teach, Peter had learned his own father, presumed dead and lost at sea, had actually been shot and thrown overboard by Teach himself.

The revelation had shocked Peter. And in his shock he lost control, abandoning the plan to expel Teach and his pirates from the island. Instead, revenge had consumed him. In that moment, killing Teach had been Peter's only desire. But Tinker Belle had brought him back, allowing reason and clear-thinking to ultimately prevail.

"I'm done killing," Peter replied at last. "With Teach, I came too close to becoming like him. I won't let that happen again."

"I'll kill him for you," Tinker Belle said, drawing her daggers. "We could still catch him. It's probably not too late."

He looked at her.

"What?" she said, her face implacable. But after a moment she smiled, unable to keep her face straight.

"I don't think so," Peter said. "The man lost a hand. He'll be off dealing with that for a long time. I doubt we'll ever see him again."

Tinker Belle whistled, sheathing her weapons. "You won't kill him, but you'll cut off his hand?"

"And feed it to a crocodile," he added, wincing.

"Shiiklah's going to love that," Tinker Belle said, giggling.

"You know, you're more like her than you know," Peter said, sitting up, the movement forcing her to take flight. "I wouldn't be surprised if you were part mer."

"I'll kill you, too," Tinker Belle threatened, drawing a dagger again and pointing it at him. But her smile betrayed the joke.

Peter smiled, then shifted his gaze back towards the waterfall.

Tinker Belle landed on his shoulder, and the pair watched the sun trace random patterns though the water. Neither of them spoke for several minutes.

"What now?" Tinker Belle asked finally.

"Peace," Peter replied, sighing. He closed his eyes again to feel the morning sun on his face. "Peace," he whispered.

A new era had come to Neverland. The morning sun had chased away all traces of the previous night's darkness. And now, with the last pirate driven away, the nightmare that had visited Neverland's shores faded. The island could finally heal without fear of attack. Her inhabitants, weary from years of strife and loss, could rebuild and rest.

But what now?

"I need a home," Peter said suddenly.

"Why?" she asked. "This is your home."

"I know, but every time I leave White Falls, I get soaking wet," he said, pointing to the falls. "I can't live like that."

"Then take the tunnel," Tinker Belle said.

"Then I'm covered in dirt," Peter countered.

Tinker Belle drummed her fingers against her chin, considering.

"I think I'll visit Shiiklah," Peter said, standing up and sending Tinker Belle into the air again. "I may be able to get some tools or something from the mers."

"What's wrong with our tools?" Tinker Belle demanded.

Peter squinted at her, then held up his thumb and index finger, indicating the general size of most things the fairies used.

Tinker Belle rolled her eyes. "I still don't trust that fish."

"You'd better, pixie," Peter said, using the slang term pirates used for fairies. "We're all friends now. And don't let her catch you calling her 'fish.'"

"I could take her," Tinker Belle sniffed, looking bored.

"Right," Peter laughed. "Sit tight. I'll be back in a bit." He dived through the falls and into the morning light.

* * *

Peter surveyed Neverland. The mountains to the west stretched out, ever looming. He zipped past the forests, ducking down under the trees to fly beneath the canopy. After a few minutes, the trees gave way to a massive black cliff. The black, glass-like obsidian stone glinted in the morning sun.

Peter landed in a clearing between the forest line and the edge of the cliff. He walked over to the edge and peered down. The waters roiled and surged, slamming against the cliff walls, as if the sea itself protested the island's existence.

This was where his ship had wrecked the night they had first come to Neverland. Somewhere at the bottom of the sea lay the vessel, along with countless others that had wrecked against the unyielding cliffs over the years.

They had found Neverland quite by accident. And by all rights, Peter never should have stepped foot on the place.

Upon hearing the news that Peter's father, William Till, had been lost at sea, Peter, along with his sister, Mara, had stowed away on the ship dispatched to find Teach.

They had finally closed in on Teach's ship when a storm struck, misdirecting them, and somehow brought them here. Their ship was hurled into the cliffs and all of the crew, save for Peter and his sister, had perished.

Mara had managed to climb the sharp cliffs, ultimately finding herself in the fairies' company, while Peter, who had fallen overboard, had been rescued by mermaids. Perhaps 'rescued' was too benevolent of a word. The truth was the mers, as they called themselves, had never seen a human child and had wanted to study him.

He hadn't been their only prisoner, though. A score of pirates had been held captive as well. And when the pirates had attempted to take a young mermaid child captive as ransom for their freedom, Peter had rescued the young mermaid, who happened to be the chieftess' daughter.

His act of heroism resulted in not only the sparing of his own life, but in receiving the Mer's highest commendation, the Pan Hakki.

Peter eventually left the mer's caves—the Enclaves of Nakkal—found his sister alive and well, and went on to unite the island against Edward Teach.

But at great cost.

Teach had murdered Peter's sister after realizing Mara would never reveal the location of the fairy's home, White Falls. Teach had known about the fairies' gift in creating things from their dust, and had wanted them for himself.

Peter looked at the grass.

He knew, from what she had told him, that this was where she had climbed up and passed out, before one of the fairies, Siene, had discovered her.

The pair had become and remained fast friends until the last. And while the fairies hadn't been able to prevent Mara from dying, Siene had managed to save her, in a sense.

Siene, after Resolving Mara – whatever that meant – became

Tinker Belle.

He didn't know much about the fairies' Resolution ritual, but it seemed that somehow part of Mara had been saved, or preserved, or joined, with Siene, and Tinker Belle had been the result.

He placed his hand on the grass and smiled, remembering that she wasn't really gone as long as he had Tinker Belle.

He stood and dived off the cliff. The water grew nearer, and eventually, he slowed his fall enough so the impact wouldn't injure or kill him.

He shot under the surface of the water. The water was deep and blue, he could dimly see the ocean floor in the distance. Countless wrecked ships littered the ocean floor, wrapped and tangled up with each other. One of them, although he had no idea which, was the ship that had brought him here, the Lion's Whelp.

He moved through the water, a combination of swimming and flying. It seemed whatever allowed him to control his flight also gave him speed in the water, although it was greatly diminished.

He searched for the section of the cliff where the stone wall angled back towards the island, creating a celling of sorts. Swimming under it, he could see several large glowing holes in the celling, dim blue light illuminating the openings in the rock.

He angled for one of the holes and shot through it, bursting out of the water to hover in the air.

It was the huge room where kelp, fish, and every other treasure from the sea the mers collected was processed.

The room was largely empty, save for a handful of mers. The time for collecting had passed, war had come to Nakkal.

And the mers couldn't be more pleased.

He landed lightly on the cold stone floor and towards one end of the massive room.

The enclaves themselves were far from abandoned. While almost all the warriors were gone, no doubt patrolling the waters for more pirates, those too young or too old to fight were still present.

To be fair, Peter had yet to meet any mer, regardless of age, who could not easily kill him. Even Kinarah, one of the clan's elders, was still as ferocious as ever. He pondered the longevity of mers as he crossed the room and walked towards one of the walls.

Peter unhooked a leather satchel from a line of pegs along one wall and slung it over his shoulder. As a Pan Hakki, he was entitled to almost anything he desired; taking a satchel would largely go unnoticed.

Peter meandered through the winding corridors, making his way to the weapons cavern. He was greeted with salutes as he encountered the few mers who remained in the caves.

Apparently, leading an assault against a fleet of pirates and defeating Edward Teach together had softened the mers to the idea of a human receiving their commendation.

Peter entered the weapons cavern and approached one of the stalls. Immediately, he recognized the old mer crafting the weapons. It was the same one who had crafted the coral dagger he received when he was made Pan Hakki.

Along one side of the wall hung a variety of finished weapons, daggers, javelins, and long, narrow swords. On the opposite wall hung strips of leather and kelp. Kelp-woven baskets hung from pegs in the wall filled with various items, among them, shiny black stones, shark and whale teeth, slender needle-like shafts, and other items.

Peter approached the mer cautiously, remembering his previous encounters with the creature. The mer's old, scaly skin clung to his body like wet linens. Slowly, Peter took a lance from the finished alcove and presented it to the old mer.

"Hi," Peter said nervously. "I was wondering if you'd be able to help me. I'm trying to make something…I'm trying to make a saw."

The mer stared at him for a long moment, then looked away.

Maybe the old mer didn't know what Peter was asking for. More likely, though, he understood perfectly and was ignoring him.

"Look," Peter said, holding out the lance and trying a different approach. "I'd like you to cut grooves along the edge, like teeth."

The old mer slowly turned his head and looked at Peter. Either he really didn't understand, or he was offended Peter was asking that one of his masterpieces be intentionally damaged.

Peter growled in frustration.

Instantly the mer rose to his full imposing height and hissed back at Peter.

Peter leapt into the air, nearly dying from fright, and bolted from the alcove.

He returned a few seconds later and dipped his hand into the basket of shark teeth.

"I'll just take some of these," he said, quickly grabbing a handful of teeth before running away. He returned a second time and snatched several leather strips from a peg on the wall, then disappeared again.

"Would it be okay if I–" he started to say, returning a third time, but an angry hiss from the mer sent him scurrying out of the chamber for good.

He quickly walked down the tunnels, reminding himself he was the Pan Hakki and was allowed to be here, when he nearly stumbled into Sarii, the merchild he had saved. The young merchild clapped her hands wildly and smiled, chirping happily at the sight of Peter.

Behind her, scraping her way long the rough stone floor was Shiiklah, the child's mother and clan chieftess.

"Pan Hakki," she said, greeting him with the honorific title.

Peter smiled and nodded a greeting to her.

"The war goes well, no?" she said.

"It's over," Peter said. "We drove the last ship away last night."

"The war is never over," Shiiklah said. "There may be moments of sssilence, but it always returns, the war is never over."

"Hmmm," Peter said, considering her words. "Okay," he said at last, having no comment.

"Come," she said, turning to continue her walk down the hall.

They walked the halls that snaked through Nakkal, reviewing their sides of the previous battle and putting together preliminary plans for restoring the island.

They passed into the Pools of Gathering, the room by which Peter had initially entered into the cavern. Turning to him, Shiiklah extended her hand, offering something to him.

Peter took the item and began to inspect it, turning it over in his hands. It was a hollow, cylindrical piece of coral. The cylinder was about the length of his forefinger. The center had been removed somehow, and all along its length a dizzy pattern of tiny holes had been drilled through it. Like all things mer, the craftsmanship was stunning. Tiny groves ran the length of the tube, winding around the holes. And at one end dangled a black strip of braided kelp.

"What is it?" Peter asked, not sure what to make of the thing, but no less impressed.

"It is a call," she replied.

"A what?" Peter asked.

"If you blow into it, we will hear, and come to your aid," she explained.

"Wow," he said, now seeing its value beyond craftsmanship alone. "Thank you. But why?"

"You proved yourself worthy of the Pan Hakki in your defeat of Teach and his pirates. You fully turned against your own kind in defense of mers," she explained. "And we can deny your honor no more. Honor has become you Peter Pan Hakki of Nakkal."

The fact that Peter, a human, had taken action and even killed other humans in defense of mers struck a deep chord. And while they still held distain for most of humanity, Peter's actions had secured him their gratitude and respect.

Peter inclined his head in thanks.

Shiiklah returned the gesture by slamming her closed fist across her chest, the mer equivalent of a salute.

He looked at the coral whistle again. He put it to his lips and blew into it.

It made no sound—at least no sound Peter could hear—but every mer in the cavernous chamber snapped their attention to him.

"Bangerang," Peter said, smiling.

He slipped the necklace over his head and hung it from his neck.

"What brings you to Nakkal?" Shiiklah asked, eying his armful of gear.

"I need tools," he said. "So I can build a house."

"You can sstay here," Shiiklah replied. "You are Pan Hakki, your place is with us."

Peter considered his response. The last thing he wanted to do was offend her. Granted, he knew she would never harm him—quite the opposite, as he had sacrificed much for all mers.

Regardless, offending a mermaid was never a good idea.

"True," he said carefully. "But I'm also a human. And I'd like to live," he paused, searching for the right word, "in the dry," he finished, using the mer's term indicating anywhere above water.

She thought, her blue eyes considering, then grunted, seeming to accept his reasoning.

"We will see you out," Shiiklah said, her tail sliding snake-like towards one of the pools that led to the sea.

You could tell a lot about how a mermaid was feeling by the color of her eyes. They changed color depending on what mood she was in. Blue meant 'thoughtful' in a I'm-not-going-to-kill-you-right-now sort of way. Green was content or passive—as passive as a mermaid could be. And black, well, the last thing you wanted was to have those terrible, black eyes fixed on you.

"Do you need assistance with your supplies?" Shiiklah asked.

"No, thank you," Peter replied, before nodding a farewell to each of them.

He jumped into the pool, then felt the water above him shudder as Sarii too, followed him in.

She swam ahead of him, her tail no more than a blur, propelling her away from him with speed any fish would envy.

Peter gave chase, but laden with supplies, he had no chance of catching the mer child.

He made his way back into the open water, then rose up to the surface and broke it, leaving it completely and entering the open air.

Sarii surfaced a few yards away and smiled, her tiny sharp teeth spreading across her face as she waved.

Peter waved back then returned to the island to scout out a place to build his house.

FOUR

Darkness. It had a way of covering things that wished to remain unseen.

James inhaled. Air squeezed past teeth that had been clenched for longer than he could recall.

He steepled his fingers.

No. Rather, he tried to steeple his fingers, then remembered his hand was gone.

Gingerly, he lowered his wounded arm.

Gone.

That dull burn in his wrist that never seemed to go away intensified, and with it, his anger. He looked down, staring into the dark where he knew his bandaged arm now rested on the table.

It burned.

It always burned.

The searing pain wrought from that boy's cruel dagger had faded into this constant burning.

That boy.

That terrible boy.

He refused to even utter the child's name, as if doing so might summon him. And he wasn't ready for that.

No, not yet.

Now all that remained was the dull, persistent burn. A burn that turned to fire whenever the barber changed his bandages. A burn that turned to fire every time he reached for something with that hand, expecting to grasp and hold, but instead jolting his wound.

The worst part wasn't the burning, or the aching, or even the fire. No, the worst part was the fact that he could still feel his hand, feel his fingers wrapped into a tight, unrelenting fist. He could feel the worn, familiar leather of the sword's hilt.

Somehow, impossibly, it remained, the muscles and tendons in his arm responding to the memory of the fist, refusing to contract. And it was this haunting pain that tortured him more than any of the others.

If he concentrated, truly concentrated, he could unclench the fist in his mind, granting him a moment of relief. But as soon as his mind wandered, as soon as his attention slipped, the ghost of a hand would seize again, returning him to agony.

James stared into the darkness where his hand would be—where his hand should be.

The darkness played tricks on his eyes. The darkness, untrustworthy, would swirl around, dark, foreign colors taking the form of fingers almost real enough to touch. But they would always disappear before becoming real enough to use.

The door opened. Sunlight exploded into the dark cabin, eviscerating the darkness from the room, the dark fingers at once disappearing.

His ghost hand once again threatened to clench into a tight, imaginary fist, but he managed to hold it at bay.

"Are you in here, Captain?" Smee's tentative voice called from the doorway.

James ignored him; instead he focused on keeping his hand unclenched.

"Are you all right?" Smee asked.

"Get out," James hissed, his teeth still clenched.

Smee paused for a moment, clearly weighing what he had to say against captain's orders.

James spared him a quick glance before returning his gaze to his bandaged arm.

"Capt'n, our supplies–" Smee pressed, choosing whatever burden had led him into the cabin despite orders to the contrary.

"Out!" James bellowed, slamming his fist, rather what should have been his fist, on the table's surface. The motion sent a bolt of agony throughout him. He screamed in pain, involuntarily leaping up, and staggered backwards over his chair. Losing his balance, he fell. He reached out to catch himself and felt the eruption of white hot pain as the full weight of his body landed on the wound.

He cried out in an animal rage, spitting and swearing as he tried to get to his feet.

He came up with a pistol in his remaining hand and fired it at Smee. His dominant hand, however, somewhere inside the belly of a crocodile, was not holding the pistol. The shot went hopelessly wide, blowing a hole in a marble statue in the far side of the cabin.

"Get out!" James screamed, hurling the discharged pistol at the pirate.

"Captain, the men," Smee insisted, ducking under the weapon.

"I don't care about the men!" James bellowed, drawing another pistol and firing it.

Again, the shot went wide, obliterating a small table next to the couch.

Smee, finally deciding that his life was worth more than whatever he had come in to tell his enraged captain, bolted for the door. He tripped over a crate filled with maps as he left. The pages flew into the air, then drifted slowly to the floor.

Smee scurried out the door, closing it hastily behind him as he left, leaving James once again in darkness.

Gasping for the air the pain had stolen from him, James found his chair, righted it, and sat down. For long minutes he stared into the darkness where his hand should be and concentrated on un-clenching his ghost hand.

With agonizing slowness, it finally relented, leaving him alone with the burning, and once again hidden in the darkness.

FIVE

It was the perfect place for a home.

Nestled between one of the many large clearings where dense, tropical jungle gave way to coniferous trees and giant oaks sat a single huge willow tree. The tree had grown in the center of the clearing, up out of some sort of depression, exposing snaking roots. All that remained of the old giant was its trunk, at least fifteen feet around, which reached skywards another twenty. Its branches were gone, broken off from wind and storms, their only remaining evidence the halo of bark that surrounded the tree.

"It's perfect," Peter said, landing in front of the tree, tossing his items collected from the mers on the ground.

"It's a dead tree," Tinker Belle said, wrinkling her nose.

"It's exactly what we need," Peter said. "It just needs some updating."

"Updating?" she scoffed. "It's dead."

The pair approached the tree. A split from the base to just beneath head-height ran up its length. Peter squeezed through and Tinker Belle followed.

The interior of the tree was cool and dark but there was still light enough to see. Above them, they could see the tree served as walls only, the top was still open to the sky, large enough for a fairy to pass through, but not Peter.

"That'll be nice when it rains," Tinker Belle muttered.

"I'll fix it," Peter said.

"And what about the door? You can hardly fit through.

"Watch," Peter said, squeezing through the crack back into the sunlight.

He sat down and emptied his satchel, spilling an assortment of shark teeth and whale leather on the ground.

He picked up a sheet of leather. It was roughly the size of a page from a book, only longer. He took a stick and drew a straight line down the center of the leather. He didn't cut hard enough to actually pierce the leather, just enough to score it.

"What are you doing?" Tinker Belle asked.

"Quiet," Peter said, without taking his eyes from his work.

He picked up one of the teeth and pushed it though the line he had scraped into the leather. He was careful not to push it all the way though. The sharp tip slid easily through the leather, protruding through the other side.

Peter took another tooth and repeated the gesture, making sure the tooth was directly in line next to the first one.

He repeated the pattern until a straight row of shark teeth stitched the length of the leather sheet.

Smiling, he reached for the short lance he had taken from the mers.

He laid the leather, tooth side up, along one end of the lance. Then, he folded one end of the leather over the other.

"You're making a saw," Tinker Belle guessed.

"I'm making a saw," Peter said, smiling.

He reached for a second sheet of leather and, using one of the teeth, managed to cut it into thin strips. Then he took one of the strips and laid it between the first two teeth in the row. He pulled the leather taut, then tied the strip in a tight knot behind the teeth, securing the teeth it sat between. He repeated the move until every shark tooth had a strip of leather securing its position on the club.

Peter hefted his makeshift saw, inspecting his work.

"Okay," Tinker Belle admitted. "That's impressive."

Peter winked at her before trotting to the tree line. Singling out a tree, he placed the tooth-filled edge of the club against one of the branches and started to saw. The branch, roughly the width of his own arm, fell from the tree as if a shark had actually attacked it.

"Woah!" Peter exclaimed, inspecting the teeth to check for damage, but the saw remained fully intact.

"Bangerang," Peter said, smirking back at Tinker Belle. "Let's get to work."

The old tree's shadow stretched out from its base, winding slowly around the clearing like a giant clock as Peter and Tinker Belle worked through the day. As daylight began to wane, the shadow dissipated, signaling both the end of the day and the completion of their task.

The old tree had been transformed.

Peter and Tink had widened the crack, shaping the hole with his saw, turning it into a workable door. Then, again with the help of his new tool, Peter had cut down several branches. Using his remaining leather thongs, he bound the branches together in a row. Finally, the pair managed to lift the door into place, hooking the ends of the leather into tiny hooks Tinker Belle had carved into the tree with her dagger.

The final touch was a branch that hung across the width of the door, extending along each side of the tree, preventing the door from swinging open.

The interior of the tree had not gone untouched. The dirt inside had been leveled and then stomped flat, providing an acceptable floor.

Along one wall of the tree lay two large logs. Resting atop the logs were dozens of smaller branches: Peter's bed. It wasn't the most comfortable bed, but it would be better than sleeping on the dirt.

A shallow pit marred the otherwise even floor in the center of the dwelling, directly under the narrow opening in the trunk.

"It sure is dark in here," Tinker Belle commented, looking over their handiwork one last time.

"Not for long," Peter said from the center of the room, his back to her. "Give me a hand, will you?"

She landed next to the small pile of twigs he had assembled in the center of the depression.

"Can you light these?" Peter asked.

"All I am is a torch to you, aren't I?" Tinker Belle said sardonically.

"Of course not," Peter said, smiling. "Torches don't complain."

Tinker Belle snorted in amusement and knelt down next to the pile of sticks.

She reached into the sticks and began to brush her fingers together as if she were removing dirt from her fingertips. But instead of dirt, golden dust sprinkled to the ground. She continued the gesture until a small pile had accumulated.

"The dust is flammable?" Peter asked.

"No," Tinker Belle replied.

"Then what are you doing?" Peter asked again.

"Making fire," Tinker Belle replied.

She gathered up a handful of dust to cup in her hands. She squeezed it tightly, her slender arms quivering in exertion. Her hands seemed to glow a deeper red, not her usual gold.

Suddenly, she hurled the handful of dust into the center of the pit.

But instead of dust, it was fire. The fire splashed, somehow, against the base of the wood, immediately igniting the sticks.

Peter's eyes widen in surprise.

Tinker Belle flew out of the small fire pit and landed on Peter's shoulder. The pair watched the small fire grow. Peter added sticks to it until it reached a size he was content with.

The dry wood cracked and popped as Tinker Belle's fire lazily spread to each stick. Outside Peter's new home, crickets and other insects chirped, exulting in a chorus of summer. Night birds joined in too, adding their own coos to the ensemble.

The moon, when it departed to wander distant skies, left Neverland's landscape void of light, save for an old tree, glowing softly—a lone watchman in a sea of darkness.

SIX

The door groaned open and someone slipped inside. It was Smee. It was always Smee. No one else was brave enough—or stupid enough—to keep attempting to enter James' cabin.

Sunlight followed Smee into the cabin, casting a long, fat shadow in front of the pirate as he padded into the dimly lit room. The soft glow of the lantern on the table did little to mute the man's dark shadow, however.

James watched the other pirate from behind half-closed eyes.

"Captain?" Smee asked.

James didn't reply. Instead he remained still, sitting in his chair, his attention split between Smee and the small flame as it shifted, dodging little currents of air.

He massaged his wrist. The burning had finally faded.

The bandages were gone, too. Now all that remained were scars. Scars, and his ghost hand, which seemed determined to haunt him, unwilling to follow the fate of his physical one.

Eaten by that crocodile.

Severed by that boy.

The thought of him threatened to close the ghost-hand, but he resisted.

He was becoming better at holding it at bay with each passing day.

"I was schooled in Camberwell," James said, finally acknowledging Smee but keeping his eyes on the flame. "In the Royal Naval School. I took first in every course. Every year."

Smee stopped walking.

"You didn't know that, did you?" James said, still massaging his wrist.

"No, sir," came Smee's nervous reply.

"No, indeed. And it's been by design I've kept my past hidden from the crew," James said. "Hidden even from you, Smee."

James rolled his head around his neck, grunting as the bones in his neck cracked.

"The purpose was two-fold," he continued. "A man with no history tends to be more frightening than the blackest monster. And on the other hand..." he trailed off, then snorted, a blend of self-deprecation and bitterness. "Subsequently," he amended, "were I ever to return to the civilized world, Captain James, well, James, could be anyone."

"Is that why you've never told us your surname?" Smee asked.

"Aye," James replied.

"So what's the plan?" Smee asked, clearly uncomfortable with the conversation.

There was no plan. Or rather, there was only a single thought that purged all the others from James' mind.

"I misjudged him, Smee," James said, ignoring the man's question. "I misjudged him, and it cost me so much."

James leaned back in his chair, his gaze shifting from the flame to his scarred wrist.

"He took so much more from me than my hand," he said.

"What do you mean?" Smee asked.

"I hear what the men say," James answered. "And I don't blame them, honest, I do not. Outwitted by a child. Bested by a little boy. Utterly humiliated."

"It's not all that bad, Captain," Smee said, stooping to pick up some of the discarded papers that littered the floor. "None of us knew what he was capable of. None of us."

"He's an anomaly, isn't he?" James said.

"The boy?" Smee asked.

"Aye, the boy," James replied.

Smee said nothing but instead shifted his attention to the clutter of goblets and uneaten food on the table.

James unclenched the ghost hand.

"Do you know the legend of Miiren, Smee?" James asked.

"Miiren, sir?" Smee replied, looking up from his work, his glasses perched on the tip of his nose, his arms full of dishes.

"Aye," James answered.

Smee's brow furrowed.

"I don't believe so, Captain," Smee said, shaking his head. He managed to balance the armful of dishes and slide his glasses back with a free hand.

"Miiren was a siren," James explained. He shifted his gaze from the flame light to stare directly at Smee.

"And as the story goes, her song was so fair that even other sirens would succumb to it," James explained. "She could entrap them and they would follow her." James leaned forward as he spoke.

"Miiren was no more remarkable in appearance than any of the other sirens, but her voice," James said, lifting a finger. "It was the song."

Smee didn't say anything.

James continued. "Upon hearing the song, sailors would flock to her, throwing their ships on the rocks that lined her shore, drowning in the process. Don't you see it?"

"So," Smee began, trying to work out his captain's point. "Miiren is Neverland?"

James rolled his eyes.

"No, you idiot," he said. "The boy is Miiren."

James rose to his feet and began to pace.

"Look," he said. "The sailors are so distracted from the danger, they're so focused on her song that they never see the real threat."

"The rocks," Smee said, finally understanding.

"The rocks," James agreed.

James dropped onto a couch, sinking back into the darkness.

"He's a child," James said. "And as such, he shouldn't have been a threat. And that, that is his song."

A spring in the couch squawked as James shifted.

"He's a stupid boy alone on an island. He should be malnourished, he should be afraid, weak. But he's not. Somehow, he's not any of those things. And that, Smee. That is what threw me on the rocks. I underestimated him, I was distracted by all of the unknowns that add up to that boy, alone on Neverland, thriving. And while I was blinded," James said. "The siren struck."

"Maybe he got lucky," Smee offered, breaking the silence.

"Luck?" James echoed. "No, that's not luck. This is not luck" he said, holding his stump up for Smee to see.

"No," he said again. "This, this was something else."

Smee shuffled, the dishes in his arms clanking as he moved.

"Is she real?" Smee asked.

"Who?" James said.

"Miiren," Smee replied. "Do you think she's real?"

James narrowed his eyes and thought.

"All legends are born from fragments of truth," he said finally. "But no, I'm sure Miiren does not exist."

"Well, now that you've figured that out I suppose you're well enough to travel?" Smee asked, changing the subject.

"Indeed," James replied. "Indeed, I am."

"So I guess we'll be leaving then," Smee said. "What port are we to make our heading?"

"Neverland," James replied.

"What?" Smee exclaimed. "We're not leaving?"

"Oh, we're not going anywhere, Smee," James replied, his voice suddenly icy.

"We're not?" Smee asked.

"No," James replied, slowly stepping into the lantern light and brandishing his stump at Smee.

"Peter Pan cut off my hand," he said, finally speaking the boy's name aloud. "And for that, Peter Pan must die."

SEVEN

It had been the best night's sleep of Peter's life. It didn't matter that his bed was no more than a pile of sticks. It was his; he had built it with his own two hands.

Peter swung his feet off the bed and hopped down. He walked to his door, pulled it open, and stepped into the morning sun.

The grass sparkled with dew. The sounds of chirping birds carried by a gentle morning breeze made the smile on his face impossible to suppress.

He spent a few minutes adjusting his door, not because there was anything wrong with it, but because now he had something of his own to fiddle with.

With his house complete, Peter spent the rest of the day with Tinker Belle, gathering food and other supplies to stock his new home. They roamed the island, gathering fruit from the various groves of citrus trees that were clustered throughout Neverland.

They collected dust-preserved fruit from White Falls' stores, and fish—that he thoroughly cooked before eating—from the mers.

By the end of his second day, the old tree was fully supplied.

By the end of his second week he had felled enough trees, cut them into pieces, and stacked the pieces next to his door, to provide him a month of fires.

When he wasn't working on his own home, he would frequent both White Falls and Nakkal, checking in with his friends and seeing how each group was progressing with restoring their own homes.

Almost every trace of the destruction that had visited White Falls the night the kites attacked was gone. The jeweled walls had all been completely repaired.

The only evidence of the battle was the large monument that had been built into the stone floor. A meter-wide circle of diamonds had been installed. In the center, made entirely of blood-red rubies, was a red kite. The monument stood as a reminder to the fairies, mers, and kites of their darkest moment—a place none of them ever wanted to revisit.

The mers made no such monument. Nothing made of stone, at least. Instead, they had returned to the dry. Mers now scouted the entire island, they could once again be seen stretched out on the rocks and boulders that lined the shores, sunning themselves while keeping vigilant watch of the seas, both above and below.

Neverland was slowly shifting, once again beginning to resemble the stories Peter had heard told in caves and under the sea.

Peter and Tinker Belle had fallen into a routine in the weeks that had passed. Every morning they would scout the island, more so for new sources of food and supplies than for threats. Then they would return to the old tree with the day's spoils.

Most evenings would find Peter and Tinker Belle on the western shore, watching the sun set. Sometimes Adelaide's retinue would join them. Sometimes Shiiklah would appear in the waves and sit with them as well.

But most of the time it was just the two of them, watching the sky. The pink clouds, like burning ships, sailed the sky's indigo seas.

After a day of adventuring, they would either return to the old tree, to White Falls, or even Nakkal. Regardless of where they ended up each day, they were always together.

Several weeks had passed, and, as often was the case, evening found Peter and Tinker Belle inside their old tree. Tinker Belle worked on the fire while Peter whittled a piece of wood with his dagger, tossing the shavings to Tinker Belle to use as kindling.

Outside, the angry sky growled. The lazy pink clouds had changed to dark, ominous things that blotted out even the most clever stars.

Peter rose and checked the door, making sure it was secured. The wind whistled through the door's slits, an eerie, mocking song that made Peter long for the morning.

It was nights like this that he was glad he wasn't alone, thankful he didn't have to face the darkness by himself.

He smiled as he adjusted the door, snugging it into place.

With Tinker Belle at his side, he could weather any storm.

EIGHT

James stepped out of the cabin and into the sunlight. The midday sun, while bright, was not as blinding as it had seemed weeks earlier.

His clear, blue eyes slid across the ship, surveying his men, the supplies on deck, and the general state of the Jolly Roger.

"The ship is in good form," James said, nodding approvingly.

"We've done our best while you were…on the mend," Smee explained.

"Hmmm," James said noncommittally. "What is our position?"

James walked to the end of the boat and peered over. The water was light blue; it shimmered and sparkled in the sunlight.

"We're at Neverland's edge," Smee said quickly.

"Good," came James' reply. "Hold fast, this place is not easy to find and I want to keep her in our sights."

"Aye, sir," Smee said. "So we're going back, then?"

"Yes," James replied.

Immediately there were murmurs of disapproval from the crew.

James knew whatever he said next would need to restore his men's faith in him or he would lose them. To succeed, he would have to play on what motivated them the most. And that would be easy— they were pirates, after all.

"Brothers," James said, spreading his arms open in an inviting gesture. "We are a mere thousand fathoms away from the richest discovery since the New World: Neverland! And every other soul who knows of its location is either dead or too much a coward to even whisper her name."

James paused, giving his words time to sink in.

He began to move throughout the gathered crowed.

"This island is a haven for those brave enough to take it from the natives," James said, remembering how Teach had originally sold them all on this venture. "Gone are the days where a humble pirate could make port anywhere he wished. We are a hunted people. But more than that, Neverland has countless riches. Caves, with walls tiled with precious gems, diamonds even," he said. "There are creatures who can create anything you desire out of dust! And gold, so much gold we could use it for bullets!"

Some of the pirates began to murmur in agreement, greed gradually overcoming fear. But a voice called from the back, "What about the mermaids?"

"True," James admitted, nodding solemnly, "there are dangers haunting Neverland's shores that are new to us, greater than what we've ever faced before."

He raised his right arm high over his head, showing them the missing hand.

"I know too well," he admitted. "But the reward greatly outweighs the cost, mark my words."

James looked over his men once more, this time, they were mostly nodding. Others were wringing their hands together. Gone were the looks of pity and doubt. He had restored his crew's faith in him with promises of riches and a handful of flowery words.

He was no defeated, broken man. Caught off guard perhaps, tricked by the siren's song, but not shipwrecked on the rocks.

"Brothers," James continued. "Together, we will pillage Neverland's spoils and take what Blackbeard could not."

But more importantly, he thought, I will have my revenge. Riches, he could find anywhere, but vengeance? Vengeance could be found on Neverland's shores alone.

James disliked misleading his men. He had led them with honesty and fairness for many years, drawing them together almost like a family. But they would not understand what he needed to do.

"Double rations!" James ordered. "Tonight we feast! And in the days to come, we will take Neverland!"

The pirates erupted into choruses of cheers and applause. A few even started chanting James' name, while others drew their pistols and fired them into the air. Even Smee joined in, suddenly finding himself in the midst of a group of pirates who had broken into dance.

Every man celebrated.

Every man exalted in the victory they believed their captain would bring them.

Every man except one.

James locked eyes with him. Tall and lanky with wild eyes and a lopsided grin that seemed to smile with more understanding than he let on.

Mad Rogue.

The pirate leaned against the mast, arms hanging loosely at his side. He stared back at James with eyes that said his ears were impervious to flowery words or promises of wealth.

A knowing smile played in the corner of Mad Rogue's mouth.

They stared at each other for a long moment before something, only seen by Mad Rogue, caught his attention and his gaze drifted away. Then he slid around the mast, disappearing from sight.

James shook the feeling of dread that came whenever the mad pirate's attention was fully directed at him, and took comfort in the fact he was once more in control of his destiny.

The next morning James found his men largely recovered from the night's celebrations. The fact that they weren't all hungover and sleeping was a testament that his speech from the day before had stirred them to action. They were preparing themselves for battle.

The ship had been cleared of debris, muskets and pistols were being cleaned, and groups of pirates were sparring on the main deck.

James watched them for a few minutes.

He looked down at his stump, made the mental effort to open the ghost hand, then exhaled as relief washed over him. He had been right-hand dominant. Now he was, well, now he was one-handed, so he supposed that meant he was left-handed. He was proficient with the sword with his left hand but had never mastered it.

"Smee!" James bellowed.

A few moments later, the stout man ran to him, his gray hair matted against his face.

Apparently not every man had been preparing himself for battle.

"My sword," James ordered.

"Aye, Captain," Smee said.

Minutes later Smee returned with his sword. This was not the ornate prized weapon he had stolen from an African prince so many years ago—no that weapon was lost, doubtless at the bottom of the swamp. For a moment, the memory of the loss of his weapon sent anger surging through James.

He could still feel the cold steel in his missing hand. He closed his eyes and unclenched, feeling his hand release the weapon. The sensation was so real that he half expected to hear the sword clattering to the decking.

Then he did hear it.

James' eyes snapped open to see Smee picking up the weapon he had brought. The clumsy fool had dropped it in his haste to return.

James sighed in exasperation and extended his left hand. Smee gave the weapon to him.

He took it, felt the weight. Like all of his weapons, it was perfectly balanced, but that didn't change the fact that holding the sword in his left hand felt off, like a boot on the wrong foot. James himself felt off-balance.

He took a few experimental swings with the sword.

Less than thrilled with how it felt, he walked into the circle of sparing pirates. At once, they stopped and turned to him.

"A pint of grog to the man who can disarm me," James announced.

No one moved to accept his challenge.

"You," James said, pointing the sword at a shirtless man with tattered pants.

The man paled but readied himself.

"En garde," James said.

The man obeyed and advanced, throwing a weak overhead strike at him.

James parried each attack with absolute ease.

"Halt," James yelled, dismissing the man with a wave of his sword. He turned to another pirate, a tall blond-haired man armed with a short sword.

"You," James said, beckoning for the man to approach. "And I'll know if you're half-hearted," he said, pointing his sword at him.

The man advanced—not with the intensity of a man trying to kill him, but neither with the lackluster effort of someone trying to protect his feelings.

The tall pirate's attack was all power and no finesse. James easily sidestepped the man's strikes, using his sword to redirect the man's blows rather than block them outright. But with each parry, James felt himself wanting to engage his right hand, wanting even more to lead with his right foot. After each strike, he would have to make a conscious effort not to strike with his dominant arm, which would slow the reaction of the left.

Then, before he realized what was happening, his shoulder

erupted in pain. His opponent had scored a touch while he had been distracted.

"Halt," James cried.

The man instantly disengaged, his face stricken.

"Good form," James said, nodding to the man. "Thank you, I needed that."

His opponent immediately disappeared into the crowd, clearly relieved to be done.

Smee was at his side a moment later, applying a wet cloth to the injury.

"'Tis nothing," James said, waving him away. "But it's shown me that this is a liability," he said, holding up his stump.

"I need…" James said, thinking out loud, "something."

He turned and left the sparring circle, the crowd parting to give him a clear path. He turned towards the stairs that led to the forecastle.

"It felt good to fight again, Smee" James admitted. "I won't deny it. But something is off, still."

The pair climbed the staircase. Without thinking, James reached out with his right hand to steady himself on the railing as he climbed. His hand touched nothing, of course, but his stump bumped something smooth and cold.

James started.

He had been expecting to feel the wood grain. He looked down. The railing was intersected with vertical posts, roughly the width of a man's arm. Covering the top of each post sat a metal cap, nearly a foot in length. The sheath was held in place with a large nail driven the top.

"Hmmm," James said aloud, stopping.

Smee, unprepared for his captain's sudden stop, walked into James, then stumbled backwards a few steps, his foot slipping off the step, nearly causing him to fall down the stairs.

"S-Sorry, captain," Smee said, regaining his balance.

"I want this cap," James said, ignoring the incident. "This metal cap, Smee. I want it."

"Captain?" came Smee's reply.

"I have an idea," was all James said.

Twenty minutes later James was holding the metal sheath, looking it over. He slipped it over his right arm. The fit felt surprisingly good. It wasn't too tight, nor did it fly off when he swung his arm around.

"Good form," James said to himself, then he spun on his heels and strode over to where the pirates continued to spar.

He waved away the pair who were fighting, dismissing one of them but keeping the second to fight him.

"Matthias," James said to the second man. "You stay."

The remaining pirate, Matthias, was a tall, stern-faced man with long black hair pulled back behind his head in a braid. He advanced on him. Matthias struck with his curved saber, a fast shoulder-height slash.

Instead of taking the blow on his sword, James threw up his right arm, the one brandishing the metal cap, and deflected the strike. The sword bounced off the cap, exposing Matthias to a quick strike from James' sword.

He struck at the pirate's side, turning his sword sideways so as to not mortally wound the man. Matthias grunted as the blow hit him. Then he took a step back, disengaging and nodded approvingly at his captain's effort.

"Again," James ordered.

Matthias came at him again. His attack was different this time but still amounted to the same power-over-form style. This time, James caught the man's sword on his own blade, reaching up to deflect the weapon above his head before spinning towards Matthias' side, bringing his metal-capped arm around to punch him in the ribs.

Everyone within earshot winched as the thud of metal crunching bone sounded through the ring. Matthias staggered back, his face a mask of pain, but did not cry out. After a moment he nodded again to James, approving of the blow, despite the injury he had sustained.

"Can you continue?" James asked.

"Aye," Matthias said, nodding, the movement sending a small wince across his face. He advanced, nonetheless, and thrust at James, who easily sidestepped the attack. The man brought his sword back in a sweeping arc; James parried the attack and again struck the man's side with the capped arm.

The blow dropped the pirate to a knee, but as he dropped, he brought his sword down. James reached up with his right arm to deflect the blow as it struck, but instead of bouncing the sword away from him, the blade skittered across the smooth cap, sending the blade towards his own face.

James threw himself to the ground, the strike sending his hat flying across the deck instead of his head.

Matthias stared at James with a mixture of agony and horror. The agony no doubt from the shattered ribs and the horror from the fact that he had nearly decapitated his captain.

"Captain," Matthias managed. "I didn't mean to–"

"'Tis nothing, well struck," James gasped, waving him off. "See to the barber for that wound."

James wasn't angry. Well he was angry, but not at Matthias. The man had given him invaluable information. His metal cap, while a formidable addition to his arsenal, was still lacking.

He pondered the dilemma as Smee, along with a few other pirates, hauled him to his feet.

"Captain, are you hurt?" Smee asked, dusting James off.

"I'm fine. This is good," he said, raising up his capped stump, "but it's still needs something. Carry on, men."

He once again left the sparring ring and let his mind wander. He needed to let the problem simmer in his mind for a while, and he knew eventually he would find a solution.

He walked towards the starboard side of the ship, where a cluster of pirates were working feverishly on something he couldn't see.

They were casting nets overboard and yelling about something. Large fish and curious dolphins tended to visit the ship from time to time, and from the degree of commotion it sounded like they had caught something large.

James reached the side just as the pirates hauled up a young dolphin. The creature wriggled in their arms. Another pirate ran past James towards the group. He was brandishing a pole with a large steel hook attached to one end.

The pirate raised the weapon, but before he could kill the dolphin, James reached out and yanked the pole from the man's grasp.

James stared at it. Technically it was a tool, not a weapon; a sharp hook used for hanging meat and fish.

The pirates who had been wrestling the dolphin all stopped to stare at James. And in their moment of confusion, the dolphin jerked free of their collective grasp, flopped over the railing, falling back into the safety of the water.

James ignored the men and carried the tool away.

"Smee!" he yelled. "Do we still have a blacksmith?"

"Aye sire, Simmons," Smee said. "He's in the hold."

Smee followed James as he ran from the forecastle down into the belly of the Jolly Roger, where he explained to the blacksmith what he had in mind.

"I want the handle removed from the hook and affixed to this," James said, slightly winded from his run. He handed the pole to Simmons, then slipped the metal cap off his arm.

"Seems easy enough," the Simmons grunted, taking the two pieces from James.

In most cases, it was ludicrous to have a working forge on a ship. But James had wanted the Jolly Roger to be as self-sustaining as possible. The blacksmith shop had all the elements of a typical shop, but scaled down in size.

Despite the relatively small size of the furnace, it still gave off a lot of heat. To help minimize the danger of burning the ship down, the walls of the shop were lined with thin sheets of metal, protecting the wooded walls from the heat.

In addition to the metal walls, channels were cut into the wood behind the metal. Whenever the furnace was in use, pirates from above would pour water into the channels from the deck above, cooling both the metal walls and the surrounding wooden planks.

Simmons removed the hook from the pole, making sure to leave a small stem still attached to the hook.

After that he placed both the hook and the metal cap into the furnace until they began to glow white.

Removing the metal cap from the furnace, he placed it on the nose of his anvil.

Then he removed the hook from the furnace and, placing the long end on the top of his anvil, he hammered the base of the stem, elongating it until it had become twice its original length.

Sparks bounced throughout the ship's hold, hissing into steam as they hit the water-cooled walls within which Simmons worked.

Smee shielded his eyes from the blistering-hot furnace, but James stared, watching the entire process as the glowing metal pieces were broken, heated, and then re-forged.

James found himself relating to the process.

The hook was placed back into the furnace and the blacksmith pumped the billows until finally James, too, had to look away.

Again, Simmons pulled the hook from the furnace, but this time, the stem, thin from being hammered, was nearly molten, threatening to drip. Quickly he brought the hook over to the metal sheath that had cooled from white-hot to a glowing red, and—before it could drip—pressed the molten end of the hook to the tip of the cap.

The stem compressed as he pushed, binding itself to the tip of the cap. He held the hook in place for a long minute then released it. The hook remained securely attacked to the metal sheath.

He waited several more minutes before freeing the weapon—for it was now a weapon—from the anvil's nose and lowering it into a bucket of water.

The weapon screamed as it dropped into the water, filling the hold with angry steam.

Simmons removed it from the water and again placed it into the furnace.

"By reheating it now as a single piece," Simmons explained. "The bond will strengthen, and the metal will harden. It'll be stronger in the end."

Finally, he removed the hook from the furnace and deposited it again into the bucket of water, where he left it until it had cooled.

"I still have to buff and polish it," Simmons said, pulling the completed hook from the water. "But she's strong as anything. I wouldn't want to be on the receiving end of this thing."

James smiled. "Bring it to me when it's completed." He left Simmons to finish his work.

NINE

The next morning, James sat in his cabin, sunlight spilling through the open windows.

The door opened.

James unclenched the ghost hand.

Smee entered. Gripped in his hands was a red box, the kind used to transport daggers.

James stood in the light. His long, black hair, usually thick with wild curls, was tamed for the moment: pulled back and tied behind his head. He was bare-chested, clad only in his customary black pants.

"Smee," James said, yanking the box from the man. "Fetch me

my affects."

"The red jacket, Captain?" Smee asked.

"Aye," James replied.

Smee scurried off to find James' clothes.

James placed the box on the table and flipped open the lid. And there it was. The hook.

With care, he reached in and lifted it out. The hook and cap had been polished to a mirror's sheen.

A smile, real and true, pulled across James' face.

He slipped the weapon over his arm and gasped in astonishment as the ghost hand disappeared.

He beamed at the weapon, rotating his arm around to examine the hook.

The grin he wore widened, then a laugh, a deep, boisterous thing, erupted from deep within his chest.

A second later, he spun on his heels, searching.

He ran to his bed and with a few quick slices with his hook, cut a rough circle of fabric from his sheets. Then, starting near the middle of the circle, he cut slices away from the center to the edge. When he was finished, he had a circular ring of fabric with strips attached to it. He pushed his hook through the center, bringing the central ring down snug with the base of the metal cap, then wrapped each strip of fabric around his arm, each strip tightening the hook to his arm, fastening it, securing it.

As he was finishing, Smee returned with his clothes. He dressed, slowly savoring each piece of his attire.

The crisp, white shirt.

The crimson jacket.

A matching hat complete with a large white feather.

Soot-black boots.

When he had finished dressing, he walked slowly towards the mirror at the end of the cabin. He stood for a long moment, watching his reflection stare at him.

"I am reborn," James whispered to the image in the mirror. "Forged in the fires of Neverland. Behold. I am the siren's fool no longer."

Grinning, he spun on his heels and strode out of the cabin.

His men, as was their custom, were sparring on the deck. The circle of men resembled the one from the day before. James marched into the center of the ring. The current match instantly ended, the combatants quickly fading into the crowd.

"I require a sparring partner," James said. He looked around for the tall man he had fought earlier.

"Smee, where is Matthias?"

"Recovering," Smee explained. "Several of his ribs were broken."

"Hmmm," James frowned, sparing was dangerous, but he still didn't like to injure his own men. He looked the crowd of men over.

"Well?" he called, spreading his arms wide. "Is there none man enough to fight me?" James taunted.

"I'll fight you, Captain Hook," a voice said from behind him.

James spun around to see Mad Rogue slinking out from the crowd, ducking and weaving as he walked.

The ship immediately fell silent.

James felt all eyes turn to him as every man held his breath, waiting to see what retribution their captain would unleash on the crazed pirate for the offensive nickname.

James ignored the slight.

"Hook wants a challenge, no?" Mad Rogue asked, entering the ring.

"He does," James replied. "Is that something you can offer me, Rogue?"

The pirate merely offered a lazy salute.

"Truly?" James asked.

Mad Rogue gave a sheepish grin and nodded his head.

"To the death?" James asked, wondering with what level of intensity the crazed pirate would fight him.

"Not mine," Mad Rogue snickered. "But yours. Then I'll be captain."

James couldn't tell if the man was kidding or not.

They began to circle each other, still talking.

"Are you afraid, Captain Hook?" Mad Rogue asked.

"Afraid?" James scoffed. "I fear nothing."

"Then you've lost," the pirate said sadly, almost whispering. "Fear is good. Fear keeps you safe. Fear reminds you of what you can lose, like friends," he said, his gaze sliding down to James' hook. "And hands."

The stillness on the ship grew even heavier as Mad Rogue once again poked fun at James' missing hand.

"Captain London was not afraid, no. And now he's slain. Peter Pan killed him," Mad Rogue explained, still ducking and weaving as he circled. "Blackbeard was not afraid, now he's gone too. Fear is our friend." Then he burst into a fit of laughter.

James was well aware both of Mad Rogue's previous captains had been bested by Peter Pan. London had been killed when the boy had escaped from his ship's hold and Blackbeard, well, his ship had been reportedly torn to pieces, barely able to make sail, but had headed due west, away from Neverland with as much speed as she could muster.

It seemed defeat awaited those who opposed Peter Pan.

"You are wise, in your own way, Mad Rogue," James said. "I wonder what else I might learn from you. I accept your challenge. En garde, Rogue."

Mad Rogue giggled, then drew one of the throwing knives that hung from the sling on his shoulder. He hurled it at James before launching himself into the air behind it.

The knife was poorly thrown, but still posed a threat. James sidestepped it easily enough then grabbed Mad Rogue by the front of his shirt and, using the pirate's own momentum, threw him into the banister.

The pirate flipped over the top of it, then jumped back to his feet, his sword clear of its scabbard and in hand.

James drew his own sword.

Mad Rogue snickered and ran towards him. The man's constant ducking and bobbing made him more difficult to track than most of the opponents James had faced.

The wild pirate struck, but James parried then riposted. Mad Rogue ducked under the strike and lashed out at James' feet, but a quick hop backwards saved him from a potentially serious wound.

Mad Rogue leapt back up and attacked from above. This was the moment James had been waiting for. He twisted his arm around and caught the blade inside his hook, then struck with his own sword.

But the crazy pirate was resourceful.

He dropped to one knee, sliding the length of his sword through James' hook as he dropped, then caught the strike on his own sword.

James twisted his sword, locking the two blades together. Mad Rogue tried to twist James' own from his grip, but the captain pivoted, decreasing the man's strength, killing his angle. The two men strained against each other for a long moment. Then Mad Rogue made a fatal mistake: he switched to a single-handed grip. But just as James thought the move would end the bout in his favor, he saw Mad Rogue's closed fist slamming into his face.

He staggered backwards, his vision double as he shook his head clear. His sword whipped around in front of him, tracing a defensive maze though the air, as he gathered himself.

"So the gloves come off eh, Rogue?" James said, spitting blood.

Mad Rogue said nothing but smiled, shaking the pain from his fist.

They reengaged, James attacking a fast one, two, one with both sword and hook. Mad Rogue blocked and pivoted, dodging the hook strikes while catching the sword blows on his own weapon.

The bout went on for several minutes, and James was surprised to find he did not outclass the pirate like he thought he would. Mad Rogue, while clearly the less trained fighter, was inventive in a way that nearly gave him the edge.

Mad Rogue slashed at James again. James deflected the blow with his hook, then inwardly flinched as the pirate threw a wild punch towards him. He ducked under it, the man's momentum carrying him off-balance.

James took advantage of the wild strike, rotating his sword around and bringing the hilt down on the pirate's shoulder like a hammer.

The pirate swore and spun away to recover. His spin continued and another dagger came flying towards James.

James threw himself to the deck, the spinning dagger zipped overhead and into the crowd, eliciting a cry of pain from someone behind him.

He ignored the cry, instead, turning his dive into a somersault. He rolled to his feet, his sword arcing up towards Mad Rogue, who was pulling another exotic weapon from inside his tunic.

This time, it was some sort of blow gun. Mad Rogue was raising the weapon to his mouth when James struck, slicing the weapon in two.

James grinned, pleased with the improving accuracy of his left hand.

Mad Rogue stumbled back, then—to James' surprise—charged towards him. A third time, the man reached into his tunic for something. But James was ready for it. He reached back and thrust with his sword towards Mad Rogue's hand.

But what James wasn't ready for was the clearing strike from Mad Rogue's sword that knocked his own weapon away, leaving himself unprotected.

The pirate skirted past James' defenses, landing a full-force punch that heaved all the air from his lungs. But James let the momentum turn his body around and he swung his own arm around as he turned, bringing his hook around where he knew some part of Mad Rogue would be.

He felt the hook make contact, heard the pirate scream in pain, then watched Mad Rogue hit the ground just as James, himself, crumbled to the deck.

Mad Rogue was holding his face, hissing, and cursing as he writhed in pain.

James, on the other hand, calmly waited for his body to remember how to breathe while watching to make sure the other man was finished fighting. After a few long moments, his breathing returned, and he rose, if shakily, to his feet.

Mad Rogue, too, had stopped thrashing and had risen to face James.

He half expected the pirate to resume the fight, but instead, he sheathed his sword and bowed deeply.

"The ship is yours, my captain," Mad Rogue said, yielding the fight to him.

"Good form, Rogue," James said, acknowledging the man with a nod. "Now see to that wound."

The wound, a gash that ran from Mad Rogue's cheek to the corner of his mouth, deepened the stupid grin the man always seemed to wear.

Mad Rogue smiled, then winced as the movement aggravated the cut. Before he left, his eye caught something and he looked towards one of the cabin portholes.

"I'm happy!" Mad Rogue exclaimed, catching his reflection in the window, and seeing the shape of the wound. "Ha-ha! I'm happy!"

The man clapped his hands and skipped away, laughing as he left.

"Well fought, Captain," Smee said, returning his hat to him.

"Hook," James added, inspecting his new appendage for damage or weak spots.

"I'm sorry?" Smee asked, confused.

"Well fought, Captain Hook," James said with a grin.

TEN

Hook didn't want to admit it, but the crazy fool was right. Mad Rogue had insisted that if they were going to return to Neverland, it would have to be without the Jolly Roger. That, and it would have to be with a smaller party, not the hundred-man army he had tried to land in the swamp.

The mission was simple: A small landing party would scout around, establish a hidden camp, and forage for supplies. Then, once the foothold was established and provisions secured, Hook would return with the full force and unleash his retribution on Peter Pan.

As far as his men knew, once they were established on the island, they would search for Neverland's treasures. Which was true, they would search for treasure.

Eventually.

Hook had underestimated Peter Pan and had paid for it. He hadn't viewed the boy as a real threat. In hindsight, he was lucky his hand was all he had lost that night.

"Lesson learned," Hook said, inspecting the gleaming, silver barb that was now a constant reminder of his failure.

The benefit was that he would always be armed.

Technically, he was already always armed, having learned years ago to always carry a blade and pistol, but now he was armed and it was always at the ready. A sword had to be drawn, a pistol had to be pulled from a belt. But his hook, well his hook needn't be drawn or readied.

"Smee," Hook said, turning to his first mate. "We've got supplies enough for five weeks. Neverland," he said pointing to the small speck on the horizon, "is our only chance to resupply. We're too far from any other port now; it's Neverland or nothing."

"But what about Peter Pan?" Smee asked.

"He must have tracked us by watching the ship," he said.

"This time, we'll return at night, and we'll drop a small party off at the wetlands and then leave right away."

"No, no, no," Mad Rogue said, shaking his head and bobbing from one foot to the other. "There is a better place."

"What?" Hook demanded, turning to the man. "If there's a better place, why did you send us to the wetlands in the first place?"

"The swamps are safer, but not better," Mad Rogue explained. "It was the best place to land a large party, but there's a better place for a small group."

"Where?" Hook asked, irritated.

"The southern point," Mad Rogue said. "But it's not safe."

Hook was growing more impatient the longer the crazed pirate spoke. "You just said it was safer, but now it's not?" Hook asked.

"Mermaids," Mad Rogue said. "They don't like the swamps because of the crocs, but they can't go to the southern point because of the current. It's too strong, and it backs up to the cliffs. It's bad for mermaids and bad for boats, but if we make it, and if we come in from the south, Peter Pan won't see us."

Hook considered his words.

"You're sure no one would see us approach?" he said finally.

"Not unless they're in the old mansion that sits atop the cliffs," Mad Rogue replied

"There's a house on the island?" Hook asked, bewildered. "Wouldn't Peter Pan be living in it? I know that's where I'd be if I were stuck on that island."

"No, no, no," Mad Rogue explained, waving his hands dismissively. "The mansion is where his sister was killed, Peter Pan won't go near it."

Hook twisted his mustache as he considered.

"Could we land forty men in secret?" Hook asked.

"At night," Mad Rogue said, nodding. "In the dark."

"Smee," Hook said slowly, still looking at Mad Rogue. "I want you and two score men to go ashore."

He gestured to Mad Rogue with his hook. "And take this one with you," Hook said. "He's proving to be a wealth of information, and I want you to keep him talking."

"Stay hidden, but I need you to secure supplies and establish a foothold and fortify it," Hook explained. "We can't afford to be driven away again before we've been properly supplied. Remember, five weeks of supplies. You've got four to set up a camp."

Smee saluted smartly. "Aye, captain."

* * *

At the southern point, atop a looming, flat-topped cliff, sat the ruins of a once impressive mansion. The old house was a mess of cracked, gray wood and dusty windows—most of which had long since been broken.

The house's walls were built flush along the cliff's edge, as if the builders were paranoid and had wanted to ensure that no one would be able to reach them from the cliff's side.

The cliffs themselves were not black like those in the mermaid's waters, but were instead an ashen gray stone. The color seemed to match the mansion. The cliffs flowed in a straight line down from the top before gaping open at their base into a huge cavern.

But it was the water that held Hook's attention more than anything.

This water was dangerous, deadly even. White, foaming waves surged from the sea, slamming into the cave rocks. The roiling water almost seemed to glow in the darkness.

"All stop," Hook called, when they had fallen within one hundred yards of the cave mouth. "Ready the longboats, Mr. Smee."

"Aye, aye, Captain Hook," Smee stammered, doubtless wishing they were closer to the opening.

The men piled into the boats, securing their gear and supplies as best they could before being lowered into the water.

Mad Rogue clapped his hands wildly, then pounded on the side of the boat.

"Off we go!" he cheered, throwing an arm around Smee, hugging him and patting him on the back excitedly. "Back to Neverland!"

"Four weeks, Mr. Smee," Hook called as the boats rowed towards the cave. "You have one month until we return."

The boats bucked and shuddered as the waves objected to their presence. But the pirates rowed on, continuing towards the island. As the party grew closer to the island, the sea grew more angry. Waves crashed into the boats from every side. Larger ones splashed over the men, forcing half of them to bail water while the rest continued to row, using all of their strength to reach the island.

"We're almost there!" Smee called, over the roar of the water.

As if on cue, Smee's longboat slammed to a stop, throwing him and every other man into the bottom of the boat. He scrambled to his feet, but as he stood, the bottom of boat dropped lower into the water, causing him to stumble.

Almost immediately, he was struck from behind as the boat, rocked by another wave, threw him off-balance once again. This time Smee was slow to rise. His head ached from being slammed into the boards.

The sea, however showed no signs of relenting.

Around him, the pirates struggled to return to their seats as they fought the raging sea. The other two longboats had moved ahead and were now thirty yards from the opening, thirty yards from safety.

Smee opened his mouth to issue a command when he felt the long boat pitch backwards before suddenly surging forward. The longboat was hurled from the water.

Everything moved in slow-motion for Smee. He saw all the men and supplies from the longboat take flight, fanning out and passing over the remaining two boats.

Beside him was Mad Rogue, arms outstretched, a ludicrous smile on his face as he flew.

He watched the longboat flip end over end and smash into the adjacent boat, shattering it and sending its occupants spinning into the sea. He watched the water surge forward into the cave, flooding the rocky shore, before the cave hissed, spitting the water back into the sea.

Suddenly, he saw the cliff wall above the cave's mouth and directly in front of him. Then he saw nothing.

Smee didn't know if he had been knocked out or just dazed by the collision with the cliff. He was being dragged out of the water and up the shore inside the cave. His rescuer deposited him roughly on the ground, then turned him over on his back.

"Silly Smee," Mad Rogue said, patting his bruised face. "You need dust to fly."

Gathering his bearings, he rose to his feet. Now in the relative safety of the cave, Smee could see the men dragging the remaining longboats out of the water and into the back of the cave. Others carefully fished what gear they could from the angry seas, while others tried to remove the bodies still in the water. The sea pulled and tossed their limp forms, almost daring the living to claim its trophies.

"A pity," Smee said, shaking his head. He turned back to the cave to inspect their landing site.

It was enormous, resembling an open mouth that tapered back to a small, narrow throat at the back. He knew from Mad Rogue's briefing that the narrow passageway wound through the cliff and into the dense jungle. There was also another passage, this one even more narrow than the throat, that wound up to the mansion.

"Mr. Smee," a man called, approaching him. "Do we light lanterns?"

Smee considered. The mouth faced due south, and with the water as rough as it was, the chance of a mermaid seeing them were next to nothing.

"I think we should be fine," Smee said at last. "But just in this cave. No lights in the mansion or jungle."

The pirates began lighting lanterns and within minutes, the entire cave was illuminated. It was a small luxury, but one that boosted their spirits.

Smee looked through the pile of supplies that had survived the trip. To his relief, he discovered more tools, ropes, weapons, and other gear as the minutes passed.

He turned to the back of the cave and trotted down the throat.

"Rogue," he called, waving the pirate over. "I suppose we should look around."

The pair made their way into the throat of the cave. The passage was too narrow for them to walk side by side, so Smee let Mad Rogue lead. After fifty paces or so, it opened up to dense foliage. The two pushed between a pair of bushes and into the jungle, the cool damp air from the cave immediately becoming thick and muggy, even in the night.

"This passage will help with air flow," Smee said to himself, then looked skyward. "And the canopy is dense, it should provide good cover." He turned back to inspect the opening. "The passage should remain hidden as long as we don't trample the bushes. I think this will do."

"Bushes can't guard, though," Mad Rogue said.

"I suppose it would make sense to post watches here," Smee said, agreeably.

The pair explored the immediate area for any signs of food, all while keeping watch over the sky for signs of Peter Pan.

They found neither.

It seemed this remote part of the island had been left untouched. Satisfied with their reconnaissance, they returned to the cave, making their way back down the throat.

As they neared the mouth, however, Smee stopped suddenly. His shoulders had been rubbing against the throat's wall as they walked and as he reached out to feel the debris on his shirt, his eyes widened.

"Rogue," he said excitedly. "Fetch me a light."

Mad Rogue trundled off to get a lantern. While he waited, Smee reached his hand out in the dark, feeling the coarse wall. Parts of it felt sandy, loose even, while other parts felt like normal stone.

Moments later Mad Rogue returned, a lantern in his hands. He passed it to Smee.

"Look, there," Smee said, pointing with the lantern. "See that stone? That's sandstone. Watch."

With his he free hand he drew his dagger and started to dig away at the wall. The stone chips easily fell away from his stabbing.

"But this," Smee said, taking a few steps into the throat and tapping a solid portion of stone with his blade. "This, is solid, probably granite I'd guess by the way it sparkles."

"How do you know this?"

Smee dismissed his question with a wave. "Just memories of the old life," he said.

Mad Rogue didn't seem impressed. Rather he looked quite bored.

"Most of this wall is sandstone," Smee explained. "We should be able to excavate it easily enough, but the veins of solid stone should prevent any cave-ins."

Mad Rogue sniffed at the sandy wall, then grunted, non-committal.

"We can carve out rooms," Smee explained. "We don't have to build a fort out in the open, we can stay hidden in here. We can build inside these caves!"

"Capital!" Mad Rogue cheered, his mood changing upon understanding.

They returned to the mouth and discovered most of their tools had been recovered.

Smee explained his plan to the rest of the men. Measurements and calculations were made by the pirates who could count. Their initial efforts went into expanding the throat to allow more than one person to walk down it at a time. While they worked on widening the throat, Smee marked the places where rooms would be hewn into the rock.

He wanted a large central room to gather and sleep in, a second chamber for keeping their stores, and a third to act as a workshop. He wanted to make sure the men sleeping wouldn't be in the same room as the men working. Especially since he was going to be scheduling work around the clock.

In addition to building out the cave, he had to come up with a way for the Jolly Roger to land without risking the lives of her crew every time.

With the initial work of transforming the cave underway, Smee, accompanied by three other men and Mad Rogue, climbed the winding tunnel that led to the mansion.

Mad Rogue, having been there before, led the way. After a few minutes of climbing, the group came to a dead end at a cobblestone wall.

"What now?" one of the pirates asked.

Mad Rogue ignored him. Instead, he busied himself with touching every stone in the wall until he found one that gave way under his touch.

The wall swung towards them, eliciting a yelp of surprise from the men. They all entered through the door and found themselves standing in some sort of cellar. The room was empty save for a few unlit lanterns.

"We'll take these with us," Smee said, pointing to the lanterns. "Leave them unlit though. We don't need to turn this place into a lighthouse."

"Look," another one of the pirates, Mardes, said, walking to the center of the room. The man knelt and inspected the stone floor. It was stained with blood.

"What happened here?" Smee asked.

"Bad things," Mad Rogue said, shaking his head. "Bad things."

Smee, having seen what happened when Mad Rogue was pressed

to share more than he wanted, let the matter slide and led the party upstairs and into another empty room.

The mansion was filled with windows, most of which were missing their panes. The full moon's light streamed through the windows, bathing the house in more than enough light with which to see.

They moved past the empty room and into a long room filled with bunks.

Everyone immediately covered their noses; the scent made Smee want to wretch.

"What is that filth?" Smee asked.

"Death," Mad Rogue replied.

Sure enough, many of the bunks were filled with pirates. Dead, rotting pirates.

"What happened here?" another man asked.

"Peter Pan," Mad Rogue said grimly. "And the others."

"If that flying boy can do this, then why the devil are we here?" Rusty, a red-bearded pirate asked.

No sooner had the man voiced his concerns then a shadow rose from one of the bunks behind him.

"Stow that gab," Smee sputtered, seeing the movement behind the man.

The shadow's eyes seemed to glow in the moonlight. Its mouth parted, exposing large, white teeth.

The Rusty's eyes widened, sensing the movement behind him. But before he could react, the shadow pounced, landing on the man's back and driving him to the ground.

The pair landed in a square of moonlight and the rest of the party could finally see the creature was a panther.

With a single bite, the panther silenced the man forever, then turned to face the rest of the party.

No one moved.

Except for Mad Rogue, who was scrambling up into a vacant bunk.

"No peeking!" he cried, burying his head under a pillow. "No peeking!"

"Shut up, Rogue," Brantley, a greasy-haired man yelled, but his words drew the panther's attention.

The cat jerked his head towards Brantley, locking eyes with him.

Trembling with fear, the man fumbled to free his pistol from his belt. He managed to pulled it free but it slipped from his grasp, clanging on the ground and bouncing out of reach before coming to a rest next to the bed Mad Rogue was occupying.

Mad Rogue uncovered his head long enough to look down at the weapon, then disappeared back under the covers.

Brantley, still shaking with terror, managed to free a second pistol, leveled it at the panther, and fired. But fear kept his aim from firing true, and the shot zipped past the cat and into another room.

"The eyes!" Mad Rogue screamed from underneath his pillow. "No peeking!"

Finally Smee understood. "Its eyes," he called forcing his gaze to the ground. "Brantley, don't stare into its eyes!"

"I can't," Brantley stammered. "It's coming. I can't look away."

Brantley kept his gaze locked on the panther's eyes, and a moment later, the party was reduced from four to three.

The panther turned to Smee. He could feel the animal's eyes on him. Using the strength within every fiber of his being, he kept his head down. Down and away.

The cat padded towards him. A deep growl grumbled from the animal. It sniffed at him then hissed loudly. The animal's hot breath moistened Smee's face, but he kept his head down.

The cat turned to the third pirate.

"Keep your head down, Mardes!" Smee ordered.

Mardes needed no second order—he carefully averted his eyes from the cat's glance. After the longest minute Smee had ever experienced, the panther leapt through the front door and was gone.

Smee breathed a sigh of relief. He looked up as Mad Rogue was climbing down from the bunk.

"Rogue," Smee said, exhaling deeply, "You're a genius."

Mardes was on his feet running towards Mad Rogue.

"Rogue, you crazy fool," he said grabbing the pirate's hand and pumping it furiously. "I'll never doubt you again."

Mad Rogue grinned, showing teeth, then winced and rubbed at his jaw.

"Cats like meat," Mad Rogue said, still idly rubbing his face. He walked over to the bunk the panther had been hiding in and cautiously peered down into it. The bed was occupied by what once had been a pirate. Mad Rogue wrinkled his nose and folded up the four corners of the sheet around the pirate's remains. He tied the corners together, forming a makeshift bag, then hauled it over to the window and threw it out.

"No meat, no cats," Mad Rogue said matter of factly, stooping to wipe his hand clean on the floor.

The three men spent the better part of an hour removing the pirate remains from the house and throwing them out of the windows.

They found six more in the main entry way. Four must have been seated at the table when they had been attacked.

Wrapping a sheet around one of the pirates slumped across the table, Mardes pulled the cards that were still gripped in the man's hands.

"That's a shame," Mardes said, eyeing the cards.

"What?" Smee asked.

"He would have won with this hand," Mardes replied.

The pirates at the table had been killed by pixies, if the tiny stab marks that peppered their bodies were any indication. But the other two nearest the door had met far more gruesome deaths. Large gashes and claw marks meant these men had encountered something worse, like mermaids, in their final moments.

An hour later, all of the bodies had been cleared from the mansion. The door that had been blown off of its hinges had been replaced and closed.

Smee stood in the master suite, peering out the large, broken bay windows. Mad Rogue lay curled up in a ball on the bed behind him surrounded by torn pillows, snoring uproariously.

The sounds of the jungle drifted up from far below like a faint aroma. Smee looked out over the island. The jungle seemed to stretch north forever, eventually graduating to forests. To the east lay the cove they had originally landed in, the shoreline eventually becoming the steep, black cliffs where the mermaids ruled. To the west, the jungle became hilly, which led to vine-wreathed cliffs with cascading waterfalls leading up to the island's twin mountains.

Neverland was not the ripe-for-the-taking jewel Edward Teach had described back in Port Royal when he had convinced James and the other captains to join him. The island's inhabitants were far from the disorganized, weak lot he had described. They were united and they were strong, led by a protector: a boy who seemed anything but.

Neverland was a wild, untamed land. And Smee was not convinced they would ever be anything more than usurpers in this foreign land.

A creak in the floor startled him from his thoughts, making him jump. Mardes walked in. The pirate spared a glance at the snoring Mad Rogue.

"We're all set up here," he said. "Everything is as locked up as it can be." He touched one of the broken panes of glass, still jutting up from the window.

"You know," Mardes said, looking again to the Mad Rogue's sleeping form, "we just watched a panther maul two men right in front of our eyes. And all I can think about is what those pixies and mermaids did to our brothers. What are we doing here?" he lamented. "No treasure is worth this much trouble."

"And what do you think the captain would do to you if he knew what you were saying?"

Mardes stared at Smee for along moment, then looked away.

"Of course," Mardes said. "I'm…I'm just rattled. I didn't mean nothing by it. What's next, sir?" he asked, changing the subject.

"I want two guards on each side of the house," Smee said. "And no more surprises."

"What about Rogue?" Mardes asked.

"Leave him," Smee said. "Head back down. Get seven more for the watch. I'll send a fresh eight to relieve you before dawn."

Mardes saluted and trotted off, leaving Smee alone with his

thoughts, Mad Rogue's snoring, and Mardes' misgivings.

He turned back to the window.

Somewhere out there was Peter Pan.

Smee didn't much care one way or the other about the boy, but Peter had bested Hook upon meeting him, and he knew his captain would not rest until his anger had been satiated. And while he'd never admit it out loud, he too shared in Mardes' fears.

There would doubtless be more blood, and Smee worried how much of it would belong to pirates.

* * *

Their work continued, and by the end of the first week, the pirates had hollowed out the main gathering area as well as several other smaller chambers.

They had quickly realized lighting fires in the main hall, or the Pit, as they had taken to calling it, was incredibly dangerous. The smoke, having nowhere to vent, threatened to suffocate them all. Extinguishing the fires had exasperated the problem, forcing the pirates to huddle in the mansion and the jungle waiting for the smoke clear.

A solution had been posed by Mad Rogue, of all people, who was proving to be quite resourceful, despite the fact that he was completely insane.

He had recommended funneling the ceiling over the top of the Pit and then digging a tunnel out through the cliff's edge. The men had promptly elected Mad Rogue himself as the one to dig the tunnel and he happily obliged. A day later, the tunnel was complete, and a fire was re-lit in the Pit, providing warmth and a means to cook.

With their living quarters in place, Smee turned his men's attention to supplies. Prudence would have led him to send scouts out while they had worked, to ensure that they had food enough to keep working, and to resupply the Jolly Roger, but he had wanted to make sure their foothold in Neverland was well established before they ventured beyond the safety of the caves.

Food was now their last challenge to overcome. And time was running out.

Getting to Neverland had cost them more than was acceptable, both in terms of lives and supplies. Smee needed to come up with a way for his captain to come ashore without risking his life.

Another benefit of having to enlarge the chambers was that the sandstone they mined literally turned to sand after being handled. The men had deposited the sand into the water in the mouth, creating a shore for landing, which tamed the water in the cave, making it much less violent than the water outside.

Smee trundled down to the water's edge. The mouth was enormous. Centuries of rough tides and southern-born winds had carved the cave into the foot of the cliffs.

Mardes joined Smee at the shore.

"I wager we could fit the Jolly Roger in here," Mardes said, looking up at the expansive ceiling. High above their heads, seabirds, with their nests in the crevasse of the ceiling darted, to and fro, their faint squeaks and caws drifting down.

"It's a shame about the depth, though," he continued, looking from the ceiling to the shallows. "I'll bet its deep enough just inside the mouth."

Smee patted Mardes excitedly on the chest, then backed away, stabbing a finger towards the man.

"Mardes, that's it!" Smee cried. "We don't need to find a way to ferry the men from the ship. All we need is to get the ship here!"

"But how?" Mardes asked, his face wrinkling in question. "She'd run aground, and with the sea as rough as it is, we'd never get her free."

"A dock," Smee said, excitedly. "We'll build a dock. That's how we'll get the Jolly Roger here!"

Smee clapped his hands before working his way around the mouth, testing protruding rocks in the shallows for stability, and marking the ones he thought might be strong enough to act as supports.

"Another success," Smee said to himself. "Now, we need to find food."

ELEVEN

Mad Rogue was a tree. He had covered himself from head to toe in black mud and pasted strips of bark to all of his exposed skin. After that, he had shoved willow branches in his shirt collar, sleeves, and belt. For all intents and purposes, Mad Rogue was a tree. And a spot-on convincing one, if he was being honest with himself.

In fact, the way the other members of the foraging party regarded him—with raised brows and jealous whispers—told him just how accurate his disguise was and how much they wished they had thought of the idea.

"Come along, boys," Mad Rogue called. "Follow me, I am the

forest."

The group had ventured through the jungle, fanning out at times, then regrouped to share information on what they had found. Or rather, hadn't found.

They had ventured several miles since leaving the safety of the cliffs and the only thing of value that they had gathered was a map of Neverland that was growing in both size and detail as the day wore on.

But now, the party had entered a clearing where the dense jungle graduated from tropical jungle to forest at the other end of the clearing.

"It's a few hours from nightfall," Jakes, a square-jawed man with light brown hair said, looking up at the sky. "Let's make camp in the clearing then explore the forest tomorrow."

The rest of the party nodded in agreement, but Mad Rogue was not convinced. With exaggerated slowness, he shifted his gaze to the sky, as if moving too quickly would invite some sort of doom.

"The sky is not safe," Mad Rogue said. He rubbed at his chin idly, a chunk of bark falling free from his face.

"Belay that gab, Rogue," Jakes said, waving his hand dismissively, unslinging his pack from his shoulders. "This'll do just fine."

The rest of the foraging party followed suit, removing their own packs and starting to make camp. A few men set to building a fire in the center of the clearing, while others scavenged for dry wood.

"Fools," Mad Rogue, muttered, slinking into the forest. He found a willow tree with low-hanging branches and climbed it. He found a branch that would hide him from prying eyes above but still give him a full view of the fool's camp below.

Evening's light eventually failed, bathing the clearing in humid darkness, save for the campfire's orange glow. The fools sat in a ring around the fire, their bodies casting shadows on the trees behind them. The shadows danced silently around the edges of the clearing, as if trying to get the attention of their owners, a silent warning that shadows in the night could not be trusted.

Mad Rogue could hear their warning clearly enough and he waved back, knowing full well the dangers open skies represented.

But the shadows had eyes for their owners alone.

The fire slowly died, and with it, the intensity of the shadow's dance. The shadows eventually resigned themselves to the sad fate only they and Mad Rogue were aware of. Mad Rogue spent the entire evening in the tree, leaving only once to find a fallen branch large enough to use as a weapon, should the need arise.

Mad Rogue was the only of them who had stepped foot on Neverland before. And Neverland was an unkind land. He knew the pirates knew the dangers mermaids represented in her waters. But there were other dangers that stalked the skies.

Pixies.

He wrinkled his nose at the memory of them, but specifically of her, the golden pixie, the one who had stolen Little Kite before showering him in dust and allowing him to tumble, helpless, into the night.

He would find that golden pixie and turn her back into dust. But lighting a beacon in the night was no way to get revenge, just to get killed. He knew the pixies patrolled the skies above their island, much like the mers patrolled the sea.

One of the fools sat up, crawled over to the fire, and put more wood on it. Moments later, the fire regained its strength and the dancing shadows began to move with renewed urgency.

Mad Rogue shook his head ruefully, dried mud flaking away as he moved. He had tried to explain the pixies patrolled at night and that fire would surely attract their attention.

"We'll be discovered for sure, Willow," Mad Rogue said to the tree he sat in. "A patrol just like that one will find us," he said, pointing to the group of pixies that had just descended to inspect the fire in the clearing.

Mad Rogue gasped, just realizing what he was seeing. The stick fell from his grasp, bouncing loudly from branch to branch as it fell. Mad Rogue sat perfectly still, thinking tree thoughts and hoping the pixies wouldn't see through his disguise.

Of course they didn't notice him. He was, after all, a tree. But one of the men did. Jakes, now awake, sat upright and looked towards the forest where Mad Rogue lay hidden.

As one, the pixies, five of them, assaulted Jakes, trying to clamp his mouth shut and force him against the ground.

In the same instant, Mad Rogue dropped from his branch, grabbed his staff, and charged towards Jakes. The pixies were doing a good job of keeping him pinned to the ground, which surprised Jakes, if the look on his face was any indication. But Mad Rogue had faced pixies before, he knew what they were capable of.

He also knew if you hit them with enough force… He brought his staff back then swung it forward as hard as he could. He connected both with a pixie and Jakes' face. The pixie erupted into a shower of dust. Jakes, on the other hand, howled in pain as Mad Rogue bludgeoned him over and over.

Mad Rogue struck a second pixie, then a third, turning each of them into bursts of golden brilliance.

The remaining two fairies took to the air as the rest of the foraging party, jolted awake by Jakes' cries, started to look around the clearing for the source of alarm.

Mad Rogue ignored Jakes' cries of pain to stoop and yank the man's pistol free from his belt, firing it and leaving only a single pixie in the air.

It flew higher, its bright glow starting to flash. No doubt it was trying to raise the alarm and get reinforcements. Mad Rogue dashed after it. He weaved between pirates waking up. Right next to the fire was a pirate. He was on his hands and knees, searching for his weapons. Mad Rogue stepped on the man's back and vaulted over the campfire. He flipped the pistol around, catching it by the barrel and swung it, handle first, at the last pixie.

He connected and the creature exploded into a spray of dust and light.

Mad Rogue landed awkwardly, a cloud of dust from his caked-on mud erupting around him. His willow branches thrashed and swayed with the motion.

"The sky is not safe," he hissed, turning to glare at each pirate as he spoke.

The pirates quickly scattered the fire, reducing it to ashes and coals.

Jakes stumbled over to him, still dazed from his beating.

"Rogue," the man gasped, looking past Mad Rogue, doubtless seeing double and unsure which Mad Rogue to address. "You saved me," he said. "You saved all of us. I'll never doubt you again."

Mad Rogue sniffed, ignoring the comment.

"Is that dust?" another pirate asked, coming up to Mad Rogue and pointing to the small specs of light that covered the top of Mad Rogue's hand.

Mad Rogue looked down at his hand; it was still caked in mud, so the dust hadn't yet soaked into his skin. He gasped and shook his hand clean, shaking the dust off.

"So what do we do now?" another pirate asked.

"We hide in the forest!" Mad Rogue ordered, scolding the rest of the party. "We dress like trees and we hide in the forest!"

The rest of the party nodded grimly, gathered up their belongings, and, without speaking, followed Mad Rogue into the forest.

An hour later, they were all trees.

* * *

The next morning the party rose. Each man had spent the night sleeping at the base of whatever tree he had taken branches from the night before for his disguise.

The party, now led by Mad Rogue, continued to make their way deeper into Neverland in search of food. Their progress was slowed considerably by the fact that every hour or so they would have to stop and reapply mud and bark to their skin as well as add fresh branches to their disguise. Considering the events of the night before, no one complained.

Morning wore into midday, and their only findings were the bulging water skins each man carried slung over a shoulder. Apart from the abundance of fresh water, however, the luscious, treasure-filled

Neverland that had been promised to all of them remained hidden.

"The trip seems busted," Jakes said, looking up at the sun through the forest canopy. "There's plants everywhere, but nothing to eat."

A few of the other men grunted in agreement but immediately fell silent as Mad Rogue raised his staff, a sign they had all come to understand meant he had new orders for them.

"Noses," Mad Rogue said, sniffing.

"He's right," one of the men exclaimed. "I smell it too!"

"Oranges!" Jakes cried, looking around for the source of the aroma.

"There!" another man cried, pointing ahead.

Through the trees, at the edge of the forest, they could see smaller trees, dotted with small, orange circles.

They ran from the forest into the grove of orange trees, bark flaking off and a cloud of dust trailing behind them as they ran.

They cheered and danced as they inspected the grove. There were at least a hundred orange trees filled with fruit, their boughs sagging under the weight of the fruit.

The sight seemed oddly cannibalistic as the pirates, still disguised as trees, began to devour the oranges. Some of them used knives to cut the fruit into pieces, while others simply bit into them, spitting out the peels, exposing the juicy flesh underneath.

Jakes walked up to Mad Rogue.

Mad Rogue was opening his mouth as wide as he could before snapping his teeth together and then massaging his jaw.

"Well done, Rouge," Jakes laughed, tossing an orange to Mad Rogue.

But the pirate ducked under the fruit, allowing it to sail past him.

"Uh uh," Mad Rogue said. "Too sticky."

Jakes shrugged then ripped the fruit in half, the sweet juice running down his arm to drip from his elbow. He smiled and bit into half the orange. The juice repeated its journey, this time down his chin and neck.

"You're an odd one, Rogue," Jakes said, patting the pirate on the back. "No doubt there, but you know your stuff."

Mad Rogue grunted noncommittally.

"What's wrong with your jaw?" Jakes asked.

"Teeth hurt," Mad Rogue replied.

"Have some oranges," Jakes insisted, chuckling. "You've got scurvy, mate."

"Scurvy?" Mad Rogue asked, eyeing the fruit hanging from the tree.

"Aye," Jakes replied. "Your teeth start to hurt, but when it gets bad, they'll fall out. Whatever's in the oranges makes it go away."

Mad Rogue yanked the half-eaten fruit from Jakes' hand, gobbling it before the man could object.

Jakes laughed again, tossing a second fruit to Mad Rogue. The man snatched the orange out of the air and set about eating it as well.

Jakes turned to survey the grove of trees again.

Dotted throughout the grove lay an assortment of willow, maple, and one unfortunate pine tree: his men. They were all lounging under the orange trees, stuffing themselves with fruit.

"Oi!" Jakes called to the rest of the party. "What say we fill our bellies and bags with oranges, then head back and tell Smee the good news. A handful of trips back here and we can just about strip this grove bare."

The foraging party ate their fill, then packed their empty sacks with oranges. The pirates, orange trees now, headed south, returning to the cave.

TWELVE

Smee couldn't be more happy. He had spent the rest of the day, and much of the night, inspecting rocks and making drawings for the dock. Now, after getting a few hours' sleep, he was back at it.

He had sent the rest of his men, the ones who were not still digging out the rooms, into the jungle in search of straight trees. And, as luck would have it, the jungle canopy was dense. He'd be able to cut down as many trees as they needed without worrying about exposing themselves to the sky.

The men busied themselves selecting the straightest and widest trees they could find. Smee would oversee, making sure each removed tree wouldn't have a detrimental impact on the overhead canopy cover.

Once the tree had been felled, it would be stripped of its branches. The branches would be cut to size and stacked in the pit to be used as kindling and firewood, depending on their sizes.

Once the tree had been de-branched, it would be cut into boards, lengthwise. Progress was slow the first couple of tries as the few saws the pirates had were not made for this type of cutting, but after fine-tuning their techniques, they managed to consistently yield five to seven four-inch thick and boards from each tree. The boards were thicker than was normally used, but it was probably for the better considering the pounding the dock would be taking by the waves. Heavier planks would stand up better against waves.

A few of the trees were not planked but were kept intact. These would be used as support struts to help balance the weight of the dock in the places were exposed stones were lacking.

In just three weeks Smee had established a foothold in Neverland, secured food sources and water sources, and designed a means by which to both land and hide the Jolly Roger on the island away from the prying eyes of fairies, mermaids, and Peter Pan.

Now all that remained was to build the dock.

It turned out that the support struts – the trees that had not been cut down into planks – still had to be cut to size. They proved to be too long to fit down the throat. The tunnel's gently winding path wouldn't allow for a thirty foot long tree to be carried through. So Smee had to have his men dig the hole in the rocky shore where the strut would be installed. Smee would make his measurements, then send a courier down the throat and into the jungle with instructions for how long to make the strut. The men would cut the strut to length, then carry it through the throat to the mouth to be delivered.

Once the strut was on the shore, Smee would instruct where it would be placed, and the men would have to dig the hole again, as the water would have filled in the hole in the time it took for the courier to make his trip, then the strut would be lowered in the hole, filled in with sand, and have rocks pilled around it.

It wasn't ideal, and added considerable time to the construction, but it worked. It took two full days to get all of the struts in place. It took another two to get the dock's frame built onto the struts and supporting rocks. The trick had been figuring out how to attach wooden planks to the rocks and struts.

They did have nails, but not nearly enough to attached everything solidly in place. There were many more available back on the Jolly Roger. The Man of War was essentially a floating town, and the Jolly Roger was no exception. She was well stocked with all manner of supplies, so all they had to do was get her to land safely in the mouth and they could secure the dock properly.

Smee focused on securing the frame to the struts. He split his remaining men in half. Half of them drove nails into the frame while the other half cut boards to length and laid them on the top of the frame.

Smee spent his time calculating lumber usage, double checking measurements and triple checking their time, making sure that they'd have time enough to finish the dock for their captain. Things were looking good. By Smee's calculations, they would be done with a day and a half to spare.

Sure enough, midday on the day before Captain Hook would

return to Neverland, the dock was done. Smee stood at the back of the throat, looking out over the mouth. The dock wrapped around the interior sides of the cave. The addition of the dock reinforced the mouth imagery of the cavern as the docks ended up resembling molars for the giant, gaping mouth.

"I can't believe it," Mardes said. "We actually did it."

Smee beamed, satisfied he had fulfilled his orders.

"And the foraging party has returned," Mardes added. "They found an orange grove, and they even managed to shoot a few birds on their way back."

Smee's smiled widened to a broad grin that trenched a path across his fat cheeks. Things were going well. So well in fact that Smee thought the men needed a reward.

"Let's take the rest of the day off," Smee said. "The dock is finished, our stores are being filled. We'll have time enough tomorrow for checking the water for errant rocks and lighting the signal fires."

Mardes nodded.

Pirates excelled at sailing, killing, pillaging and the sorts, but if there was one thing they held mastery over, it was resting. They slept, ate, drank, and made themselves utterly useless. A pirate lived for these moments. All other endeavors were either obstacles to overcome or steps to take before he could find himself drunk on a beach.

And drunk in a cave was just as good, maybe better even. There was no hot sun beating down on them.

Smee, while taking it easy, did not overindulge since he abstained from drink. He still had planning to do and someone had to remain alert.

Eventually the singing faded to snoring and the gruff snorts and coughs of sleeping men echoed through the caves.

Smee walked the pirate stronghold, from the newly-laid docks to the storerooms and up to the old mansion to look out over Neverland. He had done a fine job by his own measure and hopefully by Captain Hook's as well.

Their fortune had been good so far. Clear thinking and planning had filled their stores, won them a safe stronghold, and even kept them hidden from the island's inhabitants.

Smee stood in the master's suite and looked out over Neverland. A trio of shooting stars streaked across the sky.

He smiled at the sight.

Shooting stars were good luck. How much more luck would three bring?

He returned to the hold, confident that with their captain's return on the morrow, they were entrenched enough and ready for whatever Captain Hook had in mind.

THIRTEEN

D id you see that?" Tolan, a dark-haired and well-muscled fairy, asked.

His companions turned to see where he pointed.

It was the old mansion atop the southern rise.

"What was it?" a female fairy, Lorel, asked. She was slender, with blond hair so light it seemed white in the moonlight.

"Movement, or something," Tolan answered. "I don't know, probably nothing."

The third, Darean, clacked his tongue to get the other two's attention. Darean didn't speak, he couldn't. Instead, he pointed adamantly towards the abandoned house in the distance.

Up until very recently, the fairies had been locked in a conflict with the kites, birds of prey. The conflict had escalated over the span of several years, finally coming to a head with the kites assaulting the fairies' home en mass.

They had poured into White Falls and every fairy had hurled themselves at the invading birds.

Darean, known for his skill with the bow, had been among them, firing arrows into anything with feathers.

During the battle, however, he had been knocked to the ground from behind by a kite. He had landed roughly on the stone floor, only to have the bird land on top of him, pinning him to the ground. He had dodged beak strikes as he twisted and squirmed, managing to twist away only to sustain a slash to his neck that damaged his voice to the point where he could only whisper, but at great pains.

While fairies had the ability to mend, repair, and create nearly anything with their dust, his injuries had been largely internal, and there was no way to access and repair the wound.

Tolan pitied him, though he would never say it aloud. To have such a debilitating injury made permanent seemed unfair.

Darean raised his eyebrows and continued to point.

Tolan nodded.

"You're right, of course, Dare," he said. "We should check it out."

The trio dimmed their glow until each of their lights had disappeared completely, then adjusted their path to take them down towards the mansion.

Fairies glowed brilliantly by nature, but they had the ability to either dampen or amplify their glow. Both took considerable effort, and now that the fairies enjoyed peace between both the mers and kites, there hadn't been reason to suppress their glow on night patrols—something Tolan was very thankful for. But if there was something amiss or suspicious in the old manor, there was no reason to go flying in blazing like shooting stars.

The old mansion looked as it always did: broken windows and missing roof slats marred the once-impressive structure.

Tolan reached for his sword, a blade nearly the length of his body. It lay against his back, tucked between his wings. Twisting the hilt released the clip that held the weapon in place, freeing it.

Darean drew his bow and pulled an arrow free from the quiver, similarly secured between his wings. He notched an arrow to the string, but held it at half-taut.

Lorel, too, drew her weapons, a pair of diamond-bright daggers.

The trio parted as they came to the mansion. Tolan and Lorel slipped through a broken window into a large bedroom while Darean entered through a hole in the roof to provide support from above should anything be lurking.

Tolan looked around the bedroom.

"Nothing but torn pillows and dust," he whispered. "It seems unchanged."

"Here," Lorel hissed, nodding towards the next room.

They entered a room filled with bunks and a table. There were blood stains on the floor and in the sheets and pillows on the beds.

"These look more recent," Lorel noted, landing lightly on the side of a bunk to inspect the evidence.

"Yes," Tolan admitted, "but it's weeks old, maybe longer."

He pointed at the scratches in the floor and the damaged table.

"This is from the night we raided. When we tried to rescue Mara."

He shook his head, remembering the night Mara died. Peter,

along with a small band of fairies and mers, had blitzed the house, blowing the door off of its hinges and assaulting and killing nearly twenty pirates in less than a minute.

The boy had been consumed with grief and rage and had run his body ragged just to get there. But Mara's injuries had been too great even for the fairies' dust or the mers' medicines to overcome.

In the end, though, all had not been lost. A fairy, Siene, had resolved Mara, saving the girl's essence and merging it with her own. The process had saved Mara and changed Siene, giving birth to a new fairy: Tinker Belle, a spitfire of a fairy.

Darean flew from bunk to bunk, indicating the absence of all bodies.

"You're right, where are the bodies?" Lorel asked, catching Darean's meaning.

Tolan shrugged. "It's been weeks, a few months even. I'll bet scavengers picked this place clean within days of our assault."

The trio gave the abandoned house one more look before resuming their patrol.

FOURTEEN

Now the gaping mouth had eyes. Someone had managed to scale the cliffs above the cavern opening and chisel out two holes for lanterns, or signal fires.

"Good form, Smee," Hook whispered. "So you must have a berth for us after all."

Clearly, Smee's intent had been to help guide the Jolly Roger safely to the cave in the dark, but the lights made the cave look like a sinister creature staring Hook down, daring him to enter its mouth.

Hook found the imagery fitting.

He inhaled. The air, tinged with the salty tang of seawater and kelp, cleared his mind.

The moonlight sparkled over the blue and black waves, creating small slivers that danced along the water in erratic patterns.

"Helm is relieved," Hook said, turning to the two helmsmen on duty.

"Sir?" one of them asked.

"Dismissed," Hook insisted, his tone turning sharp.

The helmsmen gave each other a quick glance. Ships of this size required two, sometimes three, men at the helm.

"Helm is being relieved," one of them, a thin man named Bames said, trying to stifle his doubts, and clearly failing. "Rudder amidships."

"Very well," Hook replied, taking hold of the ship's wheel. "Helm has been relieved."

A night-black stained wood, inlaid with gold and ivory, the ship's wheel was the jewel of the Jolly Roger.

"Helm is in hand, rudder amidships," Hook finished.

He grunted as a shifting current pulled at the rudder. But he held fast, shifting his weight and leaning into the wheel, holding it steady and ensuring the rudder was pointed directly towards the cave in the distance. He looped his hook underneath one of the rungs, locking his arm in place, and held.

"Full sails," Hook commanded.

"Capt'n," Bames said cautiously, looking up, "I don't think that would be advisable with the wind at this speed, if we overpower the sails–"

"If the wind maintains, we can reach the cave without tacking," Hook snapped. "We don't know if anyone is watching these waters.

We need to make it to the cave as fast as possible."

"Ahh," Bames said, nodding. "So we'll make a straight run to the cave?" he asked.

"Aye," Hook grunted. "Now give my order."

"Full sails!" Bames bellowed.

The ship creaked as the southern breeze filled the remaining sails, surging the ship forward. The helm instantly fought Hook as the water pulled and yanked at the rudder.

He blinked sweat from his eyes and leaned into the helm even farther. He was determined to bring his ship into harbor, determined to be the one to lead his men back to Neverland.

The mouth lay just ahead, and the waves turned from black and strong to white and all-powerful, churning angrily around the ship. The waves smashed against the ship, almost as if Neverland herself were trying to refuse him entry.

"I will have what I will have," Hook whispered to the island. "And I will not be deterred."

He reset his footing and looped his hook a rung lower, then braced himself as the seas continued to protest his invasion.

The wind howled past him, funneling into the mouth and gaining speed.

"Sir," Bames stammered. "Our speed."

"Hold," Hook ordered.

"Sir?" he pressed.

"Hold!" Hook repeated, yelling.

Somewhere from the depths around them, a deep rumble sounded, then a tremendous boom as the surging waves rocked the ship forward.

"All stop! Furl sails!" Hook yelled, feeling the helm start to slacken in his grip.

The men scrambled to roll the sails, and within minutes the ship's breakneck speed began to slow. The ship glided through the final stretch of the foaming water and entered into the relative safety of the cavern mouth.

Along one side of the cave, starboard of the ship, was a newly built dock.

Smee had done his job well. The mouth was large enough to hide the Jolly Roger, and with the addition of the dock, getting from the ship to land would be an easy task.

Birds cried and erupted from crags in the ceiling of the cave, cawing and diving at the men rolling the sails.

"Mooring lines away!" pirates called as they hurled ropes to their fellows on the dock, who in turn fastened them to the new dock struts.

Hook released the helm and turned to see an audience had assembled to watch him single-handedly—literally—pilot the ship to safety. The officer of the watch, Bames, smiled nervously.

"Well done, sir," he stammered. "I apologize for questioning you, sir. It will never happen again."

"Think nothing of it, brother," Hook said, patting the man's shoulder as he passed by him. "We all suffer doubt on occasion."

He walked down the stairs as the ship was being secured to the dock, descended the boarding ramp, and stepped onto the dock, back onto Neverland. Smee was waiting for him.

"Mr. Smee," Hook said, taking in the dock, cavern, and lantern-lined tunnel that stretched down the back of the mouth. "I asked you to build me a foothold."

"Yes, sir. You did," Smee replied, his voice wavering.

"You did not give me a foothold, Smee," Hook accused.

"I didn't?"

"No," Hook replied, then smiled. "You built me a fortress. Good form, Mr. Smee. Jolly well done."

Color returned to Smee's face as he blew out a breath in relief. "May I show you around?" Smee asked

"Please," Hook replied.

Hook allowed himself to be lead throughout the cavern.

"Stupendous, Smee," Hook said as they made their way through the chambers. "Absolutely stupendous. This will make a fine home, and an even better one with some additions."

"Additions, sir?" Smee said.

"Indeed," Hook replied. "Your work is exceptional, but now that I'm here, now that I see the full potential of this cave, I want a more permeant presence."

"Permeant, sir?" Smee asked.

"The world is unkind to pirates," Hook explained. "And while Neverland is no safe harbor, it may prove to be a better option than ports we've visited in the past. If we can secure this place, and then recruit others, we can outlast any port that falls into British hands."

The pair walked back into the mouth, and Hook examined the wall opposite the dock.

"What if we built," Hook said, indicating with a wave of his hand the entire length of the mouth, "something, there. Some sort of dwelling there—a town, maybe. Smee, what if we built a city into these cliffs?"

"A city?" Smee asked, eyes widening.

"Aye," Hook said. "We've over a hundred men on the Jolly Roger, and we'd have room for more if we built out this place."

Smee nodded, absently, then shook his head. "But I don't know how to build a city. Docks are one thing, but whole buildings?"

"Don't fret, Smee," Hook replied, patting the top of the man's head. "We'll sort that out later."

"So what now?" Smee asked.

"It's simple," Hook said, ice creeping into his voice. "We kill Peter Pan and then reshape Neverland as we see fit. Come, we've got fires to start."

FIFTEEN

Peter watched Tinker Belle eating the giant grape. Well, it wasn't really giant, but compared to the fairy, it was enormous.

She held the purple fruit in both hands and had her head buried inside it. She reappeared from behind it, her face stained purple and dripping.

She caught his eye and grinned up at him.

"I wish I could find fruit that big for me," Peter mused, looking at the fruit in his own hands. "It would be strawberries though, not grapes."

"Nah," Tinker Belle said, pausing to pull the pit free from the grape and toss it over her shoulder. "Seeds are obnoxious. And sharp."

Peter scrutinized the strawberry he was holding.

"A strawberry seed almost killed Tolan once," Tinker Belle said.

"Really?" Peter exclaimed.

"No," Tinker Belle said, snickering.

Peter scowled at her, throwing a strawberry stem at her which she easily ducked.

Around them, fairies and kites harvested fruit from the groves, a once long-held tradition that had been interrupted by war but had resumed.

Kites and fairies would collect fruit from various groves throughout the island, then bring them to White Falls for preserving.

"How is the fruit preserved?" Peter asked, watching the kites and fairies fly overhead.

"It's actually one of the simplest things we do," Tinker Belle said. "Want to see?"

"Absolutely!" Peter said, getting to his feet.

Tinker Belle ate the final piece of grape then took off, leading the way back to White Falls.

They approached from above the falls, so rather than going through the water, they entered through the tunnels.

Tinker Belle led Peter into a chamber he had not yet explored.

The chamber was no more than a few feet deep with six shelves cut out of the stone wall no more than a foot deep. Several tiny stations lined the shelves. Each station had a long table and a tiny groove in the base of the shelf that held a cauldron. Next to the cauldron, opposite the long table, sat another table, only this one was much smaller.

Each station was occupied by several fairies—two at the table, one at the cauldron, and one behind the station, near the wall.

The tables were filled with strawberries, grapes, blackberries, raspberries, and countless other varieties, several of which Peter did not recognize.

The fairy next to the cauldron would take a piece of fruit from the end of the table and submerge it in the dust. The fairies working at the long table would move the rest of the fruit down, filling in the gap created by taking the fruit. After a few seconds, he would pull the fruit out and place it on the smaller table and inspect it, making sure it had been fully coated.

He only had a few seconds because the dust would quickly soak into the fruit, leaving it looking no different than when he had first submerged it.

Once he was satisfied with his work, he would leave the fruit on the table and walk back to the long table and grab another piece of fruit that had been moved to the edge. Then he would repeat the process.

Meanwhile, the fairy in the back would take the preserved fruit and bring it to the back wall. Depending on what type of fruit it was, she would place it inside of one of the several windows cut into the wall Peter had not noticed until now.

A pair of tiny hands would take the preserved fruit from inside the window and disappear with it.

"The stores are on the other side of those windows," Tinker Belle explained. "There are also groups of fairies who bring the fresh fruit to the tables from the main collection hall and another group of fairies who refill the cauldrons for the workers."

"Fascinating," Peter said, watching a pair of fairies fly past carrying a cauldron of dust between them.

The pair zipped past, slowed only slightly by their burden. They deposited the cauldron just as another pair removed an empty one. Another fairy dunked a piece of fruit, this one a crimson raspberry, into the new cauldron as if it had been there the whole time; his workflow unbroken.

"How long does the preserved food last?" Peter asked, seeing the similarities between the process and his own experience falling into the dust reservoir.

Tinker Belle shrugged.

"Forever," she said. "Or at least we've never had anything spoil."

"Never?" Peter asked.

"Wait here," Tinker Belle said before disappearing through one of the doors in the back of the shelf.

She returned a minute later, holding a ripe strawberry with one hand by the leaves. She grabbed an identical strawberry from one of the long tables, carrying both over to Peter.

"Close your eyes," she ordered.

He closed them.

"Open them," she ordered again.

In front of him sat the two strawberries.

"One was picked today," she explained. "The other was not."

Peter looked from one to the other. They looked like both had come from the grove today.

"Which one is preserved?" Tinker Belle asked.

Peter picked up both pieces of fruit, hefting their weight in his hands, testing to see if dust added any additional weight to the fruit.

It didn't.

He sniffed each strawberry, checking to see if the dust changed the fruit's smell, or, even, if the dust itself had an unique smell.

It didn't.

Finally, he tasted each fruit. Both were equally juicy and full of flavor. There was absolutely no difference between the two of them.

"I have no idea," Peter laughed. "Which one is preserved?"

Tinker Belle pointed to the half-eaten fruit in his right hand.

"That one," she said.

Peter inspected the fruit more closely.

"It's no different," Peter said, amazed. "How old is it?"

"Very," Tinker Belle said, winking.

"So," Peter said. "What about me?"

He looked around at the fruit being dipped in the dust.

"I fell in the dust just like all of these," he continued. "Am I 'preserved' now too?"

Tinker Belle shrugged, seemingly unconcerned.

"I guess we'll know in fifty years or so," she said.

"Never changing?" Peter said, considering the possibility. "Never growing up?"

"That would be difficult," Tinker Belle said, nodding solemnly.

"Difficult?" Peter asked. "That would be amazing!"

"But, you were only in the reservoir a few seconds," Tinker Belle explained. "And you're much bigger than a strawberry."

"True," Peter agreed. "You're probably right, being able to fly is probably the only effect from the dust."

He popped the preserved fruit into his mouth. "It's a fun thought," he said as he chewed, and imagined never growing old and living forever.

The pair left the shelves and made their way back to the main cavern.

Peter was surprised to find Shiiklah in the main hall. She towered over the passing fairies, none of who paid her any heed. Her pale skin, normally a gray and green tint, took on a metallic glow as it reflected the light from the fairies.

She stood in the center of the room, on top of the monument to the kite, and conversed with Adelaide. The fairy queen's normal retinue was gone, leaving only the two of them.

"Pan Hakki," Shiiklah said, nodding to him as he approached.

"Shiiklah?" Peter said, returning the nod. "Is everything all right?"

"Everything is fine," Adelaide reassured. "We were actually discussing you."

"Me?" Peter asked. "What about me?"

Adelaide looked to Shiiklah, who, after a long moment, nodded once.

"Come with me," Adelaide said.

She led the group through the narrow, winding confines of White Falls towards the very back of the cave. The smooth, gem-studded walls gave way to rough, unfinished stone abruptly.

Stalagmites thrust up from the ground in increasing number as they made their way to the back of the cave.

"What is this place?" Peter asked.

No one answered. Instead they continued deeper into the cave.

The hall narrowed into a small corridor. It was wide enough for Peter and Shiiklah to fit sideways and more than wide enough for the two fairies to fly though, but for some reason, Tinker Belle and

Adelaide did not fly through. Instead, they landed on deep shelves cut into the wall that held tiny spikes.

The fairies walked slowly, weaving through the spikes.

Peter drew closer and realized the tiny stone spikes were not spikes at all. They were statues of fairies.

Peter leaned in to inspect one. Whoever had made these possessed a mastery in their craft beyond anything Peter had ever seen.

The fairy's face was flawless; the tiny mouth and perfectly pointed nose almost life-like.

"These statues," Peter said, awestruck. "They're incredible."

"They're not statues," Adelaide said, sadly. "They're fairies."

Peter staggered backwards.

"What?" he said, his eyes wide with shock.

Adelaide walked across the shelf she had landed on, winding around the stone creatures.

"Dust," Adelaide said, extending her hand and sprinkling her fingertips. Almost immediately, the golden dust began to flake away from her.

"It's what we're made of," she explained. "And it regenerates within us, but if we expel too much of it…" She trailed off, her eyes sliding from her own hand to one of the stone fairies.

The figure was on one knee, stooped slightly. Her right hand was fully extended, fingers splayed as if reaching out for something.

Adelaide slid to her knees and reached out, lacing her own fingers between the stone figure's ones.

"Sister," she said to the statue, almost in a whisper. "Have I led them well?"

It was a rare, unguarded moment for the composed fairy queen.

"Yesss," Shiiklah replied, answering her as she squeezed through the narrow passage.

Adelaide blinked and looked away, a sad smile tracing her lips as her normal composure returned. She rose to her feet and continued down the path.

Peter looked around the hall, or crypt, now that he knew what it really was. There were thousands upon thousands of stone fairies all around him. No two figures held the same pose. They all wore expressions varying from violent and angry to peaceful and resigned. Some of them stood, facing off against some unseen threat, while others knelt or sat, much like the one Adelaide had stopped by.

Peter could have spent the rest of the day inspecting each figure, but the party continued to make its way through the narrow tunnel.

"Each figure," Adelaide explained, as she continued to wind through the army of stone fairies "shows the fairy's final moment of life. Frozen in time forever."

She gently touched each one as she passed by.

"Every pose, every expression is different," she said. "But the constant they all share is they surrendered their life in a final moment of sacrifice. Each of them died saving someone or something else."

Peter watched in wonder as he walked past the remainder of the stone fairies. He was struck by the fact that although he was physically larger than all of them, each of them were so much greater than he could ever hope to be.

The passage narrowed even more. The stone walls nearly touching in places, making it difficult for Shiiklah to pass though, but she managed to get through and Peter had the sense she had been this way many times before.

Only now did Tinker Belle and Adelaide take off again and fly through the narrow opening.

Peter squeezed through the passage. It went on for a few more feet, then turned sharply to the left.

Peter followed the turn then stumbled.

The narrow rough stone hall gave way to a large, golden room. The gold, somehow glowing, lined the ceiling and the exposed section of wall. What lined most of the walls was the last thing Peter expected to find.

Books.

"What is this place?" Peter asked, unsure what to make of the place.

"A library of our histories," Adelaide replied.

Peter walked up to one of the walls. It was lined from floor to ceiling in small books.

"May I touch them?" Peter asked.

"Of course," Adelaide said.

Peter pulled one of the books from the shelf. Its spine was a rich brown with a gold-inlaid title: The First Time.

Peter brushed his fingers over the words. The lettering was masterfully done, inlaid with real gold, and it gave off a slight glow, much like the walls. The book was slightly larger than a man's hand, making it just large enough for him to hold and read comfortably, but not too big that a pair of fairies couldn't lift it.

"What are these?" Peter asked.

"They are the records," Adelaide said. "All of our histories, everything we know. All of our victories, all of our sins." She gingerly touched the spine of a book titled The Just.

"You'll find," she said, "that we record our own failings with better accuracy than our adversaries." She stared at the book with sadness and longing.

"The world is much more than darkness and light, instinct and intentionality," she said. "The failings of man are not his alone to bear as others would have you believe. We share in your likeness in that regard."

Adelaide didn't elaborate, and Peter felt uninclined to press her.

"Why are the books so large?" Peter asked, pulling another tome from the shelf. This one, titled Making contained pages of elaborate diagrams with explanations written in what Peter assumed was Fae—the fairies' own written script—English, and what he guessed was Spanish.

The pictures depicted fairies creating various items: writing utensils, torches, chairs. The book seemed to be a basic explanation of crafting with dust.

"And why include languages other than your own?" Peter asked.

Adelaide smiled.

"We don't write for our sake," she answered, "but for yours."

"For me?" Peter asked, surprised, closing the book.

"Neverland is the last corner of a world that once was," she said, a sad smile creasing her features.

"What happened?" Peter asked.

Adelaide merely smiled that sad smile.

He thought about pressing her for more information, but something else caught his eye.

The rest of White Falls' floor was stone, like any cave's should be, but the library's floor was gold layered with what looked like glass or quartz. The floor under the glass had been hollowed out, leaving a shallow depression. The walls and floor of the depression were lined with the same glowing gold that made up the rest of the room, but in the center, visually distinct to its surroundings in every way, lay a black square box.

Peter knelt down to look more closely and realized that it wasn't a box at all but a book tightly bound by oily black leather.

"What's this?" Peter asked, squinting at the entombed book.

"You are fair, Peter," Adelaide said. "Fairer than most. But not even you may read that book. Some songs must remain unlearned forever."

"Then why keep it at all?" Peter said, still staring at the black mass buried in the floor. "If no one can read it."

"Because we are the keepers of history, and that is part of our history; perhaps the most vital of all parts," Adelaide said.

"But it's just a book," Peter said, confused. "How dangerous could it be?" He ran his hand along the surface of the glass that separated him from the mysterious black book. It seemed no more conspicuous than any of the other books.

The sounds of scales sliding along the ground drew his attention. He twisted his neck around to see Shiiklah towering over him. Her eyes, black like the book in the floor, bore into his.

"If you touch that book, I will kill you," she said, speaking for the first time since they had entered the room.

Peter was instantly transported back to the first time he had met Shiiklah, and for an instant all the fear and terror from that encounter rushed into him.

Instinctively, he backed away both from the book and the mermaid. He couldn't believe there was anything that could make the mermaid chieftess hostile towards him again. But if whatever was in this book was enough for that, Peter had no intentions of ever touching it, let alone reading its contents.

"There's a reason it's buried beneath stone," Adelaide said, flying next to Peter. She looked up at Shiiklah and the mer's eyes softened ever so slightly.

"You promised to help protect our home," Adelaide said. "Above all else, this is what must be protected."

Peter eyed the book suspiciously.

"But you can't tell me what it is," he said. "Or what happens if someone reads it."

"Therein lies the greatest of all questions," Adelaide said. "Does your promise require sight?"

Peter looked up at her.

"Or can your faith remain blind?" Adelaide asked.

Peter considered. He wasn't thrilled they were keeping something from him, but he knew they could be trusted.

"I think we've all been through enough for me to take you on your word," he said after a moment, shifting his gaze from Adelaide to peer into Shiiklah's still-black eyes .

"I told you he was ready," Shiiklah said at last.

Adelaide smiled at the mermaid, nodding in agreement.

"And cut it out with the black eyes," Peter said, nodding towards the mermaid. "You're freaking me out."

Adelaide sniffed in amusement as Shiiklah's eyes graduated from black to a less-dangerous green.

"And Peter," Adelaide said, "you are free to read any other book in this room."

"I'd like that," Peter said, purposefully not looking at the book in the floor, lest they thought he had any desire to read it, which he soundly did not.

"I have one more question, though," Peter said, looking down at the book in the floor again.

"Yes?" Adelaide said.

"The black book," Peter said, carefully. "How long has it been buried?"

The fairy looked to the mermaid.

"Not long enough," was Shiiklah's reply.

Peter thought she might elaborate, but a cry from the room's entrance drew their attention.

"Cousin!" Tinker Belle yelled from the hall.

"What is it?" Adelaide demanded.

"Kite Nest," Tinker Belle said, panting for breath.

"What happened?" she asked.

"It's burning!" Tinker Belle said.

SIXTEEN

Peter accompanied the score of fairies, with Adelaide in the lead, towards the smoke. They soared over the tops of the giant pine trees that thrived in the northern wood. After what felt like forever, they arrived at the source of the smoke.

Kite Nest was engulfed in fire and smoke.

Adelaide stopped, her retinue of attendants and guards fanning out in a protective ring around her.

She looked from the flames to the surrounding forest, not yet burning,

Peter followed her gaze. He saw the smoke swelling from the trees. He looked to the coast, but fog covered the shore so that he couldn't make out the coast, only that the trees ended.

Dark clouds sagged in the sky.

"Lorel," Adelaide said, staring up at the sky. "Return to the falls and come back with every maker you can find."

"Majesty," Lorel started to object.

"Do not make me ask twice," Adelaide said, still looking up at the clouds.

The fairy inclined her head then shot off towards White Falls.

"Tinker Belle," Adelaide said, turning towards the fairy.

"Yes, cousin?" Tinker Belle answered, moving closer to her.

"Can you still make water?" Adelaide asked quickly.

"It's been a long time," Tinker Belle said, considering. "Siene could, but I haven't tried."

"Try," Adelaide said.

Tinker Bell stared at her hand, then began to work her fingers together, almost as if trying to rub them clean. Her hand glowed as she worked. A moment later, she opened her hand, exposing wet fingers.

"I guess so," Tinker Belle said, grinning.

"Come," Adelaide said, flying higher into the clouds, leaving the remaining fairies behind.

Peter followed her up towards the drooping clouds.

The trio reached the clouds.

Peter reached into the dark cloud. His hand disappeared into it. It felt like cotton, but much lighter. And cool to the touch—not freezing, but cool like rain.

He pulled his hand out.

The cloud remained largely unchanged, but his hand was damp.

He could hear little claps coming from inside the cloud.

He flew into the cloud to investigate.

Immediately, his clothes became damp and clung awkwardly to his body. He flew into its interior, which was hollow save for the two fairies, Tinker Belle and Adelaide, in the center. The two of them were hovering in the middle of the clouds, working their fingers and rubbing their hands and then clapping.

When Tinker Belle clapped, a few sprinkles of water splashed from her hands and fell into the mass of clouds below, darkening them ever so slightly. When Adelaide clapped, a small, white flash would erupt from her hands as even more droplets of water fell from her hands.

"You're making rain," Peter surmised, watching the clouds gradually grow darker with each contribution.

"If we can get these clouds full enough," Adelaide said, grunting between hand claps. "We might be able to make it rain and maybe put out the fires."

"You can do that?" Peter asked, shaking his head in disbelief. "What can't you guys do?"

"Raise the dead," Tinker Belle quipped.

Minutes passed and other fairies began to enter the cloud. The makers, as Peter guessed due to their lack of weapons and plain dress, joined their queen and began to work their hands and clap as well.

At first, Peter thought the clapping of their tiny hands was the only sound being made, but after several white flashes, he could make out a snapping sound that accompanied the white flash.

More and more makers joined the cloud, all working their hands together and clapping.

Increasingly, one of the white flashes would arc from one maker's hands to another if they clapped at the same time. The fairies, however, didn't seem to be hurt by the flash, or even notice it.

"It's lightning," Peter said.

Tinker Belle, who had returned to his side, nodded.

"It happens when a real maker creates water," she said.

The arcs of electricity were now ever-present in the ball of fairies. It grew in intensity, almost reaching the clouds around them.

Eventually, one of the arcs contacted the surrounding cloud, and when it did, electricity shot through the entire cloud, illuminating them all.

"Faster!" Adelaide yelled.

More makers added to the group to create water. The mass of fairies began to glow white, and thick arcs of lighting began to fire in all directions.

What sounded like a blast from a thousand cannons accompanied the flash. It jolted through Peter, momentarily deafening him. He covered his ears and his vision seared to white.

The lighting continued, unaided by the fairies.

"What can I do?" Peter asked, shouting to be heard over the crackle of lightning.

"Let's check the nest," Tinker Belle said quickly.

The pair dropped through the cloud, then flew to the nest.

Kite Nest was an impressive sight. It was a single giant nest with smaller nests honeycombed throughout the main structure. It was nearly fifteen feet in diameter and fashioned from sticks and mud. Within the giant nest sat countless individual nests, some empty, others filled with eggs or small, white hatchlings.

Peter could make out the adult birds, Red Kites, frantically grabbing younglings who were too young to fly and carrying them from the nest to the shoreline several hundred yards away.

"The hatchlings!" Tinker Belle yelled. But Peter was already thinking the same thing and soared towards the nest.

He landed next to a nest filled with eggs and a startled mother jumped, clacking her beak at him.

"I'll carry the nest to safety," Peter explained. As carefully as he could, he lifted the nest and flew towards the shore. The flight took less than a minute.

Upon reaching the shore, he found the kites' temporary camp at the edge of the tree line. Several kites were standing guard over the younglings, ensuring that no forest creatures would try and take advantage of the grounded birds.

Peter gently lowered the nest to the ground, being careful not to crack any of the eggs, then turned to return to the nest. But a sound from behind him halted him in his tracks.

It was the sound of a ship.

His head whipped towards the sea, looking for the source of the noise. The northern shore was blanketed in a heavy fog. He couldn't see more than a few feet into the water, but he had heard something.

Having lived his entire life near the docks, Peter was intimately familiar with every sight, smell, and sound of ships.

And he could have sworn he had just heard the sound of creaking oars.

He squinted into the fog, but fog liked to play tricks on the mind. He saw everything from giant sea monsters to haunted ships swirling through it.

He ignored them and closed his eyes, turning his head slightly to listen, but all he could hear was the snapping and popping of burning trees behind him.

More than anything, he wanted to fly into the fog and investigate. But he knew had to keep evacuating the kites.

Opening his eyes, he turned back to the nest. The pillar of smoke was growing darker with each passing minute.

Another creak from the direction of the sea spun him around and again he found himself walking towards the water.

But Peter knew he only had precious minutes before Kite Nest was engulfed with flames. The only prudent course of action was to save what he could from the nest. Growling in frustration, he took to the sky and flew back to the nest.

He arrived to see the clouds above were flashing tiny bursts of white. Clearly most of the makers from White Falls had arrived and were busy making water in the clouds.

He landed in the nest just as Tinker Belle flew past him, a black-spotted hatchling squawking and protesting in her arms as she flew it to safety. She winced and grumbled as the bird landed errant wing strikes in her face.

"Ungrateful beast," she muttered as she flew past him.

Peter smirked despite the situation, found another nest filled with eggs, picked it up, and flew it to the shore.

Ten minutes later the nest was empty and the flames were starting to lick the top of the nest. The last of the birds had either been rescued from Kite Nest or had flown away on their own.

All but one.

Kite Grath.

The stubborn bird, fully capable of flight, screeched in defiance at the smoke that snaked up through cracks in his nest. He was hopping around the now-empty nest, stomping out tiny fires that were beginning to ignite throughout the nest.

"Grath, get out of there!" Peter yelled.

But the bird ignored him. Instead it continued to stomp out the fires as they appeared. He seemed well decided that he was going to save the nest or die with it.

Peter considered grabbing the bird and leaving, but thought better of it and instead joined the foolish bird.

A moment later, Tinker Belle appeared.

"What are you doing?" she cried, landing in the nest between the pair. "Everyone here can fly, let's go!"

"Grath won't leave," Peter explained, scuffing out a flame with his foot.

"So of course you're staying," Tinker Belle said, rolling her eyes.

"Check on Adelaide. See how much more time they need," Peter said.

Tinker Belle ignored him and started working her hands together and clapping, then drying her hands on parts of the nest that had not yet caught fire.

"If you get us killed," Tinker Belle grumbled, "I'll never forgive you."

"This is what friends do," Peter said, winking at her. "And besides, this'll make for an awfully exciting chapter in the histories."

The trio made their way throughout the nest, stomping, drying, and putting out fires where they ignited. But after a few minutes, the fires started appearing faster than they could be extinguished.

Peter felt the branches beneath him grow warmer. His eyes began to water and sting, and his lungs burned as more smoke rose up through the nest floor. Tiny coughs squeaked out of Tinker Belle and her work slowed.

Grath's feathers, normally golden red, were now singed and stained black and starting to smoke.

Peter looked up at the clouds. They were flashing with so much lighting now he wondered if it all came from the fairies.

He could fly up. Not more than thirty feet away was clean air and safety, but Grath and his kites had come to his aid when he had needed him the most, and Peter wasn't about to abandon him now.

Grath cawed at Peter and Tinker Belle, nodding his soot-stained face to the sky, but Peter shook his head adamantly and carried on extinguishing fires. Peter felt himself getting dizzy and dropped to the floor of the nest. The mud and sticks were hot against his face.

His head swam as the combination of overheating and breathing smoke took a toll on his body.

Then he felt it: a single drop splashed on top of his hand.

He thought it was his imagination, but as he stared at the droplet of water, watched it run down off his hand then drip into the dried mud below, he knew it was real.

A flash of lighting, the biggest one yet, ripped through the clouds overhead. It was followed by a peel of thunder that shook Peter's chest. Then the clouds emptied themselves on the forest. Rain poured on the trio, almost immediately cooling the branches and combatting the fires.

Peter sat up, his fortitude bolstered by the rain.

Tinker Belle, too, was on her feet. Moments later she was in the air. Grath cawed in delight as the rain fell, soaking them all.

Peter and Tinker Belle laughed and cheered, skipping around the nest. Grath too, joined them, hopping around in victory.

The smoke began to dissipate as bird, boy, and fairy danced atop Kite Nest.

The fairies followed the rain, dropping down from inside the cloud. They descended to the nest, then around and into the forest below, making sure that the fires were indeed dying.

Grath sat perched on the edge of the nest, watching the fairies rush into smoke and flame in an effort to save his home.

Peter walked up to the bird and sat down across from him.

"You came to our aid when we needed you, now we come to yours," he said to the soot-stained bird. "That's what friends do. Don't ever doubt that, Grath."

The bird nodded slowly, then clacked his beak.

Adelaide joined the trio at the nest.

"Lord Grath," she said, placing her closed hand over her heart in greeting. "It pleases me to see you."

Grath clacked his beak, his head dipping in greeting.

The fairy queen was soaked, her wings sprayed tiny droplets of water into the air as she hovered.

"Your feathers are damaged," Adelaide continued, looking over the bird. "May we attend to you?"

The bird clacked, shaking his head, then twisted his neck, peering towards the shore.

"Of course," Adelaide said, nodding. "Once the fires have been fully quelled, we'll help return your clan to the nest and then attend to you."

Grath snapped his beak in agreement.

The fairies, with Peter's help, returned nests and hatchlings to Kite Nest. Most of the surrounding trees were either smoking or still burning. Smoldering branches fell from their trunks, crashing into the forest floor, exploding into smoke and burning coals as they hit the ground.

Suddenly, an entire tree shuddered, then fell, erupting in a spray of smoke and sparks. Kites and fairies flew in all directions.

But as the noise subsided, a cry could be heard from below. It was an angry, fearful squawking.

Peter, along with a handful of fairies, Tinker Belle and Adelaide among them, flew down to the sound.

Next to the fallen tree was a young kite. She was flapping and hopping from foot to foot, kicking helplessly at a burning branch.

Peter sighed in relief. The bird had just escaped the branch.

"Tolan!" Tinker Belle cried.

Peter looked more closely and saw that pinned between the burning branch and the ground lay Tolan, unmoving.

Peter was at his side in a heartbeat. He grabbed the branch with both hands and lifted. He felt it burn into his hands. Ignoring the pain, he focused on freeing the fairy.

The branch shifted—barely, but enough for the frantic bird to move Tolan clear of the branch. The bird dragged Tolan by the leg with one talon, hopping as it pulled him to safety. Peter released the branch then immediately began to shake and blow his hands to cool them.

Fairies swarmed around Tolan, inspecting his wounds and lifting him from the ground.

"Take him back to the falls" Adelaide ordered, coming abreast of

Peter. "You're a brave and foolish boy, Peter," she said, sprinkling dust into his hands. "Thankfully your burns appear minor."

She examined his hands as they absorbed the dust. "Tolan's injuries..." she said, her face a portrait of concern. "We will have to see what we can do."

The bird continued to hop about, watching Tolan being carried away.

"I think he saved her," Peter said, nodding towards the bird as he inspected his healing hands.

Adelaide landed next to the bird.

"You're injured," she said, inspecting the bird's wings. "May I help?"

The bird, finally looking away from Tolan, looked at Adelaide just long enough to nod, then snapped her gaze back towards the departing fairies.

Peter landed quietly next to the pair and watched her work. Tinker Belle landed on his shoulder and sat, her tiny legs dangling.

"Oh, you're in for a treat," Tinker Belle said, leaning forward.

"How so?" Peter asked.

"Watch," she said. "Adelaide is a master."

Adelaide walked around the young kite, taking note of missing and burned feathers. She laid a hand on the bird's wing. The bird flinched, then relaxed. The fairy rubbed her fingers together and white golden flecks began to drizzle from her fingertips. She caught the dust in her other hand, then began rubbing her hands together, almost as if she were washing them. She then began to brush the bird's red feathers with her hands, and every section of feather she touched became imbued with dust, causing the golden red feather to glow.

Peter gasped.

"Oh, that's nothing," Tinker Belle said, smiling. "That's just repairing, wait until she starts making."

Adelaide continued to work her way around the bird, repeating her sprinkle, wash, and rub technique as she moved. And after a few minutes most of the bird's back, head, and chest plumage had been fully restored. Almost the entire bird glowed. The fairy then turned her attention to the bird's wings. The kite's flight feathers were charred ruins. Nothing remained but splintered parts of the hollow shaft.

Out of the corer of his eyes, Peter saw Tinker Belle lean closer.

Adelaide was sprinkling a large ball of dust in her hands now. She cupped her hands together, compressing the pile into a ball. She kneaded and rolled the ball, much like Peter's Aunt Ellie had done with dough back home.

The sudden realization that he hadn't given so much as a thought to his old life, or remaining family, shocked him, but he had work to do here. There'd be time for that later. He pushed the thoughts out of his mind and continued to watch.

Adelaide continued to roll the dust into a small, dense ball, then worked it into what looked like a long tube.

"Tinker Belle," she called over her shoulder.

Tinker Belle hopped down from Peter's shoulder and flew to her cousin's side. Adelaide handed the cylinder of dust to her then reached past her, pulling one of Tinker Belle's daggers from their sheath.

The bird hopped back at the sight of the blade.

"Do not fear, my friend," Adelaide said, her voice soft and soothing. "I'm only going to cut away the damaged feather."

The bird clacked her beak in understanding and opened her wing to the fairy.

Adelaide ducked under it and found the damaged flight feathers. Running her hand up along the damaged stems, she found where they graduated from scorched and brittle to strong. She cut the damaged portions off, discarding the burned pieces.

Adelaide returned to Tinker Belle. She cut a section of tube, then handed the blade back to Tinker Belle.

She inserted the piece of now-hardened, condensed dust into the hollow of the feather shaft, then pulled. The dust stretched out, thinning as it grew in length until it was as long as the rest of the feathers.

Again, she sprinkled dust into her hand, but this time she didn't work it into a ball, she kept it a light, fluffy pile. Then, dipping her fingers into the dust, she brushed her fingers through the remaining feather, combing her fingers between the blades of feather. As she worked, the existing feather became stronger, and the missing segments grew. She worked her way down the broken feathers, painting new feathers where moments before there had been nothing.

Adelaide stepped back to inspect her work. She circled the bird, dipping her hand back into the fine dust and touching up places she had missed, then finally smiled, satisfied with her work.

"That's incredible," Peter said, captivated with the fairy's work.

Tinker Belle turned to him and smiled, clearly equally impressed with her queen.

"You're all set, my friend," Adelaide said to the bird, stroking its wing.

The bird inspected her new feathers, then without a second look, shot off into the sky, dirt and leaves swirling around the trio as it left.

"Ungrateful little beast," Tinker Belle muttered.

But a look from Adelaide silenced any further grumblings.

"If our actions were guided by other's responses, we might never do good," Adelaide chided her gently.

"Of course, Majesty," Tinker Belle admitted.

Adelaide inspected the remaining dust in her hands. Instead of brushing her hands clean, she knelt and used the remaining dust to repair broken blades of grass that had been crushed by fallen branches. And with the last bit she created a few flowers, painting stems and pedals seemingly from nothing.

Her hands clean and her work complete, she rose into the air.

The trio returned to the nest. Upon their arrival, they found the remaining small nests and hatchlings returned, and Grath finally accepting aid from the makers. With the fires extinguished and Kite Nest's repair well underway, they headed back to White Falls.

Upon their return, the typically serene enclave was anything but. Fairy scouts and warriors were everywhere, swarming around the healers' quarter.

"What's going on?" Peter asked, taken aback by the chaos.

"There!" Tinker Belle exclaimed, pointing.

Trying furiously to get into one of the rooms was a kite. In fact, it was the same kite Adelaide had just mended.

The bird fluttered and flipped, avoiding fairies brave enough to try and pull it away from the room that held the still unconscious Tolan.

The musical tapping of beak and talon on glass rang though the hall. Her wings, new feathers still glowing, batted unlucky fairies out of her way.

Rike, a well-armed fairy, presented himself before Adelaide and explained the situation.

"It's this bird," he explained between breaths. "She came out of nowhere, flew down here and has been trying to get to Tolan since we brought him back. May we use force to subdue her?"

Adelaide pursed her lips, considering.

"No," she said at last. "Call them off."

"As you wish, Majesty," he replied, placing his right hand over his heart in salute.

Rike whistled and immediately all fairies engaged with the kite drifted away, giving the bird space.

The bird, frantic in its efforts, finally managed to break through the glass wall, chipping away until it had widened a hole large enough for her to get in. She climbed inside and settled down next to the unmoving form of Tolan.

"He saved her," Peter said, finally gathering the bird's intent. "So she's watching over him."

"I think Peter is right," Adelaide agreed, nodding. "How is Tolan?"

"Not good, from what I hear," Rike admitted. "But Evee can explain better."

The trio moved to the healers' quarter. Adelaide and Tinker Belle entered the room while Peter watched from outside.

"How is he?" Tinker Belle asked, concern etched on her tiny face.

"He's been burned badly," Evee explained. "The branch must

have been incredibly hot; most of his back has been burned away, his wings were completely destroyed."

"They can be rebuilt though, right?" Peter asked from outside.

"The problem is not repairing the wings," Evee said, turning to Peter. "His injuries were largely internal, and while we can repair the skin and even give him new wings, but he wouldn't be able to use them."

Tinker Belle gasped. "But how can he fly? Adelaide, do something, he needs wings. Wings that work."

"Can you do anything?" Peter asked, picking up, based on Tinker Belle's reaction, how devastating this news was.

Evee shrugged. "We don't even know if he'll wake up," she said. "Life, at this point, is what we're hoping for. We'll address flying if we get that far."

"When," Tinker Belle corrected, glaring at Evee.

"If," Evee replied, unruffled by Tinker Belle's rage. "I deal in certainties, Tinker Belle, and this is what we have right now."

* * *

The next few hours passed without event. Tolan seemed no closer to waking than the young kite seemed willing to leave his side. Tinker Belle, too, refused to leave the healer's quarter, which meant Peter remained as well.

The makers had managed to repair all of Tolan's external injuries and the limited internal ones they could reach. With the exception of his wings, he was healed, but he would need to wake up before they could ascertain how severe his internal injuries were.

It was well into the night before Tolan stirred. A faint groan brought Peter to full wakefulness and Tinker Belle to her feet instantly.

"Tolan?" Tinker Belle said, squatting down to his eye level.

"Tinker Belle," Tolan answered, wincing. "Where am I?"

"The healer's quarter," she answered.

Tolan moved his head, but his movements were stiff and slow. He turned his head, then jerked in surprised, clearly not expecting to see a kite lying next to him.

"Hello, there," he said, smiling, recognizing the bird. "What are you doing here? You should be home."

The bird clicked her beak in disagreement and settled deeper into her place against the wall.

"How are you feeling, Tolan?" Evee asked, coming up next to him.

"Sore," he said. "Sore and a little numb."

Evee and Tinker Belle exchanged a quick glance, then Evee placed her hand on Tolan's back between his shoulder blades, right where his wings would be.

"Tolan, I'm going to put my hand on your back, let me know what you feel," she explained.

"Go ahead," he replied.

A bolt of fear and sadness shot through Peter.

"Can you feel my hand?" Evee asked.

"You're not touching me," Tolan replied.

Evee breathed out slowly.

"I am," she replied.

"What?" he said. "No you're not, I can't feel you."

Tolan twisted his neck around to see behind him, then started.

"Where are my wings?" he asked, sounding more confused than upset.

"Tolan," Evee started.

He was instantly on his feet, his footing weak and unstable from being unconscious for so long.

Where are my wings?" he demanded, this time angry.

"You were very badly burned," Adelaide explained, entering in to the conversation for the first time. "We're not sure what the extent of your internal injuries are."

"Fix them!" Tolan demanded, staring directly at Evee, not daring to speak to his queen with a raised voice, regardless of his situation.

"You have no feeling in your back," she explained. "You couldn't use them. You couldn't control them"

"No, no, no," Tolan said, rubbing his face and hair.

"You're alive," Peter said.

"Alive?" Tolan spat. "A fairy without wings is...is not a fairy! I'm a scout, how can I scout if I can't fly?"

"There is still much you can do," Evee said.

Tolan merely glared at her.

"I'm going home," was all he said. He turned and walked towards the ledge. He looked out across the expanse. His apartment was almost directly across the cavern hall, on the opposite wall; only a few seconds flight away, much farther if you had to walk.

Peter considered offering to carry Tolan across the gap but guessed the offer probably wouldn't be well-received.

Tolan peered over the edge, looking for a place to climb down, when suddenly, his legs kicked out from under him. The kite, still

and motionless a moment before, shot forward, ducking under Tolan, seating him on her back. She flew the distance to Tolan's apartment, faster than any fairy could, and stopped, hovering just outside
his golden alcove.

He leaped from the bird to his ledge.

"Is that why you're here?" he asked the bird. "Repaying some
sort debt?"

The bird clacked her beak in acknowledgement.

"Don't bother," he said. "You don't owe me anything."

The bird screeched, clearly disagreeing with him, then climbed
into the empty alcove next to Tolan's and settled down.

"Don't you get it?" Tolan yelled, addressing anyone and everyone
in earshot. "Now I'm nothing. Without wings, I'm useless."

SEVENTEEN

The next morning found White Falls humming with activity. Fairies in every corner of the cave were busy with various tasks—even more so than normal.

Those assigned to food preservation were working overtime, preserving even more food than immediately needed. Scouts and warriors were busy carrying buckets of dust from the reservoir in the ceiling out of White Falls. The makers fairies, however, were nowhere to be found.

"What's happening?" Peter asked a passing fairy.

"We're resupplying Kite Nest and helping with repairs," the fairy answered.

"Ah," Peter said. "Have you seen Tink?"

The fairy smiled, then nodded, indicating past Peter's shoulder.

"She's watching, just like everyone else not assigned to the nest," he replied.

"Watching what?" Peter asked.

But the fairy merely smiled and hooked a thumb over his shoulder.

"See for yourself," was all he said, before flying away.

Curious, Peter turned and headed in the direction the fairy had indicated.

Off to the side, near one end of the falls, hovered a cloud of fairies. These fairies, obviously not part of the rebuilding efforts taking place in the north, cheered and yelled at whatever was happening in the center.

Carefully, he made his way through the cloud of fairies, pressing in just far enough to see through the dazzle of light their collective bodies gave off.

They were circled around Tolan's alcove.

Tolan, wingless, stood at the lip of the edge and peered down to the stone floor below. It was no more than six or seven feet high, a painful fall for someone Peter's sized, but crippling, maybe even fatal, to a fairy.

The fairy walked back inside his home, reached the back wall, then sprinted back towards the ledge. When he reached the edge, he dived into the air, arms outstretched. His momentum carried him several feet forward before he started to fall.

But before his tiny body's momentum pitched downward, a golden-red blur shot from one corner of the cave. Before Peter could figure out what had happened, Tolan was back standing on his ledge.

The fairies watching erupted in cheers and applause.

"What happened?" Peter asked, not sure what he had just seen.

"It's the kite Tolan saved," Tinker Belle explained, still clapping. "She's his wings now."

"Wow," Peter said, whistling. "She's fast."

"She's lightning," Tinker Belle added, shaking her head. "I've never seen anything move so quickly. Crim is determined to keep Tolan safe."

"Crim?" Peter asked.

"Crimson," Tinker Belle replied. "The name Tolan gave her."

Tolan was once again in the back of the room. He sprinted towards the ledge, but this time he came to a quick stop, then stepped off the edge.

The bird hadn't flinched. It still remained in the corner of the cave, seemingly unconcerned. But the instant Tolan stepped off the ledge, Crim appeared under him, catching him neatly on her back. He landed squarely between her shoulder blades, one leg draped on either side of her neck.

She hovered for a moment while, once again, the fairies erupted in shouts and cheers.

Peter joined in with them this time, shaking his head in amazement.

After the cheering had died down, Peter turned to Tinker Belle.

"I want to go back to Kite Nest," he said.

"You want to help with the rebuilding?" she asked.

"No, something doesn't make sense," he explained. "I want to see where the fire started."

"It was lightning," Tinker Belle said. "It happens from time to time."

"Did they see the lightning?" Peter asked.

"Probably," Tinker Belle said. "But I don't know for sure."

"But lightning would have ignited the nest itself," he explained. "The fire started at the base of the tree. The nest wasn't in danger until after the fire had climbed it."

Tinker Belle shrugged, unconcerned.

"If you say so," she said. "But I think it's a waste of time."

"Let's go," Peter said.

The pair left White Falls and headed north.

As they flew, Peter tried to remember everything he knew about lightning, which, regrettably, was not much. He had heard stories of lightning strikes and had even witnessed one himself.

The ship that had brought him to Neverland had been struck by lightning right before she had crashed into the black cliffs. The bolt had struck the main mast. But there had been no fires in that instance. In fact, the mast had exploded, showering everyone with debris.

If Kite Nest had been struck by lightning, it should have been obliterated instantly.

Something didn't feel right about the fire.

They arrived at the nest and found fairies and kites working to repair the nest as well as parts of the tree, which had been weakened by the fire.

Scouts and warriors were chipping away at burned parts of the tree while Maker fairies were rebuilding the wood using their dust.

The pair went largely ignored as they flew down to the base of the tree.

Peter walked around it, inspecting it.

Unfortunately, most of the burned wood had already been re-moved so Peter had no way of knowing if wood had been piled around the base of the tree to start the fire or not. But one thing did draw his attention.

"Why is this the only tree that caught fire?" Peter asked.

"Because the lightning only hit this tree," Tinker Belle said, growing increasingly bored as the minutes passed.

"But the other trees would have been affected," Peter insisted, remembering the sheer force of the bolt that had struck his own ship.

"The surrounding trees only started to burn after this tree's fire grew hot enough. None of the grass around any of the other trees has been burned."

He walked from the tree towards the shoreline, searching for signs of anything out of the ordinary. He couldn't find any footprints; the rain the fairies had triggered to quell the fire had washed away any potential tracks.

Other than the damage done to Kite Nest, the area seemed large-ly unmolested.

He ran onto the beach, hoping to find signs of activity there, but the rains and tide had washed away any evidence there as well.

"I heard something," Peter said, replaying the events from the day before in his mind. "I could have sworn I heard something yes-terday."

Tinker Belle laughed behind him.

"What?" he demanded, spinning on her.

"I think you're bored," she said, shrugging.

"What do you mean?" he repeated.

"I think you want there to be someone out there," Tinker Belle explained.

Peter scowled at her.

"Silly boy," she said, smiling. "There are no more pirates to fight. You'll have to find something else to do with your time now they're all gone."

He ignored her and turned back to the sea. He scanned the entire horizon, searching, aching to find a speck.

Nothing.

"I know you're out there," he whispered. "I don't know who you are, but I will find you."

"Come on," Tinker Belle whined. "There's nothing here."

"Fine," Peter said, casting one final glance at the sea.

But Peter spent the rest of the day consumed by the circumstances of the fire. So much so he did nothing but sit in his tree for the remainder of the day, thinking and replaying everything that had happened.

And when Tinker Belle returned that night to light their fire, she found him pacing, still trying to work out how lightning could have struck the nest without damaging the surrounding trees.

Peter spent the next few days returning to Kite Nest to further inspect the tree, but at that point, all the damage had been repaired and the ocean yielded fewer answers than the forest. Eventually, having exhausted every possible angle, Peter was forced to abandon his investigation.

EIGHTEEN

Micah was strong—stronger than most. But not in a brute force kind of way. His was a quiet strength, a strength that required no pronouncements. His abilities spoke plainly on their own, nor would he have ever considered speaking on their behalf.

But in addition to his physical strength, he had a strength of heart and of mind, all of which were required of warden fairies.

Warden fairies, of which there were only a few, were keepers of the island.

Their patrol routes were less defined than those of standard scouts. And where scouts searched for threats to Neverland, wardens were tasked with exploring and preserving the secrets and mysteries of the island.

Even though fairies had lived on Neverland for longer than even their own histories recorded, the island was ever-changing. New mysteries could always be found, and hidden parts of the island needed to be uncovered.

And wardens did just that.

Their patrols ranged across long distances. Therefore, their assignments were more open-ended and took longer to complete.

So whenever something did go wrong—which was exceptionally rare —it was difficult to track down missing parties or to know if a group was actually in trouble, instead of just taking longer than normal to complete a task.

This was one of those times.

And Micah didn't like when a party of his wardens went missing.

"When were they due back?" Adelaide was asking.

"What's going on?" Peter asked, dropping down from the reservoir entrance.

"Have you solved the mystery of the burning tree?" Tinker Belle joked.

"Quiet, you," Peter said, offering her a half-hearted glare.

She smiled at him, then landed on his shoulder.

"We've lost a patrol," Adelaide answered, still looking at Micah.

"Three days ago," Micah replied, answering her previous question.

"Three days?" Peter exclaimed. "And you're just now worried?"

"Three days is not long for my wardens," Micah explained. "This wasn't a standard night patrol. They were tasked with finding new fruit groves in the southlands."

"And normally, I'd give them a few more days," Micah said, "but since their assignment was largely devoid of danger…Well, there's no reason they should be delayed."

"What if one of them is hurt?" Adelaide asked.

"There are five in the party," he said. "Two would have stayed with the injured fairy while two would have returned for help."

"So you think something's wrong?" Peter asked.

Micah's blue eyes narrowed in thought.

"All I know is they're too late in returning for everything to be fine," he said with a shrug. "It could be they found a large grove, and they're still cataloging it, in which case we should send others to help with the task. Or something's gone wrong."

He addressed Adelaide again. "Regardless, I would like to send additional fairies to the jungles in the south, but I wanted to inform you of the situation."

"I trust your judgment," Adelaide said. "And I agree with your decision. When will you send the next patrol?"

"I'd like to assemble them now," Micah said.

"I'll go with," Peter offered.

"Me too," Tinker Belle chimed in.

Micah nodded at them.

"Let's go," Peter said, turning to Tinker Belle.

The party, six fairies and Peter, flew south. They spent the better part of an hour fanning out then regrouping to discuss what they had found, or rather, hadn't found.

An hour later Peter spotted something.

"There," Peter yelled. "What's that?"

In the distance, the thick jungle gave way to rows of trees dotted with specks of orange.

"An orange grove," Micah called, then nodded towards the trees.

The party adjusted their course and landed among several dozen orange trees.

"Who planted these?" Peter asked. "They're all grouped in one area."

Tinker Belle shrugged.

"People used to live here, long ago," she said. "When they left, the trees stayed behind."

"Groves like these also spring up in random places," Micah explained. "Animals spread the seeds throughout the island, and eventually one tree gives birth to another. And given enough time…" he waved his arm, indicating the grove they were in. "We have a new grove. It's not uncommon for a grove to appear and remain undiscovered for several years."

Peter pulled an orange free from a tree and smelled it. The rind smelled sweet and bright.

He pocketed the fruit and walked through the trees.

Something seemed off about the grove, but he couldn't name it.

"What is it?" Tinker Belle asked, seeing the confusion on his face.

"I don't know," Peter said, squinting in thought. "Did you know about this grove?"

Tinker Belle shrugged, then looked to Micah for an answer.

"There are many such groves," he explained. "But this one is farther south than we usually venture. Oranges are large and more difficult to bring back to White Falls. We would probably leave this one alone because of the distance."

Peter fished the orange from his pocket.

"It's perfectly ripe," he said, inspecting it again.

"So?" Tinker Belle asked.

Peter looked around at the surrounding trees.

"Shouldn't there be more fruit on the trees?" Peter asked. "And if fairies aren't harvesting the oranges, who is?"

Peter looked from Tinker Belle to Micah.

Micah said nothing. Instead, he drew his sword and looked around. The weapon was much larger than the daggers Tinker Belle used but smaller than Tolan's broadsword.

"There should be more fruit here," he said after a long moment, still scanning the grove. "Either in the trees or at least on the ground."

"Kites?" Tinker Belle offered.

"It's possible," Micah replied. "But it's far for them. And they'll only eat fruit if they can't find animals or fish. And we saw plenty of life on our way here."

Micah continuously shifted his position as he hovered, his blond head constantly moving, always looking around him.

"Sharp eyes," Micah cautioned. "But let us continue."

The party took to the sky again.

Peter's eyes moved constantly, searching for any sign of life.

He left the fairies and flew straight up for several minutes until he could see the entire island. At this height the wind gusts were strong. And cold: the air was a sharp contrast to the tropical temperatures he enjoyed closer to land. But from this altitude, he could see the entire island. More importantly, he could see the surrounding water for miles in all directions.

But water was all he saw.

No ships.

No pirates.

He sighed and descended back towards the group. Micah looked at him expectantly as Peter rejoined the group.

"Nothing," Peter said, still shivering from the cold winds.

"Maybe it's just a bad harvest," Micah said. "It's uncommon but not unheard of."

"Maybe," Peter said.

"There's still the question of our missing fairies, though," Micah said. "I think we need to head back and formalize an organized search."

"I agree," Tinker Belle said, nodding her tiny head. "I think if we–"

"What's that?" Peter asked, interrupting her.

The others followed Peter's eyes to a clearing in the distance.

"It's a clearing," one of the fairies answered him. "Where the jungle turns to forest."

"No, that," Peter said, pointing. "In the middle of the clearing.

Peter flew towards the clearing, the party fairies trailing just behind him, and landed in the center of the clearing.

"What's this?" Peter asked, running towards the center.

In the middle of the clearing were the remains of a fire. Peter stooped to inspect the charred logs.

"They've been extinguished," Peter said, poking at them.

"What do you mean?" Tinker Belle asked.

"This fire was put out, it didn't burn out," Peter explained. "Look at the logs. Parts of them are still unburned. Whoever was here didn't stay here. They lit a fire, put it out after a while, then left."

"So what?" Tinker Belle said. "It's a fire,"

"But who lit it?" Peter asked. "It's too large for fairies, it wasn't me, and mers wouldn't have been this far inland."

Peter stood, wiping his hands clean. "We're not alone," Peter said.

"Yes, you keep saying that," Tinker Belle said.

"Then explain this!" Peter said, pointing to the fire.

"Look, Peter," Tinker Belle said. "We've searched the entire island, there's no one else here."

Peter shook his head then started counting off on his fingers.

"First, the missing patrol. Second, the fire at Kite Nest. Third, the orange trees with no oranges. And finally, this camp," he said. "Apart from each other, none of them matter much, but add them all up? Something is going on here."

Peter turned to examine the edge of the forest and found himself staring down the barrel of a pistol. Peter stared wide-eyed at the gun, then at the man holding the gun.

"Something indeed is going on here," the man said.

It was the captain from the beach, surrounded by a half dozen other pirates.

"Hello again, my young friend," the captain said, smiling.

"You!" Peter shouted.

"Indeed," the man replied coolly.

Peter tensed to spring, but the man took a step forward, then shifted his aim, centering the gun at Peter's chest.

"Ah, ah, ah," the captain chided. "You're fast, but you're not that fast."

Peter looked from the gun to the man's face, then thought better of starting the fight.

"What do you want?" Peter demanded.

"An answer," the man said. "On the beach, when we first met, you didn't attack. Why?"

Peter shrugged, feigning disinterest. He looked up at the man without tilting his head back.

The truth was Peter was tired of killing pirates. He had just spent much of the previous night fighting for his life and the life of every being on the island. He had always been taught that fighting should be the last resort, and killing the final course of action when no other remained.

However, Peter had always romanticized the idea of killing. His own father had been a renown warrior, celebrated for his fighting skills. But when Peter had been forced to take his first life, near death himself in the bowels of a ship where he had been tortured, the veil of glory had been removed, leaving a hollow pit in the place where the fantasy had once lived.

But it was more than weariness. Peter was afraid.

The foreign, unnatural act of killing had quickly become palatable, but when he had faced Edward Teach for the last time, he wasn't just okay with killing the man, he had wanted to kill him. The man had killed Peter's sister, and Peter wanted to make him pay.

Slowly.

Painfully.

More than anything, Peter had wanted to kill him.

But it had been Tinker Belle who had pulled him back from the brink. And it was that encounter that showed him just how easily one could fall into the darkness.

So when this captain had wandered on to his shores, the last thing he wanted to do was kill him.

But Peter couldn't tell this man that.

"You didn't seem worth the trouble," Peter lied.

The man narrowed his eyes.

"I should kill you," the man said.

Peter watched the man.

The man reached across his pistol to pull back the hammer. With a gleaming silver hook.

"Fancy," Peter mocked.

"We had it lying around," the man retorted.

"Be careful, Captain Hook," an all too familiar voice rang out. "This one's clever."

Peter shifted his gaze to see a pirate, obviously disguised as a tree and even more obviously failing, with branches thrust in his shirt, belt, and pants.

Mad Rogue.

"Searching for some missing fairies?" Mad Rogue asked, miming an explosion with his hands before bursting into a fit of giggles.

This was the pirate who had helped torture Peter in the hold of the ship. An electric jolt of terror shot through him and, for an instant, Peter was transported back into the dark hold of the ship. Again he was tied to the mast, the heavy, itchy ropes digging into his arms while Mad Rogue danced around him, singing and throwing buckets of icy water on him as Captain London tortured him.

"Wakey, wakey, Peter Pan," Mad Rogue called, apparently sensing Peter's distraction.

Peter pushed the fear away and put on a mischievous grin, inwardly cursing himself for allowing an enemy to read him. He slid his gaze from Mad Rogue back to the captain. Captain Hook.

"You should listen to your tree," Peter said, with more confidence than he felt.

"There's an old saying," Hook said, ignoring the verbal jab. "An eye for and eye."

Peter stared at him, unblinking.

"I refuse to be indebted to anyone," Hook said. "For whatever reason, you spared me. It was a mistake, but you did it none the less. Now we are even. But the next time we meet," Hook hissed, his breath hot, "I will kill you."

"Words," Peter replied.

"Yes," Hook said, "but sleep with the knowledge the promise those words carry is but the harbinger of my vengeance. Peace is a memory."

Peter burned with fear and anger. But he kept his face impassive. He shifted his gaze over to Mad Rogue.

The crazed pirate was glaring hatred at Tinker Belle.

Peter waited until the pirate felt his gaze, then offered the pirate a knowing smile.

"Where's Little Kite?" Peter asked, knowing full well Tinker Belle had stolen Mad Rogue's most prized possession, a large kite feather, when they had last fought.

Mad Rogue gasped, then covered his mouth with his hands.

"Captain!" he cried. "Kill them all!"

"Hold fast, Rogue," Hook ordered. "Their time will come. Very soon."

The pirates began to slip back into the jungle.

Hook, too, backed into the jungle.

"Remember with fondness the days you ruled Neverland," Hook said, now just a voice from within the trees. "For they are gone, cast in the fires of my retribution."

No one moved or spoke for a long moment. Tinker Belle was the first to speak.

"I'm sorry," she said, speaking to Peter. "I should have believed you."

He looked at her, smiled, then winked.

He opened his mouth to offer a reply when gunfire erupted from the jungle. Everyone hurtled to the ground as angry bullets thudded into the trees behind them.

"Retreat!" Micah cried and everyone obeyed, taking flight and soaring back to White Falls.

* * *

"I knew it!" Peter cried, upon entering White Falls. "I knew there was someone here."

"Who?" Adelaide asked, joining the group.

"He was the last pirate to come ashore," Tinker Belle explained. "The morning after the battle."

Adelaide shifted her attention from her cousin to Peter.

"Forgive me," she said. "I should have given your concerns more weight."

Peter waved her off, more concerned with the pirate who had infiltrated Neverland than being proved right.

"Where is he, then?" Adelaide asked, looking from face to face. "If he is indeed the one responsible for burning Kite Nest in the north, and for the missing patrols, and the bare orchard in the south, where can he be? Neither our scouts nor the Mers have seen him until now."

"His ship must come at night," Rike said, shrugging. "It's the only way. We would have easily spotted a ship during the day, so he must make landfall in the night, make trips throughout the island, and then leave before anyone can trace their location."

"That would explain how he's managed to traverse so many parts of Neverland without being spotted," Adelaide said. "He lands in the north at night to start fires, hides in the forest until the following night, and then leaves."

"That would explain his activity in the south as well," Rike said. "His party gets dropped off, gathers food, then departs."

"It works for now," Peter said, finally cooling down enough to join the conversation. "But it's a bad long-term plan. His men would be exhausted from the constant back and forth. And his ship would need to make port eventually for substantial supplies."

He narrowed his eyes thoughtfully.

"It doesn't make sense," he said. "He has to be here, on the is-land."

"It's impossible," Tolan sad, shaking his head. Crim clacked her beak in agreement.

"I don't know," Peter said, his brow furrowed. "It doesn't feel right."

"What we do know," Adelaide said, "is he's here now, today."

Everyone nodded in agreement.

"Which means he has a specific reason for being here," she surmised. "Whether he's established a presence on the island or is making trips from the sea doesn't matter at the moment. He's here. Now."

"But why reveal himself now?" Rike asked.

"Peter," Tinker Belle said, nodding towards him. "He wants Peter."

Peter felt all eyes turned towards him.

"He could have killed us," Peter said, agreeing. "But he thinks the fact I didn't attack him on the beach meant he owed me something. So he wanted to show himself first. To make us even."

"So you're 'even,'" Tolan said. "What now?"

"He kills Peter," Tinker Belle answered.

"She's right," he said "He wants revenge for what I did to him."

"Then why burn Kite Nest?" Tolan asked.

"He wants you to suffer," Micah replied. "And what better way to cause you pain than to cause pain to the ones you care about."

"I think you're right," Peter said, nodding. "But eventually he's going to stop trying to hurt others and come after me."

"Which is why I think, for now, you should remain here," Adelaide said. "It's far safer here than in your tree."

"No," Peter said emphatically. "He's not going to send me into hiding. That would just be another victory for him."

"As you wish," Adelaide relented, seeing Peter would not be dissuaded. "In any event, we now have much to plan and discuss, no?"

The group spent the rest of the day planning new patrol routes and making new plans to try and track the pirates' movements. Before nightfall, parties were sent to Kite Nest and Nakkal to share the news: pirates had returned to Neverland.

The peace they had enjoyed seemed more like the eye of the storm than its conclusion.

Back in their tree, Peter secured the makeshift bolt that held his door secure while Tinker Belle lit the small fire in the center of the room.

He returned to the fire and stretched out on his stomach on the packed soil floor. Tinker Belle landed on his shoulder, and the pair watched the fire.

Neither spoke. The soft hiss and crack of the fire carried the conversation on its own and Peter and Tinker Belle were content to listen—listen and ponder the coming days.

NINETEEN

My boy!" William Till yelled, jumping from the ship to land on the dock.

"Father!" Peter cried running towards him but stopping short of embracing his father as fear and shame of the memory of losing his sister crashed into him.

"What's wrong?" William asked, concern tracing the lines on his weathered face. "What is it?"

"I..." Peter stammered, his eyes suddenly filling with tears. "Oh, Father. I failed. I couldn't do it. I couldn't protect her."

William closed the distance between them, but Peter just stared at the ground, not daring to meet his father's gaze.

He felt the deck boards shift as his father sat down next to him.

William didn't speak. Words were hollow and meaningless when it came to grief.

"It was Teach," Peter finally managed to say. "He…He was going to destroy Neverland and everyone in it unless we told him where the fairies lived."

Peter looked at his hands, still stained from his sister's blood.

"I was about to tell him, I had no choice. I couldn't bear to see her in pain, but she wouldn't let me," Peter said. "Mara wouldn't let me give them up."

A fiery evening sun hung low in the sky as Peter told his father everything that had happened.

William's gaze never broke from Peter. His sad smile spoke of understanding only fathers knew.

"How many did you save?" William asked a few minutes later. "How many still live because Mara died?"

Peter didn't answer right away. The pungency of nearby fires wafted through the docks as Peter considered.

His father had always been more concerned with lives saved than lives lost. But this was Peter's sister, William's own daughter. Didn't that change things?

"Thousands," he said at last. "I don't know, maybe more—maybe everyone in Neverland. But not her."

Suddenly he grew angry.

"When does it stop being about numbers?" Peter demanded, angry tears pooling in his eyes. "When is one life worth more than the others? Why didn't she let me save her?"

"She made the choice." William said, his own calm voice a sharp contrast to Peter's.

"What?" Peter asked, taken aback.

"She chose to die. She chose to protect the others."

"But I could have saved her," Peter insisted. "I could have told Teach what he wanted to hear and saved her."

"And you would have traded thousands of lives to save the person you had just betrayed," William countered. "In the end, you would have lost everything and gained nothing."

A weight Peter hadn't realized he was carrying, shifted. Something inside panicked and held on tighter, not wanting to release the burden of guilt.

"You did not fail her," William continued. "Denying Mara her choice would have been failing her."

Peter exhaled, releasing a breath he hadn't known he was holding.

William put his hand on Peter's shoulder.

"My boy," William said. "In no manner of the word have you failed. Your sister chose her path, now you must walk yours."

Peter finally raised his head and stared into his father's green eyes.

"Her burdens are not yours to carry," he said.

Peter could still feel the weight: the burden of Mara's death. He wore it like a cloak. It was the standard he weighed all he did against. But his father was right. To continue carrying it was not fair to himself and definitely was not fair to Mara's memory.

He closed his eyes and mentally, with painstaking care, removed the cloak, letting it slip off his shoulders and fall behind him.

He still hurt for Mara, he guessed he always would, but the guilt and shame that had followed the pain was less now.

"My boy," William said, a smile in his voice.

Peter opened his eyes.

The sky, hazy from the fire's smoke made the sun look like a giant fireball.

He inhaled, breathing what felt like the first real breath he'd ever taken.

He straightened his back, looked down, and saw Mara.

She was walking towards him, her brown hair blowing behind her as she strode towards him.

"Mara!" he exclaimed, jumping to his feet, not believing his eyes.

But something was wrong. She was angry.

"Peter!" she yelled, clearly upset about something.

"What is it?" he asked, still not believing his eyes. He looked to his father who was watching Mara without any hint of surprise.

"Peter, they're here!" she yelled again.

"What?" he asked, looking back to his sister. "Who?"

She marched right up to him and slapped him hard in the face. It hurt much less then he thought it would. The blow was light and soft.

"Peter Pan, get up," she screamed in his face. "Hook is here!"

Then she erupted in a cloud of smoke.

The smoke gagged and choked him. He reached for his dagger— his father's weapon—but it wasn't on his belt. He searched wildly around, looking for his weapon.

"Peter," William said sternly, spinning him around to face him. "Think, then act. Then think of nothing else."

Peter calmed, sobered by his father's words, then nodded.

"And remember, you are my joy," William smiled, his hands on Peter's shoulders.

Then the smile faded.

"Now fight, my son."

The dream evaporated into full wakefulness as Peter's eyes snapped open.

Immediately they began to sting.

He rolled off his makeshift bed, grabbing his daggers off the log as he rolled.

"It's about time!" Tinker Belle yelled as he fell. He hit the ground and came up in a crouch, brandishing both weapons.

"What's happening?" Peter asked, coughing. Smoke filled his vision as he looked around the tree.

"It's Hook," she explained, her glow drawn in to almost nothing. "They've piled up debris around the tree. The door and windows are blocked."

Peter looked at the entrance. Large branches and bushes had been piled up, blocking any escape. Flames roared around the outside of the tree, sending slivers of light through the various cracks in the tree. Peter knew he only had minutes before the smoke suffocated him. He looked up through the center of the tree.

He hadn't gotten around to widening the opening enough for him to fit through yet.

"I really wish I'd have done that earlier," Peter said, annoyed.

"No kidding," Tinker Belle quipped.

"You can get out through here," he said, pointing up. "I'll figure something out."

"Shut up," was all she said.

"Tink," Peter started.

"Do you really think I'm going to leave?" she spat. "Do you want to waste breath arguing?"

Peter could see she wasn't going anywhere. And neither would he had their situations been reversed. He looked around again. The only exits were the main entrance he had cut and a few smaller window-sized holes, all of which were now stuffed with debris and burning.

He snapped his fingers as an idea came to mind and flew to the back of the hollow and started to dig around the roots, clearing the rich, black soil from around the roots. He broke the surface, but as soon as his hand broke through, the dirt exploded in front of him as gun fire shot through.

He dived backwards, barely dodging the angry bullets that zipped into the hollow after him.

"It's time to die, Peter Pan!" a familiar, crazed voice yelled from outside the tree.

Mad Rogue.

Peter ignored the jest, knowing to answer it would do nothing to improve his situation. He looked back at Tinker Belle. She stared at him, hovering in the air, waiting for him to act.

"Boom, boom, Peter Pan!" Mad Rogue called from outside.

A sharp hissing sound brought his attention back to his feet. He looked down and saw a black orb with a burning fuse attached to it.

He sprinted away from the explosive. He ran towards Tinker Belle, snatched her out of the air, then hurled her towards a trench he had been digging earlier.

His intent had been to divert part of one of the nearby streams for water, but hadn't gotten around to connecting it. In this moment, he was grateful he hadn't.

Tinker Belle landed roughly in the hold, yelling in protest, then Peter was throwing himself on top of her, pulling his makeshift bed over the both of them.

A second later, the world exploded.

Debris and smoke erupted from every opening in the tree, showering the pirates with dirt and ash. Mad Rogue was the first to rise.

"Ha-ha!" he laughed, pumping his arms into the air and clapping.

"Check it out," Hook yelled. "You and you, make sure it's done."

Two pirates stood on each side of the tree's opening and peered in.

Nothing.

They exchanged glances, then the one to the right stepped into the smoking tree.

"Ollie?" the second man called. "What do you see?"

An instant later the man came hurtling back through the opening; he flew into the clearing and slid on the ground face first. Peter Pan rode on the man's back, driving the man's face into the ground.

In the same instant, a golden spark shot into the other pirate, striking him in the throat and sending him crashing to the ground.

Peter flipped backwards off the dazed pirate's back, taking his weapon with him, and threw himself into the nearest mob of pirates. He spun in a dizzy circle, cutting anything near him. Pirates screamed in surprise and pain as the boy's hungry blade bit into flesh and leather. Belts fell from waists as the boy spun, sending pirates stumbling over each other as they tried to get clear of the boy's blade.

Mad Rogue charged into the fray and dived, knocking the boy

off balance, but Peter recovered quickly. Instead of being driven into the ground, he took flight, moving in the direction Mad Rogue's blow had sent him. He grabbed the pirate and hurled him into the group of pirates coming towards them.

Hook, however, made no effort to assist his men. Instead, he watched them from the edge of the clearing.

The boy certainly could fight, there was no doubt of that. Whoever had taught him must have been a master himself. The boy's form, while far from perfect, was years ahead of any skill someone of his age should possess.

His tutor had even gone as far as to prepare him for combat against multiple opponents—a skill which the boy generously employed now.

Peter would engage with a pirate for one, maybe two strikes, and if he didn't land a substantial blow in that time, he'd disengage and attack someone else. It was the perfect tactic for this situation.

"Fascinating," Hook admitted, muttering to himself. "Fascinating, but I've seen enough."

He drew his pistol and leveled it at the boy. Just as he squeezed the trigger, his arm was shoved out of the line of Peter and towards one of his men.

The gun discharged, and the man crumpled to the ground. More upset over his missed shot than over wounding one of his own men, Hook dropped the pistol and drew another, but it discharged before it had cleared his belt. He looked down in surprise to see that a pixie, doubtless the same one who followed Peter around, had somehow fired the gun.

Before he could move, she was at another gun, a little spark of fire in her hand igniting the charge. The gun fired, and Hook instinctively spun away from the blast. The movement did nothing since the gun was still firmly thrust in his belt. Immediately, the pixie was on the fourth gun, then the fifth and sixth, firing them as Hook yelled and batted at her, jumping away from each shot.

Then, once all of his weapons had been fired, she was gone, hurling herself back into the fray.

A surge of frustration ignited in Hook. His perfectly executed ambush had not delivered to him the lifeless body of Peter Pan. Instead, the boy was making them pay dearly for entering his domain.

Hook narrowed his eyes and walked back into the forest.

"Very well," he muttered to himself. "We'll just have to wear you down a bit more."

After all, these little encounters continued to show him things about the boy. And while Hook left each encounter with more valuable information, Peter Pan, no doubt, left each encounter more and more frustrated and beaten down.

Inevitably, the boy would tire, falter, and fail.

Hook smiled to himself, then put his thumb and index finger between his lips and whistled.

Immediately, his men disengaged and returned into the forest.

* * *

Peter fell to his hands and knees gasping for breath, then rolled over to his back. His chest heaved as he sucked air into his lungs. He stared at the night sky as he fought to regain his breath.

After several long minutes, he sat up. His tree was gone. The flames had died, extinguished from the violent explosion that had rocked it, but his nearly completed home was now nothing more than a smoking, black crater.

"It was a rotten house anyways," Peter said, wiping his still-stinging eyes clear.

"We'll make another one," Tinker Belle said.

"Forget it," Peter said, hurling a piece of debris into the crater. "Let's get out of here."

TWENTY

Peter was livid. He had spent the rest of the night flying across every part of Neverland, searching for Hook. It was only after the first sliver of the morning sun appeared that he returned to White Falls. Upon entering the falls, he collapsed into sleep almost immediately. He awoke a few hours later in time to join the afternoon patrols.

When the patrols returned that evening with nothing but spent time to show for their efforts, Peter rested again, only to rise again to join the night patrols.

Peter continued joining on the patrols for several days until, near exhaustion, Adelaide forbade her fairies to allow Peter to join them on patrols.

Peter objected, furious at being denied, but ultimately relented after being pinned to the ground by a score of fairies and pricked by arrows coated in one of their weaker sedatives.

After two full days of drug-assisted sleep, Peter, fully rested, was allowed to resume patrols with the fairies.

Peter and Tinker Belle's patrol had brought them within hailing distance of the mermaid's Obsidian Cliffs.

Tonight, however, they were not alone. Tolan, perched atop Crim, had joined them. Always looking for opportunities to strengthen the bond between himself and the bird, he had offered to accompany Peter and Tinker Belle on their patrol. The pair had become quite adept at working together.

The odd group zipped and darted through trees, all the time checking for any sign of pirates.

It had been over a week since Hook had bombed Peter's tree. And while others were starting to think the pirates had left, resulting in search patrols more or less returning to their normal patterns, Peter remained unconvinced.

So he and Tinker Belle continued to patrol the farthest reaches of Neverland, hoping to catch sight of the man who now always seemed one step ahead of them.

"We were just out here," Tinker Belle was saying, her eyes constantly taking in her surroundings.

"I know," Peter replied. "But if we become predictable, we'll never find him."

"I don't know," Tolan said, slowing Crim's speed to match Peter's. "I'm starting to think Hook may have left."

"He wouldn't leave after I wounded him," Peter said. "He won't leave until he has what he wants. And that's me."

Suddenly, a silver glint in a clearing about a hundred yards away caught Peter's eye.

"Look!" Peter exclaimed, pointing in the direction.

Far below he saw five men stepping into a clearing, the light glinting off their blades as they stepped into the moonlight.

"There!" Tinker Belle exclaimed, seeing it too.

And without another word, they shot towards the clearing.

The pirates never saw them coming.

The first pirate was thrown to the ground as Crim and Tolan crashed into him. The man went sprawling, deep talon and sword wounds on his neck, leaving no doubt he'd never rise again.

Tinker Belle shot past the second one, setting off the man's holstered pistol in the process.

The gun discharged, firing point-blank into the man's leg. The pirate howled in pain, and although Peter couldn't see her face, he knew Tinker Belle was grinning at the man's pain.

Despite the agony the man was in, to his credit, he still managed to pull his sword free and block her first two strikes.

But it was the third strike that sent him to the dirt. And the fourth that ensured he'd never leave it.

Landing, Peter drew his own dagger and struck at the leader, a low slash that would certainly injure but not kill the man.

The man pivoted away, blocking the attack, then riposted with a fast overhead strike. Peter caught the blow then twisted his dagger, forcing the man to lower his sword or risk having his own wrist broken.

Around him, Peter could hear the sound of battle diminishing as Tinker Belle killed another pirate, leaving herself and Tolan to contend with the last one together.

Peter continued to twist, drawing the man's arm completely behind him. Peter yanked the sword free of the man's grasp and kicked him hard behind the leg, forcing him to his knees.

"Where is he?" Peter demanded, twisting the arm even more.

The man grunted in pain but didn't move to answer.

"Where is he?" Peter repeated, yelling this time.

"Go rot, boy," the pirate spat.

Peter opened his mouth to reply when the muzzle flash of a gun erupted a few yards from him.

The pirate Peter had been fighting lurched over and began screaming in pain.

Rather than discharging the shot into the ground, Tinker Belle had directed the man's aim towards the one Peter had been fighting.

"No!" Peter cried as Tinker Belle and Tolan killed the pirate they were engaged with.

"We can't afford to play nice," Tinker Belle snapped, flying now towards Peter's attacker.

But Peter stepped between Tinker Belle and the man, blocking her way.

"We can't kill him," he insisted. "We need him to tell us where Hook is."

"Fine," Tinker Belle snapped. "Then he dies."

"That's not your decision," Peter said.

Tinker Belle didn't answer. Instead she just glared at him.

Behind him, the man thrashed in agony.

Peter turned and walked towards the injured man who was trying to pull himself towards the tree line.

"Where is he?" Peter demanded, seizing the man by the leg and dragging him back into the clearing.

The man howled in agony as Peter pulled him. The pirate's once tan shirt was stained dark with blood. Peter took one look at the man's wound and knew at once the severity of the injury.

"Where is he?" Peter asked again, squatting down so the pirate could look at him.

The man said nothing and continued to writhe in pain.

"I could help you," Peter offered.

"I'm dying," the man managed, a painful laugh. "Wot could you do?"

"Where is he hiding?" Peter asked again, ignoring the question.

The man, shaking from pain or fear or both, shook his head, muttering to himself between gasps.

Peter watched the man. He looked from his face to the man's wound then back to the man's face. Then finally he turned to Tinker Belle.

"Enough of this," Peter said, turning to Tinker Belle. "Tink, get it."

"Are you serious?!" she demanded.

"Just do it!" Peter ordered.

Without another word, Tinker Belle drew a dagger and shot towards the pirate. The man's eyes widened as she approached, and he raised his hands to cover his face. Tinker Belle landed on the man's chest, and with a single strike, cut his shirt open, and plunged both the dagger and her hand into the man's wound. He howled in pain, but before he could fend her off, Peter was on top of him, using his weight and a good deal of flight to keep him pressed to the ground.

After a few long minutes, Tinker Belle withdrew a round bullet from the man's gut.

His cries of pain lessened but didn't dissipate fully.

"Where is he?" Peter asked a third time.

This time, the man answered.

"Do ye think pulling a bullet out of moi gut suddenly makes us into pals?" he managed. "Captain Hook is a ghost, he is. And no amount of flying about or grand ole speeches will help you find him."

The pirate coughed; blood and spit covered his mouth as he did.

"Fair enough," Peter said, rising to his feet and turning to leave.

"That's it?" the pirate scoffed. "No witty retort?"

"I'd give you a message to deliver," Peter said, turning once more to address the pirate. "But between that wound, the patrols in the sky, and the mers on the coast," Peter said. "Hook would never get it."

"Wot's that supposed to mean?" the man called as Peter walked away.

"Get out of here," Peter ordered, turning back to face the man.

"What?" Tinker Belle sputtered. "He's a pirate! He dies!"

"No!" Peter bellowed. "No more killing! There are other ways."

Tinker Belle just shook her head.

"No. You're wrong, you're so wrong. Killing is all they know," she said, pointing to the man who had gotten to his feet and was scurrying to the tree line. "If you're going to protect us, then you have to actually protect us. And that means killing the people who are trying to murder us."

"I agree with Tinker Belle," Tolan said, joining the conversation and hovering between Peter and Tinker Belle. "We can't afford to–"

Tolan erupted into golden brilliance.

Peter went cold and hollow inside.

One moment he was talking to Tolan, the next instant the fairy was gone. And through the shower of dust, Peter saw Tinker Belle. Her mouth gaping open as she stared at the shimmering cloud of dust that had once been her friend.

Her daggers slipped from her hands and fell to the ground.

"No," she pleaded. "No, no, no, no."

Helplessly, she began snatching handfuls of dust from the air, and stuffing them into a small bag on her hip. But the dust had already begun to drift to the ground.

She continued to gather what dust she could. She moved as quickly as she could, gathering small handfuls. But the golden disappeared, soaking into the ground, into the grass, into Peter's feet, faster than she could collect it.

Peter looked to the tree line where the shot had come from and saw the injured pirate—the one he had let go—dropping a pistol and fleeing into the forest.

He looked back and saw Crim, dazed, her wings fluttering madly as she rolled around the ground a few yards away.

Then he looked back at Tinker Belle. Now she was staring at him; her small, furious eyes bore into him with enough intensity to stop a mermaid.

She rose to her feet, her hands still coated in Tolan's dust. She opened her mouth to speak, or scream, or call down fire on Peter, when Crim zipped past her, screeching in rage and sorrow, flying towards the tree line where the pirate had fled.

Tinker Belle immediately deposited her final handfuls of dust in her pouch, picked up her daggers, then shot after the bird.

Peter stared at the ground, watching the remaining dust that had once been Tolan soak into the ground. His once bright light faded as the dust disappeared, until all traces of him vanished, leaving Peter alone in the dark.

Numbly, he followed after the pirate, not really in pursuit of him, but allowing the task to occupy a small part of his mind.

He saw the pirate, more stumbling than running. The man's arms flailed behind him as he ran, no doubt trying to fend off the bird that now relentlessly attacked him. His path would lead him to the edge of the cliffs, and in the dark he would never see the edge.

Peter had no emotion for that fact.

He saw Tinker Belle, a white-golden streak, flying arrow-straight towards the man.

She intercepted him while he was still ten paces from the cliff's edge. She moved around him, attacking him with such speed and ferocity, he looked like he was being wrapped up by a bright, golden rope.

The man shrieked in pain and horror and sprinted with what little energy he must have had left.

He ran off the edge of the cliff and must have dropped twenty feet before realizing he was falling.

The kite and fairy, neither of which needed solid ground or sure footing, pursued the man as he plummeted towards the dark waters.

Just before the trio hit the water, Crim disengaged and flew up. A heartbeat later, Tinker Belle broke off her attack, leaving the man to fall the final few seconds alone before crashing into the sea.

Peter knew the man had died before he hit the water.

Peter watched the pair return to the top of the cliffs. They flew towards him. He half expected, even hoped, they would turn and attack him, but they streaked past him without slowing.

Peter dropped to the ground, curling into a ball. He pounded his fists against the cold grass as the wind carried his cries out to sea.

When his body would give up tears no longer, he stared out at the sea. And with puffy, burning eyes, Peter watched the waves and envied the dead.

TWENTY ONE

Morning brought an end to the ignorance that only sleep could offer. Peter woke, soaking wet from dew and trembling uncontrollably.

He opened his eyes to a gray, featureless sky.

Neverland seemed dull and muted, as if the island itself was affected by Tolan's death.

No, death was the wrong word.

Tolan hadn't died.

Tolan had been obliterated.

In the blink of an eye, he had gone from that strong, smart fairy to dust.

The worst part was that Tolan had been voicing his concern over

Peter freeing the pirate when that very pirate had drawn a pistol and fired it, instantly killing him.

It would have been no different had Peter himself fired the weapon.

He crawled to the edge of the cliffs and peered down. The water seemed impossibly far. He reached for one of the head-sized rocks that lay nearby, then rolled off the edge with it.

He let himself fall towards the water at full speed. Part of him wished the dust that imbued his body, enabling him to fly, would fade away.

No luck.

He slowed his fall and repositioned his body so he hit the water feet first and at a manageable speed.

He let the rock pull him deeper into the water, down below where the sheer cliffs ended and jutted inland.

Mers were in the water, some leaving the cavern base, others returning, carrying kelp, fish, and whatever else they had found in the sea that morning.

Peter released the rock and swam under the cliff, angling towards one of the dozens of round glowing openings in the stone.

He reached one of the pools and pulled himself up out of the water. He could have easily flown, but he chose not to.

Mers were leaping in and out of the pool.

Peter largely ignored them and walked over to the far wall where various fish had been stacked and where whale hides were stretched out, drying in the cave.

He leaned against the wall, then slid down until he was sitting.

Peter watched the commotion without interest as the activity of maintaining the Nakkal proceeded around him.

A small figure entered the cave and meandered its way through the various stalls, stopping to inspect new crafts or taste freshly prepared food. The small mer child stopped at one such stall and picked up something then continued on her tour.

After a few minutes she noticed Peter and, abandoning her wandering, angled straight for him.

She grinned as she approached him, her huge emerald eyes revealing the pleasure she felt seeing him again.

"Peter," she chirped happily.

"Sarii," Peter said, smiling, despite himself.

She nestled next to him, settling herself close to him, watching the activity of the cave with him.

Peter looked down at her and, feeling his gaze, she looked up and smiled, her young, sharp teeth almost glowing white.

In her hands, she held a fillet, freshly removed from an unlucky fish. She pulled it apart, tearing it in two, a few sinews stretching taut before snapping free. She handed half of the fish to him.

Peter accepted the gift and bit into the raw flesh.

He was more or less used to food like this now, and to be honest, he was grateful to not have to forage food on his own today.

The pair sat, sharing their meal and watching the morning hum in silence.

"Pan Hakki," a voice said, from above him.

Peter looked up to see Shiiklah towering over him.

"Come," she said.

Peter and Sarii both rose and followed.

The trio wandered through the caverns, as was their custom

whenever Peter would visit. After a few minutes Shiiklah stopped to look at him, staring at him with those eyes.

Those eyes that always seemed to stare into him, rather than at him. Those eyes that demanded answers to unspoken questions.

"I've done something terrible," Peter answered.

"Leave us," Shiiklah said, turning to Sarii.

The mer child yipped in acknowledgement then turned and wandered back the way they had come, just as happy to explore on her own as with the rest of the group.

Hot tears welled in Peter's eyes. He closed them. He shook his head, then, taking a deep breath, he opened them and spoke.

He told her everything.

Starting with his unwillingness to kill and his countless arguments with Tinker Belle and finally the events of the night before.

He finished explaining and realized he was out of breath.

Peter pulled his coral dagger free from behind him and inspected it.

"I must be the worst Pan Hakki ever," Peter said, running his hand over the engraving in the weapon.

The pair walked in silence for a few minutes. The only sounds were those of the mermaid's scales scraping along the ground, and the ever-present sound of water dripped and echoing.

"Your first kill," Shiiklah said, speaking for the first time since Sarii had left them. "It troubles you."

Peter nodded. "Yes."

"Good," Shiiklah said. "If it did not, you would be undeserving of that," she said, pointing to the blade in his hands.

"But people keep dying," Peter said. "No matter what I do..." he trailed off.

He heaved a sigh.

"It's…it's too much," he said.

"The weight iss our burden," Shiiklah said, surprising Peter with how open she was.

Peter looked up at her.

"We kill to protect thossse who cannot from falling."

Peter considered her words, brief as they were. He thought about his father and wondered how someone who had killed so many could still have so much joy. Peter had no idea how many men William Till had killed. But he knew it had to have been a lot.

Once Peter had asked his father how many lives he had taken, but William hadn't answered. Instead, William had had told him it wasn't about lives taken, it was about lives saved.

Death wasn't the focus for William Till.

It was something else.

"We know of sacrifice," Shiiklah said, her blue eyes focusing on something in the past. "And we know of death."

Shaking her head and blinking back to the present, she stooped down and closed Peter's hand around the hilt of the weapon, an extremely intimate gesture, considering the lack of affection mers tended to display.

"Fear not, Pan Hakki," she said. "Your course is true."

Fear.

That was it.

Peter was afraid.

More than that, he was terrified that if he killed again, he would become like the men his father had died hunting.

Fear had paralyzed him, deceiving him into thinking his inaction had been anything but. He had been a fool, and others had paid for his mistake.

Peter blinked the tears away.

"Good," Shiiklah purred, her eyes melting from blue to black.

She pushed the weapon towards Peter.

"There is a poison in Neverland, Pan Hakki," she said. "Drive it out."

Peter looked up at her and nodded, spurned on both by his own revelation and Shiiklah's faith in him.

Turning, he began walking back towards the pools.

He paused after a few steps.

"Mermaid," Peter said, turning back to face her again.

She looked back at him.

"I may call on you," he said.

Her eyes flicked down the mer-call that still hung around his neck, then back up to him. She nodded, the whisper of an expectant smile tugged at the corners of her mouth.

Peter walked down the hall and into the chamber of craftsmen.

Each alcove was filled with mers, busy crafting. He reached the stall with the ancient mer who always seemed to be crafting weapons. Today, though, he was working on something Peter had never seen.

It resembled the mer's common thin, long swords, but it was even longer. It was white—as were all mer weapons. But instead of a single, leather grip at one end, it had two. A single grip at the end, and then a second one almost mid-way up the shaft. It was a weapon meant for large prey.

The old mer looked up from his work and, recognizing Peter, bared his teeth and hissed.

This time, though, instead of recoiling in fear or running away, Peter growled back at the old mer, showing his own teeth. And to his surprise, the mer's snarl twisted into the slightest smirk and then he gave Peter the faintest of nods before returning to his work.

Peter continued to wind through the cavern labyrinth he now knew so well. Arriving at the pools that served as portals to the sea, Peter looked around the cavernous room one more time, then dived through the hole that would take him into the sea. Then back to the dry. Then back to duty.

TWENTY TWO

Peter decided to walk back to White Falls rather than fly. The time it added to his trip allowed him to consider what would come next. He knew he had learned a precious lesson in Tolan's death, but he doubted the other fairies would view Tolan's unwitting sacrifice an acceptable payment for Peter's lesson. Peter himself knew he didn't.

He continued to walk and consider every possible reaction they might have—ranging from him simply being declared an outcast to Tinker Belle leading the cloud of angry fairies that would skin him alive.

About an hour later, he found himself staring up at the cascading water. He lifted off the ground and drifted towards the place in the falls where the cavern interior hid.

Tiny sparks of cold water pricked his skin as he grew closer. The sparks turned to mist which turned into the full down-pouring weight of the falling water. He had to adjust mentally to keep from being swept away, and for a small instant he considered letting the torrent carry him away. Dying would have been easier than facing the fairies' wrath.

He clamped down on the thought, taking it captive and driving it from his mind. Life or death, he would face Adelaide and her fairies.

He slipped from the waterfall and into the cave. Any activity that had been happening had stopped completely. The absolute silence was painfully at odds with the roaring waterfall he had just passed through.

The water gave way to the dazzling interior of White Falls and immediately every fairy stopped and stared at him.

Someone moving towards him caught his eye and he looked up to see Tinker Belle, her yellow hair a mess and her tiny eyes red and puffy. She said nothing to him but instead flew right up to him and landed on his shoulder.

Immediately, Peter felt his eyes fill with tears.

Searching for something to say, but failing, Peter opened his mouth to speak anyways.

"You've returned?" a voice above him said.

He looked up to see Adelaide, her long, golden staff in hand, approaching him.

Peter nodded, again opening his mouth to find something to say.

But Adelaide held up a hand.

"We do not require perfection, my friend," she said. "Only your best. And you've given us nothing less."

The tears streamed, unchecked down Peter's cheek. He dropped to his knees and buried his face in his hands.

"Tolan's loss was profound," Adelaide continued, landing on the ground beside him. "As is every fairy I lose in this conflict. But remember, Peter, we are at war."

He looked up and found her standing right in front of him.

"Oh, my dear friend," she said, smiling down at him. "There are still a great many things you do not know about us."

Peter frowned in confusion.

Adelaide's eyes slid from Peter to one corner of the cave.

Peter followed her gaze and gasped.

A fairy walked towards him. He was as pale as the moon and bare-chested, clad only in simple white shorts.

Tolan.

"What?" Peter exclaimed, stumbling forward. "Tolan!"

"Tinker Belle managed to save enough of him and return to White Falls in time for the makers to restore him," Adelaide explained. "The bag she carried was made to contain dust, not absorb it."

"Still no wings," Tolan replied, hooking a thumb over his shoulder. "Well, none without feathers at least," he added with a smile.

Crim, perched on the ledge next to Tolan's apartment, clacked her beak in agreement.

"How?" Peter stammered. "I don't understand."

"Sometimes we get lucky," Tinker Belle said, speaking for the first time.

"Tolan," Peter said, crawling towards the fairy.

He was careful not to touch him, unsure of how to act.

"I was so wrong," Peter said. "Please forgive me."

Tolan smiled back at him and nodded his head.

"We move forward," Tolan said. "And we finish this."

Peter sniffed, wiped his eyes dry, and nodded.

"We still have much to do, my friend," Adelaide said. "Are you ready, Peter?"

He was ready.

Free of guilt and shame.

Free to defend Neverland.

And confident in who he was but more importantly, who he would never become.

Peter rose to his feet, placed his hands on his hips, and smiled.

"Yeah," he said. "I'm ready now."

TWENTY THREE

They have to be somewhere," Peter insisted.

"But we've searched the entire island," Tinker Belle said.

"And they've left no trace. They strike where they strike and then they're gone. Maybe they just head back out to sea each time after all."

"Their ssship has not been in our waters," Shiiklah said. "Nor in any of the outlying islands. We would have felt it."

The topic of Captain Hook's whereabouts had become a daily, sometimes hourly, focus of discussion. The entire island's populous had banded together and searched from the northern wood to the southern forest and from the eastern shores over the mountains to the Obsidian Cliffs that lined the western edge of Neverland.

"Okay," Peter started, pacing back and forth. "Either they sail to Neverland, launch their attack, and then sail away—all without a single mer seeing them–"

An angry hiss from Shiiklah interrupted him.

"Which is incredibly unlikely," Peter finished, holding up his hands to her. "Or they're here and the ship is hidden somewhere so well we can't find it, or it's gone and the pirates are traveling on foot."

No one objected.

"Either way," Micah said, "a group has to be here. Hook is clever; he's no fool."

"Agreed. He was largely successful at avoiding us in the cove," Shiiklah explained, referring to the winding route along the shallows Hook had taken to shore when he first arrived.

"I agree," Adelaide said. "I think to search for the ship is an unwise use of our efforts."

"Then we need to find the core group," Micah said, agreeing with Peter.

"Agreed," Rike said, nodding.

"There were the remnants of camp fire in the clearing," Tinker Belle offered.

"The one in the south?" Tolan asked.

"Yes," she replied, her ponytail swaying behind her as she nodded.

"He has to be close," Peter said. "He burned Kite Nest, then right after that, he showed himself in the clearing. That night, he blew up my tree. You're right, he's moving too quickly to be leaving the island and returning each time. His actions are too close together. He has to be here."

Peter rubbed the heels of his hands into his eyes. He was weary. Weary of searching and finding nothing.

"Any large camp or new buildings would stand out, we would have found it by now," Tolan insisted. "The island is large, but not so large we would miss something large enough to hold a ship's crew if they'd have built something."

"If they had built it…" Peter said, trailing off. "Wait a minute." Peter's eyes lit with sudden comprehension.

"What if they didn't build a camp?" he asked, looking up. "What if they didn't build anything? We're looking for any new indication that they're here. What if there isn't any?"

"I don't understand," Rike said, frowning.

"What's the one place large enough to hold that many pirates?" Peter asked. "And what's the one place I haven't searched?"

"You mean…?" Adelaide asked.

But Peter was looking at Tinker Belle, who was nodding slowly to him.

"The mansion," Peter stated.

Tinker Belle nodded faster.

"But we checked the mansion," Tolan said.

"All of it?" Peter asked, turning towards him. "It's huge."

Tolan didn't reply. Instead, he clenched his jaw and growled in frustration, then stepped off the ledge where Crim caught him on her back.

"Lorel, Micah, assemble your patrols and meet us in the air," Rike commanded.

The pair flared into golden brilliance and whistled, each whistle distinct. Fairies from various parts of the cave flew towards their respective leader. The scouts flew to Rike and Lorel while the wardens assembled around Micah.

"Let's go!" Peter yelled, then hurled himself through the water fall.

* * *

A quarter of an hour later the mansion was in view.

It was as dark and foreboding as it ever had been—an old, blind watchman overseeing the island, unaware that its charge had long since overgrown.

The fairies diminished their glows to avoid prying pirate eyes. The group landed noiselessly in what appeared to be a ground floor bedroom. The large bay window had long since been shattered. Stale pillows lay strewn around the room, hanging off the bed.

"Spread out?" Tinker Belle whispered.

Peter shook his head.

The party moved from the bedroom out into a long hallway that had been converted to a dormitory of sorts, but long ago. The beds, roughhewn planks nailed—sometimes roped—together appeared anything but comfortable. The old splintered wood smelled stale and dank.

They made their way noiselessly through the hall, the fairies slowly hovering over and under the beds, checking for any sign of use.

"There are blankets in some of these," Micah whispered. "But who could know when they're from."

Peter was about to answer when the squeak of wood halted and silenced everyone.

Pirate or old house? Tinker Belle's stare asked Peter.

Peter shrugged, but drew his dagger anyway.

The hall opened up to a larger one, squared and intersected by conjoined rooms. Before them arched a narrow doorway. Whatever lie beyond must have been for servants or slaves since the doorway was wide enough only to permit a single person at a time. That and it was unremarkable in appearance. Beyond the opening was utter darkness and Peter felt less than inclined to venture forward. To his right was a much larger doorway. The wide panels that framed the door had deep, ornate patterns carved in them. Peter couldn't make out exactly what the designs were, but he could tell guests had been permitted into that room.

To the left was a staircase that led beneath the main level. The smell of cold, damp air hinted this was a cellar.

But Peter didn't need any of his senses to tell him what lie at the bottom of the stairs. Down those stairs was the cellar, the place where Edward Teach had brought his sister to die.

"Down?" Rike asked.

"No," Peter said immediately, making eye contact with Tinker Belle then looking away. "Not yet."

He turned, wanting to do anything to keep from replaying the events of that night in his head. He had never wanted to return to this house in the first place. Now he was here, every step he took was languid, as if each of those steps cost him something. And he was afraid if he went down those stairs, he might disappear before ever reaching the bottom.

He looked at the narrow doorway, facing the darkness, then turned away and led the party through the large entryway.

The doorway opened up to an expansive room. It was long like the dormitory hall but wider and with expansive cathedral ceilings. There were cracks and broken tiles in the celling that let splinters of moonlight sneak through, their narrow beams long and thin like bamboo shoots.

Countless flakes of dust danced together in the small spotlights for a few moments before drifting out of the light, making room for others to take their place.

The streams of light offered just enough illumination to see they had entered a grand dining room. Whoever had built this place had been wealthier than anyone Peter had ever heard of. The table, huge by any standards, stretched out before him. Cobwebs and dust coated what few remaining goblets and candelabra dotted the table. High above the table, rafters braced the roof, stretching up from the walls to the ceiling's peak.

The party made their way through the dining hall, inspecting items that appeared to have been untouched for decades.

"There's nothing here," Rike said, annoyance creeping into his voice.

Peter opened his mouth to agree when a faint, metallic snap echoed through the room. Instantly, he recognized the sound of a pistol's hammer clicking into place.

"Down!" he screamed.

The cloud of fairies—still suppressing their glows—dispersed, scattering in all directions. Peter, despite his own order, hurled himself up into the rafters.

Gunfire flashed from the far wall, illuminating a handful—six, maybe ten—pirates hiding in the shadows. A war cry sounded from the men as they rushed towards where the group had been assembled a moment before.

Peter stopped himself just short of the ceiling, then pressed his back against it, one hand above him on the ceiling, the other gripping one of the supporting beams.

"Did you get 'em?" one of the pirates asked.

"No, you didn't get 'em," Tinker Belle mocked quietly, more to herself than to Peter. She hovered next to him for a moment before landing on the beam to dig something out of her tunic.

"I dunno, the shot was true, but that one is clever," another pirate replied.

The pirates were all gathered in the center of the room now, almost directly below Peter and Tinker Belle. Peter split his attention between listening to the pirates below and watching Tinker Belle, who had now found whatever she had been searching for. It was a small, leather pouch. She had unrolled it on one of the wooden beams and was fitting what seemed to be a small dart into a blowgun.

She looked up at him and, he couldn't tell in the dark, but she might have winked at him. Then she leaned out over the beam, paused, then brought the tube to her lips and exhaled sharply.

There was the faintest 'puff' as she blew, followed by a startled cry from below.

The man slapped the back of his neck, as if killing an offending bug, then pulled his hand away and squinted at the tiny dart in his hand.

"I've been bandaged!" the man cried.

His comrades all turned to him.

"What?" several of them asked, clearly confused.

"There's porridge in my boot!" the man insisted, holding the tiny dart up for them to see. But it was too dark and the dart was too small for the others to see.

"Blue!" the man cried, trying in vain to explain to his fellows that he had been poisoned. He suddenly stopped talking then dropped to the floor and stopped moving. The rest of the pirates recoiled in horror, then, realizing they were now the ones in danger, drew their weapons and began firing them blindly in all directions.

In response, the fairies from around the room flared into light and flew towards the pirates like guns returning fire.

Peter dropped from the ceiling and landed on a pirate, slowing not to injure himself when he landed, but still with enough speed the man crumpled to the ground upon impact.

He dived across the table to avoid an attack coming his way. He then found himself leaping backwards to avoid a strike from a second pirate. The man's knife sank deep into the wood. The pirate tugged at the blade, but Peter lashed out with his foot, catching the pirate squarely in the face. The man's eyes rolled backwards, and he sank to the floor.

Peter leapt to his feet and quickly scanned the room. It was alight with the muzzle-blast of discharging guns and glowing fairies. The din of battle must have alerted other pirates to the fray, because reinforcements were now pouring through the gaping doorway. The only difference was these pirates, in addition to their standard armament, were brandishing torches and lanterns.

Most of the pirates were busy fighting fairies, but one, a bearded man with black hair and a long rapier in his hand, strode through the battle towards Peter. Peter watched him approach. He adjusted the grip on his dagger. He shifted his weight, making sure it was evenly balanced on his feet.

The pirate swung his sword around, a showy display meant to intimidate opponents.

But Peter was not afraid. Instead, he waited until the pirate's sword play brought his weapon farther from Peter. Then he shot forward.

The pirate's eyes widened in surprise, then in pain as Peter's dagger appeared in the man's chest.

Peter let the pirate fall to the floor, then retrieved his weapon and scanned the room for the next threat. He was alive and the pirate was not. And he gave his actions no further thought. Peter flew back up to the rafters and began to inspect the ceiling. There were plenty of cracks and holes—nothing large enough for Peter to fit through, but the fairies would be able to escape easily.

"What are you doing?" Tinker Belle demanded, arriving at his side.

"The cracks," Peter yelled. "They should be large enough for all of you to escape."

She glared at him and opened her mouth to speak when the rafter exploded next to them, struck by a bullet. Her scowl deepened as she scanned the crowed for the shooter. Finding him, she zipped towards him.

"She's not going to leave me here, is she," Peter said to himself.

"Nope!" came Tinker Belle's response, hearing what he had said.

Peter laughed, despite the situation and dived back into the fray.

He threaded through the pirates engaged with fairies, sometimes knocking one off balance, granting a fairy a momentary advantage.

Concerned that his tactics may be becoming predicable, he sheathed his dagger and flew erratically, throwing himself into the backs and sides of the pirates engaged in battle. Once again, the fairies took advantage of their attackers being knocked off balance and struck. Their diminutive size gave them another advantage, they were almost always underestimated, a mistake that no foe ever made twice.

Peter threw himself against a particularly fat pirate. The man stumbled forward a few steps before being overwhelmed by a trio of warden fairies he had been trying to fend off with a lantern. The pirate crashed into the floor and did not rise.

He turned to start another pass and made it half way down the length of the table when something seized his ankle. Before he knew what was happening, he had reversed direction and was being swung like a hammer towards the table. He tried to change his direction, but his momentum was too great. He slammed through the table. Thankfully, the table was brittle, weakened by time, and the collision merely jarred him rather than severely injuring him.

He landed on his back and looked up at the biggest foot he had ever seen. Peter's gaze quickly traced up the leg and body and saw the visage of the man. His giant blond head was peering down at Peter. The man shook his head at Peter.

"No fly," the pirate said, his voice thick with an accent Peter did not recognize. The man raised his impossibly large foot and brought it down towards him. Peter rolled to his side, crashing through pieces of table and tarnished dishes, then scurried under a section of table that was more or less still standing.

He paused for a few heartbeats to catch his breath before the table above him exploded as a giant blade burst through the wood, burying itself in the floor.

The blade was as wide as Peter's own head and polished to a mirror-shine. Peter watched himself gaping at his own reflection in the weapon then shook his head in an effort to clear his mind and scurried under the table towards the end. The smashing and chopping of wood resounded behind him as the blond pirate hacked and stomped at the table to reach Peter. To avoid the blade, he half-crawled, half-flew through the table debris, trying to get free. He reached the end of the table and took off into the air, but once again, the Pirate's vice-like grip yanked him from the air and threw him to the ground.

His head slammed against the ground and when he looked up, he didn't know if the light he was seeing came from his injured head or from nearby fairies.

"No fly," the man repeated, swinging his large sword above his head. Peter leapt to his feet and drew his own weapon. The dagger was hilariously small compared to the pirate's weapon.

The man brought his sword down where Peter stood. He dived out of the way, then came up in a crouch and lashed out with his blade, slicing a furrow into the man's wrist.

Expecting the man to recoil in pain, Peter took a precious second to regain his footing.

It was the wrong move.

The man didn't even seem to notice or care about the injury. Instead, he released his grip on his weapon and backhanded Peter hard across the face. Peter staggered backwards, then tripped and fell hard on his tailbone. He scurried backwards on all fours out of the dining hall and through the doorway that led opened up into another hallway. He struck again, but the pirate deflected the blow with his massive weapon. The force knocked the dagger from Peter's grip and sent it flying, burying itself to the hilt in the doorway above him. It was an embarrassing reminder that skilled as he might be, Peter was still fighting men who possessed several times his own strength.

He gathered himself to leap for the weapon but an overhead slash from the pirate changed his mind. He stumbled back, falling again. The blows were much faster and farther-reaching than Peter had thought possible. The sword sheared through doorways, carving deep furrows into the walls. Peter scrambled to his feet and hurtled down the hall. Several lanterns, both lit and unlit, dotted the long hallway. Peter ignored them as he flew.

The hall dead ended into a large floor-to-ceiling window. It was ornate, various stained glass panes depicting a battle of some sort. At one end sat an elegant mansion atop a cliff. All around the mansion were men in armor with crossbows and swords. They were being attacked by mermaids with glowing eyes, led from the rear by a much larger, sinister-looking mermaid with black eyes.

For a precious second, Peter did a double take at the being. She was clearly a mermaid, but something was terribly wrong with her somehow.

The sound of the massive, blond pirate thundering down the hall behind him chased all thoughts of soldiers and mermaids from his mind as he slammed his fist against the glass.

Nothing happened.

He hit it again and a few cracks appeared in the glass. The sound of charging footsteps grew closer as Peter, seized by panic, hammered at the stained glass window. The cracks expanded, and smaller panes began to break free of their moldings and shatter on the ground. The musical sound of breaking glass collided with the pirate's thunderous pounding.

He turned and saw the man closing within ten spaces.

"Tink!" he yelled, desperate to get help.

But no help came.

Peter grabbed one of the few lit lanterns and hurled it just in front of the man, a desperate attempt to buy a few more seconds. The lantern smashed into the floor, breaking, and spilling its oil on the floor and on his attacker. The puddle instantly ignited, bathing the hallway in a golden light.

Peter turned back to the window and pounded on it, and again each time chips and pieces fell from the glass, but they exposed the multi-layer of glass.

Peter looked behind him and started. The man was standing there, towering above him, legs smoking from where they had been burned. He had leapt over or possibly even walked through the fire. A helpless, defeated cry slipped through his lips and he waited for the final blow.

Instead, the man smiled down at him, a cruel, hideous thing that snaked across his face.

"Yes, fly." The man smiled down at him, speaking in his heavy accent.

Peter squinted in confusion, then his confusion turned to fear as the pirate raised one of his enormous feet and kicked Peter with more force than he thought possible. Dimly, as darkness wrapped him in cold, nothingness, he wondered if those men in the glass had survived the dark mermaid's attack.

The next thing Peter realized he was in water. His entire body ached. He was being thrown around violently. The surf hammered at him and tore at him, pulling him underwater.

He broke the surface of the water. He rubbed seawater from his eyes then looked up to see how far he had fallen.

The mansion was burning. No doubt his own doing from the lantern. The fire encompassed the entire side of the building. Flames reached up from the house, clawing at the dark sky, hurling sparks at the moon.

The old wood began to crack and groan as the flames consumed it. A large cross beam, burning, broke free of the house and tumbled towards the sea, fire trailing behind it like a comet. It crashed into the sea thirty yards in front of Peter, but he hadn't followed it all the way to the sea. Something else had caught his eye.

Below the burning house, carved out of the cliff was an enormous cave. It looked like a giant, gaping mouth. And just above the mouth, on each side hung lanterns, giving eyes to the giant face.

And there she was.

The ship.

The ship that he had nearly lost his mind trying to find.

"There's a cave here?" Peter cried, spitting another mouthful of seawater. And punching the waves in anger.

He stayed in the water but moved out of sight of any potential watchmen. The water was rough near the opening of the mouth, so he rose out of the water and quickly flew to the side of the cliff.

The motion sent a wave of dizziness rolling through him, and for a moment everything started to spin. He tried to ignore it and flew up along the side of the cliff, careful to stay out of view of any onlookers. He passed the left eye and realized the light sources were not lanterns, but rather, bowls of pitch or oil resting in holes carved into the wall. A tunnel of sorts seemed to wind down behind the fire. Probably carved to access the lights. Which had to be signal lights. Peter guessed the ship would only make port under the cover of night, and her helmsmen needed to be able to see where to go. Two lights on each side of the opening would give them a clear target. And with this cliff being the southernmost point of the island, no one else would ever see the fires.

Peter peeked over the top lip of the mouth and surveyed the interior.

The ship was berthed at a dock along one side of the mouth, almost like a row of teeth. And the ship was tethered to it. Along the opposite side, pirates were busy building another dock. It looked like it would eventually stretch along the back of the mouth and connect to the other side. But this dock would stick out farther, and additional framework was being built—what for, Peter couldn't tell.

"You've been busy," Peter whispered. "While we've been chasing shadows, you've been building."

Other pirates carried wooden planks from the back of the mouth to the construction zone.

Peter shook with fury. How was it that no one knew about a giant cave? A cave large enough to harbor a ship. He seethed as he surveyed the pirate's work. They were firmly established in the cave, and who knew how deep the cave stretched back. His head began to swim again, the various cuts making themselves known as his shock began to wear off.

He realigned himself upright as a wave of dizziness washed over him. He pressed himself flat against the cliff wall and closed his eyes, pressing his hands against his face. He pulled his hands away and in the bright moonlight could see that they were bloody.

"I am tired of pirates making me bleed," he said between clenched teeth.

He peered back over the lip of the mouth and glared at the ship in her berth.

"You stay put," he said to the ship, then shot back up to the mansion.

He re-entered through the window he had been kicked through. He expected to find the giant pirate waiting for him, but he was nowhere to be found. The entire hallway was on fire. The wood was so old and dry the fire gave off almost no smoke, which made breathing much easier. Nonetheless, he backed out of the house into open air, took a deep breath, and shot back into the house and down the hall.

Peter landed and staggered into the dining room, one hand holding a wound on his side. With the other he reached up to the dagger, wincing with the motion. With an effort, he pulled the weapon free and surveyed the room.

The battle still raged on in the dining room. Many pirates lay on the floor, unmoving. Others writhed in pain, clutching legs, arms, or necks where small fairy blades had done their work. Splashes of glowing dust could be seen in various parts of the rooms as well, sprayed against walls and furniture—the fading remnants of slain fairies.

A crack overhead drew Peter's attention. He looked up to see chunks of the rafters breaking away from the ceiling and crashing into the floor around them.

"Tink!" Peter yelled, punching an approaching pirate in the stomach just before a passing fairy killed the man.

Almost immediately, she was at his side.

"Where have you been?" she shouted.

"Busy," came Peter's retort. "We've got problems."

He spun away from an attack, Tinker Belle mirroring him like a shadow.

"This place isn't going to last long, we've got to get out of here," he said, as he parried the attacker's blade in time for Tinker Belle to put the man down. He stepped back, giving the pirate room to fall, then looked up, sparing the ceiling another glance.

Tinker Belle followed his gaze, a fresh layer of alarm coating her face as the cracks in the ceiling, white from the moonlight, now glowed orange as fire hurriedly devoured the old house.

"How'd that happen?" Tinker Belle asked, her tiny eyes reflecting the fire's orange glow.

"Well," Peter started, grimacing as he spoke.

"You set the house on fire?" Tinker Belle accused.

"It couldn't be helped!" Peter replied, indignant. "But we've got bigger problems. I found the ship."

A moment later, a pirate crashed to the ground, then tried to rise but couldn't as Rike, somehow, impossibly, managed to pin the pirate to the ground.

Tinker Belle zipped to the pirate, and a moment later the struggle was over. Rike nodded his thanks, then smiled up at Peter, the fairy's eyes bright with battle.

"Do you smell smoke?" Rike asked.

"Peter torched the mansion," Tinker Belle explained.

"A bit heavy-handed," Rike said, frowning. "We're managing well enough,"

"Look-" Peter started but was interrupted as Micah joined the group, his sword gripped between his hands, ready to strike.

The fairy moved constantly, scanning the room around him as he spoke.

"This house is on fire," Micah said calmly, as he turned, constantly scanning his surroundings.

"It was Peter," Tinker Belle said.

"Look," Peter began again, but a thunderous crack, this one larger than the first, sounded from above as one of the central beams broke free from its housings and tumbled to the ground with a crash.

Peter looked again at the scattered bodies and glowing piles of dust that stained the table, walls, and floorboards.

He sobered instantly.

"This wasn't supposed to go like this," he managed, his voice tightening.

Rike nodded.

Micah offered a reply, but Peter didn't hear him. Instead, he stared across the burning beams that littered the floor and out into the doorway. He stared back at the man who had been watching him.

Hook.

Peter watched the pirate, framed by fire and death. The pirate captain stared back at him.

"I never wanted this!" Peter yelled, taking a step forward.

Hook's gaze shifted from Peter to the burning house around him then back to Peter.

"I did," he said, his black mustache curling up as he smiled. He turned and disappeared into the darkness.

"We need to leave," Micah said, coming up to Peter's side.

"How about down there?" Rike asked, indicating the hallway Peter had just come down.

"Not anymore," Peter said, looking at the ever-growing brightness from the fire. "It's way too hot now. You'll never make it."

"Then it's a fight," Tinker Belle said.

"Let's rally," Rike said.

He put words to action. He didn't say anything, but his glow began to stutter then flash bright. Almost immediately, the fairies still fighting disengaged and flew to the center, surrounding Peter and the others.

"Ready?" Rike asked.

No sooner had he spoken the words than a crack resounded from above, and a huge section of celling broke away, opening a gaping hole. Several more beams broke free and fell to the ground. One of them smashed through the remaining table debris, breaking through the dining room floor and into the sublevels of the house.

"Sometimes we get lucky," Rike said, glancing at the now open roof.

The surviving party ascended through the roof and Peter was thankful that at least part of the day had favored them. Now that he knew where Hook and his ship were hiding, the real work was about to begin.

TWENTY FOUR

The following night found Peter and Tinker Belle at the mouth of the cave, taking turns stealing glances inside. Above them, the smoke still trailed into the sky, remnants of the previous night's events.

Peter's anger, like the house above them, still smoldered. He was angry Hook had eluded him for so long, and not only that, but that he had been so close for so long.

Peter pressed himself against the wall and, hanging upside down, peered into the cave.

He winced as the injuries sustained from the night before reminded him they weren't quite finished with him. He did his best to put the pain aside and inspect the pirate den.

Things were much the same as before: pirates mulled about, some working, some sleeping. Peter quickly scanned the area, then the roof of the cave.

"Look!" Peter hissed, pointing to a dark hole in the ceiling.

"Is that a cave?" Tinker Belle asked, squinting at the small opening.

"Let's check it out," Peter said.

"You stay, I'll go," Tinker Belle said.

Making sure her glow was fully extinguished, she zipped over to the hole and flew up. A moment later she reappeared, waving Peter to follow her.

Peter quickly scanned the cavern floor, the ship, and the construction for signs of prying eyes, then, satisfied that no one was watching, quickly flew up and into the hole.

The hole was just large enough for him and Tinker Belle to fit inside, if he curled into a ball.

"Not much room in here," Peter complained.

"No, but watch," Tinker Belle said drawing her dagger and flying towards the cave wall. She began stabbing it and little chips of stone began to fall away.

"We could tunnel to the outside wall and enter from there," Tinker Belle said.

"Brilliant!" Peter said. "We should see if Rike will add this spot to his patrol routes too."

Tinker Belle nodded, then added, "We should expand it and make it a permeant outpost. We'll always have at least three fairies stationed here. Two to watch and one to raise the alarm if something happens."

"I like it," Peter said. "You start digging, I'll pitch it to Adelaide."

"It'll be an easy sell," she said as he slipped back into the main cavern and flew back to White Falls.

* * *

A few days later, the outpost was fully excavated, cleared, stocked, and supplied. The outpost Peter had christened Fae Watch was always manned by at least three fairies, as Tinker Belle had suggested: one to report and two to watch.

Today, the watch duty fell to Peter and Tinker Belle, and they were joined by Tolan and Crim.

Crim was curled up next to Tolan, eyes closed and motionless.

"Here's a question," Peter was saying. "The kite's leader is Grath."

"Mhm," Tinker Belle answered, nodding her tiny head.

Crim, motionless until now, lifted her head in recognition of Grath's name and clacked her beak in affirmation, as if the question had been for her.

"But they can't speak," Peter continued.

"Well," Tinker Belle said, correcting him. "They can't speak like we do, but they do communicate with each other. And they can understand us."

"Right," Peter said. "But my point is, if they can't talk to us, how do we know their names?"

"How do you think, stupid," Tinker Belle said laughing. "We name them."

"Ah," Peter said.

"What does–" Peter started to say, but the sounds of yelling and heavy mooring lines being cast off stopped him.

Peter and Tinker Belle instantly looked at each other then flew to the small dinner plate–sized hole that served as their main window to the cavern mouth below.

"The ship's leaving," Tinker Belle said.

"What are you up to now, Hook?" Peter asked the ship.

"Tolan," Tinker Belle snapped, turning to the fairy. "Alert the Falls, Hook is on the move."

Without a word Tolan sprinted up the tunnel that led to the sea side wall. Reaching the outside lip, he leapt out, arms and legs splayed out. The kite exploded into action, traveling the distance to the outside wall in a fraction of the time and flying down to catch Tolan, seating him on her back then adjusting her course up and towards White Falls.

Peter turned away from watching the ship leave the dock long enough to see that Tolan was gone.

"Good, he's gone," Peter said.

"What?" Tinker Belle asked.

"Let's go," Peter replied, slipping his legs over the lip of the hole and dropped down into the open air.

"What?" Tinker Belle cried as she followed him out. "What are you doing?" she hissed.

Peter fell ten meters, landing noiselessly into the crow's nest then crouched down.

"What are you doing?" Tinker Belle demanded.

"We've got to see where he goes," Peter explained. "What better way than inside the ship?"

"This is a bad idea," Tinker Belle said. "Now no one will know where we are."

"And if we stay in the cave we won't know what Hook is up to," he said. "And after blowing up my tree and nearly killing every kite on the island…now that I know where he is, I'm not letting him out of my sight."

"Fine," she said, crossing her arms. "Just don't do anything stupid."

He winked at her and slowly got to his feet to peer down over the crow's nest.

The ship was in open water now, heading due south out of the cave's mouth. The warm ocean breeze tousled his hair, and with an overwhelming rush, he remembered how much he loved ships.

He closed his eyes and breathed in; the air was saturated with a salty tang. He felt the sun's heat through his hair, the rhythmic rocking of the ship.

Then a sharp pain in his arm jolted him back.

"Ow," he exclaimed.

He looked down to see Tinker Belle, her dagger in hand glaring at him.

"Focus," she scolded. "What's wrong with you?"

"Sorry," he said sheepishly.

The crow's nest creaked and swayed as furrowed sails began to swell and increase the ship's speed.

"What's the plan?"

Peter was about to reply, when a gruff voice, faint at first, then growing louder, brought their conversation to a halt.

The pair exchanged glances as Peter slowly drew his dagger from his belt. He pressed a finger to his lips and crouched down. The voice grew louder, and they could make out muttering and complaining.

"Sticking me in the nest. It's not even my shift, but no, Mad Rogue is scared of heights," the voice complained as it grew nearer to the top.

One thick hand grasped a hold of the top of the crow's nest, followed by a second. Then a large head appeared and the pirate heaved one leg over the edge.

The man, having no reason to expect to find anyone in the crow's nest, was completely taken unawares. He must have been doubly surprised to find Peter's dagger protruding from his chest.

The man crumpled and fell into the crow's nest.

Peter pulled his blade free, shook it clean, and slipped over the edge of the crow's nest. Only falling a few feet, he quickly righted himself and pressed himself against the underside of the crow's nest.

A moment later, Tinker Belle was at his side, her glow drawn in so tightly Peter could hardly see her light.

"Are you crazy?" she exclaimed. "They can see us."

"No," Peter insisted. "They can't. It's noon; the sun is directly overhead. There's no way anyone can see us. We're hidden in the shadow."

"Well, what now?" Tinker Belle asked.

"We watch," Peter said. "Hook is up to something, and I need to know what."

The ship groaned as sails were unfurrowed, pushing the ship's speed forward. Peter and Tinker Belle had to adjust themselves to stay under the crow's nest.

"I don't know how much we're going to learn from here. It's just a bunch of pirates running around."

"You're right," Peter agreed.

No sooner had he spoken the words than he dropped down from his hiding place and fell twenty feet before landing atop the topsail yard. He pressed himself flat against the wooden beam, stretching himself out, hiding himself along the top of it.

He looked up towards the crow's nest and smiled. The blinding sun obscured any chance of seeing Tinker Belle hiding.

"You're going to get us killed," a voice snapped at him.

Peter jerked in surprise, nearly falling off the yard as Tinker Belle landed in front of him.

"I need to find out what he's up to," Peter shot back. "I won't let him start any more fires."

"What's the plan?" she asked.

"We drop down, take him by surprise," Peter said.

"Then what?" Tinker Belle.

"Then we carry him off the ship," Peter explained. "Without a captain, the crew will have no choice but to give up."

"That's a bad plan," Tinker Belle said. "We need to think this through."

"No," Peter insisted. "We don't have time. Besides, with Hook out of the picture, the rest of his crew will have no idea what to do."

He returned his gaze to the ship's deck and found Hook. The pirate captain was on the deck, staring out at nothing in the ocean.

Peter could drop down and catch him unawares.

"Watch this, Tink," Peter said winking, then drew his dagger and rolled off the mast.

He landed directly behind Hook, grabbing the pirate and pressing his dagger to the man's neck.

"I told you to leave," Peter hissed into the man's ear.

"I wondered when you'd make your move," Hook said, unsurprised, "after that whole sneaky bit with jumping into the crow's nest."

"What?" Peter gasped.

"We've been watching you up in your little cave for the last week, wondering when you'd make your move," Hook said with a chuckle. "So I figured we'd cast off and draw you out. And here we are," he said, motioning with his arms.

"You're done with Neverland," Peter said. "You're going to-" he started, but before he could finish, his dagger was wrenched from his hand and something sharp and piercing grabbed him from behind. The next thing he knew, he was flipping over Hook's shoulder and was lying on his back, staring up at the man.

"Are you quite finished?" Hook asked, his voice now cold and angry, all sense of lightheartedness gone.

Peter saw his dagger a few feet away and flew towards it. But Hook was faster. Just as Peter's fingers curled around the hilt, Hook stomped his boot on Peter's hand.

Peter howled in pain, the sound echoing across the water. He tried to blink the pain way, tried to stay focused, but Hook twisted his boot, grinding Peter's fingers into the decking, which elicited another scream.

"I think you've played soldier long enough, no?" Hook hissed. "Do you feel like a child yet, Peter Pan?"

Peter tried to pull free, but the man had all his weight pressed down on Peter's hand.

"The reality of war," Hook said, pulling his sword free of its scabbard and raising it above his head to strike.

In the instant before Hook's sword removed Peter's hand, Peter yanked away with every ounce of strength and flew backwards with all of his might, finally freeing himself just as the sword cut a deep gash into the deck where his hand had been a moment earlier. But the momentum sent him hurtling backwards out of control, his weapon bouncing away, out of reach.

Tinker Belle, who had been streaking down towards him, angled her approach and intercepted the dagger, her arms and legs wrapping around the hilt as she flew it back to Peter. He grabbed it with his uninjured hand then looked up to see Hook charging after him, his gleaming metal hook raised to strike, his other hand, now empty of his sword, pressing two fingers between his lips and whistling.

"You were right," Peter mumbled, deciding enough was enough.

"Forget it," Tinker Belle said, hovering right next to him. "Let's get out of here."

"Agreed," Peter replied.

Peter rocked straight up—right into a net. The weight of the net threw him back to the deck. It had obviously been thrown in response to Hook's whistle.

He started to climb free of it, but saw Hook was nearly upon him. Instead, he flew up again, this time preparing to lift the extra weight. He flew into the air, more slowly than normal, but still quick enough to escape. But his efforts were slowed as pirates began leaping on to the edges of the net.

Tinker Belle was soon hacking and sawing at the ropes, attempting to weaken them enough for him to break through.

He still rose, but as more and more pirates joined their fellows, his progress slowed. And for an agonizing second, he hung, suspended twenty feet in the air as pirates threw themselves from rigging and masts to cling to the net.

Suddenly, something glass slammed around Tinker Belle with a tiny door that slammed shut, trapping her inside.

It was a lantern. Held by Mad Rogue.

"The golden pixie!" he cheered, letting go of the outside of the net he had clung to. He tumbled to the deck with his prize, ignoring the rough landing. Then standing to his feet, he raised the lantern over his head in triumph.

"Golden pixie!" he bellowed, dancing around, ignoring the struggle above him.

Peter began to descend. Slowly, inexorably, he was drawn towards the deck. He gritted his teeth and screamed as he strained to fly, but the overwhelming combined weight of the pirates was too much.

Exhausted, and soaked in sweat, Peter collapsed to the deck, panting.

"I tried to turn you away. But you wouldn't have it," Peter gasped, as Hook walked towards him. "The mers, the fairies, they'll crush you."

"Words," Hook mocked.

The net, itchy and heavy, pressed Peter hard against the deck.

"What comes next is on your hands," Peter managed.

"Just the one, I'm afraid," Hook retorted, waggling his hook at the boy.

Then the man raised his boot, and Peter knew no more.

TWENTY FIVE

Peter was dreaming again. He knew it was a dream even though the reality of it was so inescapable. But it had to be a dream. Because there was no way Peter was tied to a mast in Captain London's ship.

The man was dead. Peter should know. London was his first kill.

Taking a life was such an unnatural event that it made perfect sense his mind would return to this moment over and over to try and find some kind of reason.

Peter knew the reason, of course: it was kill or be killed, and Peter had been unwilling to die.

Still, reason and logic rarely offered peace to a troubled mind.

And that's why his dreams continued to bring him here.

He was both participating in and watching the events unfold – a sort of duality that only dreams could offer.

Once again his ropes were cut, his body tumbling to the decking.

Peter watched himself marshal what little courage, or foolishness, or whatever had given him the strength, to do what came next.

And then it was done.

William Till's blades had claimed another life, the only difference was, this time it was at the hands of his son.

Peter watched himself standing over the unmoving body, his own chest heaving as he sucked air into his lungs.

Then with a jerk, Peter was awake, a loud gasp escaping his mouth as he exhaled the breath his body had been holding.

His clothes were wet with sweat. The normally warm tropical air felt cold against his clammy skin.

He opened his eyes.

And fear, again, gripped him. For a heartbeat, he thought he was back in the hold of Till's ship.

"Killing is easy," said Mad Rogue, giggling. "It's what comes after that's hard, no?"

The crazed pirate had been watching him as he slept.

Despite his new attitude towards taking a life, despite the reassurances from Shiiklah, and despite the fact he had no doubt in his mind he had made the only and right choice, the memory of his first kill still followed Peter, waiting for moments where he had ceased to think about it, reminding him of it in repetitious, agonizing clarity.

Peter followed the man's gaze, craning his neck to look above him. Just over his shoulder, hung on a nail in the mast, swung a lantern. Its light, glowing more brilliantly than the other lanterns around, told Peter it could only be Tinker Belle's prison.

The pirate snickered again and walked away, but not before shifting his gaze above Peter and smiling cruelly.

"Leave her alone, Rogue," Peter said.

Mad Rogue looked back to Peter, brow wrinkled as he noticed something. He approached, then pulled out the mer call from under Peter's shirt. The man yanked it free, the thin, braided kelp twine snapping as he pulled.

"This is mine now," Mad Rogue said

Peter groaned inwardly, remembering the mer call for the first time since being captured.

The pirate snickered, sauntering off and admiring his new prize to leave Peter and Tinker Belle alone.

When the pirate had left, Peter gathered his bearings. He was leaning against the mast, but, thankfully, he wasn't tied to it this time. Rather, a long chain, maybe ten feet long, was shackled to one ankle. He followed the other end of the chain; its links ran a few feet away and was secured to a large iron ring in the middle of the deck.

He gave the chain an experimental tug and quickly surmised there was no chance in breaking it.

"Hi, Tink," Peter said at last, returning his gaze to the glowing lantern.

"Hi, Peter," Tinker Belle replied.

"So, that went poorly," Peter admitted.

Tinker Belle laughed despite their situation.

"Yes," she agreed. "Yes, it did."

"This is going to be a tough one to get out of," Peter said. "Can you get out?"

"No," Tinker Belle said. "The door is sealed tight."

"Could you make something to break the glass?" Peter asked.

"No," she said, dousing his hope. "I'm not a skilled enough maker to create anything hard enough to break glass."

"Maybe I can break you out," Peter said, still searching for options. He rose to his feet and reached for the lantern, but the chain kept her just out of reach.

He searched for something he could use to free Tinker Belle, but nothing was near. Dejected, he slumped back down to the deck.

He tried to think of something, anything, he could do to free himself and Tinker Belle.

But his thinking was interrupted by footsteps.

He looked up to see a fat man waddling up, stool in one hand, a cup of tea in the other.

The man set his stool up a few yards from Peter, placed his tea on it, and then settled down on the deck next to it.

He gave Peter an awkward wave, then looked up at Tinker Belle.

"Ma'am," he said, offering the fairy a nod, then shifted his gaze back to his tea.

Peter watched him.

"Who are you?" Peter asked after a moment.

"Who, me? Oh, Smee," the man said, nodding again. "Mr. Smee."

Peter watched the man prepare his tea for several minutes.

He had never seen a tea-drinking pirate before. In fact, the man seemed no more a pirate than Peter himself did. Perhaps less so, as he seemed completely unarmed.

"Why are you here?" Peter asked after a few minutes of silence.

"It's my watch," Smee replied without looking up, blowing on his tea.

"No," Peter said. "Why are you here, with them?"

"Where else would I be?" Smee asked, looking from Peter to Tinker Belle.

"I don't know," Peter explained. "At home, in the navy. You don't seem much like a pirate."

"Ah, right," Smee said, chuckling, then sobered. "Do you know what a pirate is?"

Peter didn't reply.

"Well?" Smee asked.

"Someone who steals," Peter replied. "Someone who breaks the law, someone who pillages and kills."

"That's actually not true," Smee said. "By definition, a pirate is anyone who takes violent action without authorization by a higher authority," Smee explained.

"Okay," Peter agreed. "And that makes you a pirate."

"And who is the higher authority?" Smee pressed.

"Easy," Peter said. "The King."

The response elicited a squeal of laughter, the motion causing his tea to slosh from the cup, burning his hand.

"The King?" Smee scoffed, shaking the tea from his hand. "The king who ordered the bombardment of the towns along the French coast?"

"I'm sure he didn't know," Peter offered.

"Oh, there was no mistake," Smee said. "'Soften them up', the king said. And it wasn't just the forts, it was the towns, the schools, the churches. Hundreds of deaths, among them, my wife. And even more would have been slain had Captain Hook not been there to stop them from killing everyone."

Peter didn't reply.

"And I'm supposed to accept that man to tell me what's right and wrong?" Smee asked, interrupting Peter's thoughts. "No. He's not my king, not anymore. There is a higher moral authority than him, and no king on any throne can tell me otherwise."

Peter considered the man's argument. Technically, what he was saying made sense. Of course someone who ordered the deaths of women and children would be on the side of wrong, not right. He followed the man's argument and came to the alarming conclusion that if it were true, that would mean that the pirates were, if not on the side of right, themselves, neutral.

The logic would also put England, her navy, and even Peter on the side of wrong.

Peter was growing more uneasy as the conversation progressed.

"The way I see it," Smee surmised, leaning towards Peter and stabbing a chubby finger at him. "You're the pirate, not me."

"I'm nothing like you!" Peter spat, his own conflicting thoughts translating to rage. "You take what's not yours, and you torture and kill people who get in your way."

"How many people have you killed, Peter Pan?" Smee asked, leaning in towards Peter. "How many lives have you taken?"

"That's not what this is about," Peter said.

"Says the killer," Smee said. "Me? I've never killed a man."

Peter shook his head.

"That's not," Peter stammered, searching for the right words. "No, you're twisting my words."

"Am I?" Smee asked. "Suddenly the fairy tale makes less sense.

It's getting difficult to see which way is up and which way is down, eh?"

Smee smiled coldly, taking a sip from his tea.

"Things get confusing when the hero is the killer, and the villain has never taken a life. Seems awful confusing to me."

"You're wrong," Peter said. "You're so wrong."

Smee chuckled.

"Well, maybe you're right after all," he said. "Maybe we are the villains."

He smiled again and leaned back.

"However, I've never cut off another man's hand either," he said, looking at his own hand. He inspected the fingers then made a fist.

Peter glared at the man. "That was mercy," Peter said at last.

"Mercy?" Smee scoffed. "English mercy at its finest!" he said applauding.

"I could have killed him," Peter said.

"Well, my boy," Smee said. "That was probably your first mistake. And clearly not your last if those chains are evidence. But, it won't be long before you experience the fruit of that mercy."

He tipped his head back, emptying the last of his tea. Then rising to his feet, he picked up his stool and began to walk away.

"You'll have to excuse me," Smee said. "I think I've had more than a comfort's share of English charm for one night."

Peter watched him leave.

"I'd try and get some rest, pirate," Smee called to Peter as he left. "Tomorrow will be…" he paused, searching for the word. "Merciful," he chuckled.

Then he offered Peter a mock salute and walked off.

TWENTY SIX

G ood morning," Hook said.

Peter jerked awake, disorientated at how quickly morning had come.

"What do you want?" Peter asked.

"Straight to the point," Hook said. "I admire that."

The pirate paced as he spoke, as if he were discovering each word for the first time.

"You gave me a gift, Peter Pan," he said. "You made me aware of a weakness. Lesser men, more prideful men, would have balked at learning from one such as yourself, but not I."

Peter had no idea what he was talking about.

"I underestimated you, Peter," he explained. "You're young, too young to be a threat, but a threat you were. You see, I've come to enjoy the position I'm in because I've been able to identify threats in all forms. But I'd grown accustom to a specific flavor of danger."

Hook pointed out to sea.

"A hidden reef, an oncoming storm, disgruntled crewmen," he said pointing to one of the pirates who had gathered around to watch. "Years of searching for obvious threats had narrowed my vision," he said. "I saw a child on a beach and considered him nothing more than a child on a beach—no threat."

Hook inspected the sliver barb that had taken the place of his hand.

"A hard lesson," he said. "But one I've taken to heart. That's why I let them call me 'Hook,' why I make them call me 'Hook.' Every time I am called, every time I am talked about, every time I hear my name, I remember the pain. And I remember the lesson. But most of all, most of all, my young friend, I remember what you took from me," Hook snarled.

The man was in Peter's face now, his hook pressed hard against Peter's face.

"Killing you quickly would not be justice for this," Hook said, brandishing the hook. "No, for this, you must suffer."

His mood turned, suddenly.

"But there is hope," he said. "I will allow you to escape, in a sense. You will fight some of my men, and if you defeat them, I will kill you quickly."

"And if I don't?" Peter asked.

"Then I will burn Neverland to the ground, killing your friends as punishment," Hook said. "And when everyone you care about is gone, then I will turn my attention to you. Then I will take my time, and I will make your torment last until I draw forth your final breath from within your chest."

A wooden sword was dropped in front of Peter. He started at it, then at the bare-chested pirate, then at the man's iron cutlass in his hand.

He considered doing nothing, just allowing the man to strike him down. He was chained to the ship, with no hopes of escaping. And Tinker Belle was locked up in her own prison. They were on their own, with no options.

Except one.

Think, then act.

It was a saying his father had repeated so often it had driven him and his sister crazy.

Think, then act.

It was a simple phrase, and he had hated how vague and meaningless it always seemed. But now, and like all the other times his father's seemingly pointless sayings had saved his life, it had meaning. As long as he drew breath, there was a chance to escape. Once he was dead, that chance was gone.

Peter marshalled his strength and picked up the sword. A joke of a weapon: it was unbalanced and made entirely out of wood. He'd sparred with better weapons back home with Mara.

The thought of his sister drew his eyes to Tinker Belle. She was standing inside her prison, her hands pressed against the glass, watching him.

He shot her a crooked smile and then stood up. His ankle shackles jingled as he rose. Only his right leg was chained, but the chains would be far too heavy to snap if he tried to fly away.

He looked from the chains to Hook, meeting the pirate captain's eyes. The man stared back, the hint of a smile tugging at the corners of his wicked mouth. Hook looked at someone in the crowd and dipped his head in an unspoken order.

A pirate nodded back, then drew a cutlass and entered the circle.

Peter studied the man's form—or rather, lack of form. He held his weapon like a club, without any sense of strategy, other than that he intended to hack to bits whatever he came against. It was a joke. Granted the man could easily overpower Peter and kill him and Peter was still in mortal danger, but his technique was laughable.

Peter backed away from the man to get a feel for maneuvering while wearing a chain. And to give him time. The pirate sneered at him. It was an ugly, toothless thing. He quickened his advance on Peter. Peter let the man close the distance, then jumped up and slammed back down on the deck, jerking his chained leg down in the process. The sudden slack in the chain attached to his leg traveled the length of the chain, catching the pirate square in the face and sending several of his precious few teeth bouncing away. The man stumbled backwards, then tripped and fell into a heap on the ground.

A few of his fellow pirates came forward and helped him out of the circle.

Peter looked around, feigning boredom, then picked at his fingernails.

"Next," Peter taunted, his voice thick with sarcasm.

Another pirate came.

And after that one fell, came another.

And another.

He had fought ten men and had defeated them all, armed with only a wooden sword and his father's lessons. But the skill of each pirate had increased as Peter fought through the gauntlet Hook had arranged for him.

Peter was starting to wonder if any of Hook's men posed a real threat to him.

Then came Mad Rogue.

The pirate bobbed and ducked into the circle, smiling that crazed half-smile he always seemed to be wearing and muttering to himself.

"Hold my oranges," Mad Rogue said, thrusting a satchel filled with fruit towards another pirate.

The sight of the pirate turned Peter's blood to ice, the way it always did. And for a second, he was transported back into the hold of the ship where he had first met Mad Rogue. Where he had been tortured at the hands of Captain London with Mad Rogue at his side.

He blinked the images away, returning to the present.

"Wakey, wakey, Peter Pan," Mad Rogue taunted, clearly seeing the drift of Peter's attention.

Peter's focus fully snapped to attention.

"I see you, Peter Pan," Mad Rogue said, as the two began to circle.

Peter ignored him, instead watching the man's hands: one lay deceptively relaxed at his side, while the other was curled around the hilt of a rapier.

Peter forced himself to relax and balanced his weight evenly on the balls of his feet.

The pirate struck, an overhead slash Peter had practiced against so many times the block he raised took almost no effort. Peter deflected the blow, then stepped back, not disengaging but keeping himself from getting drawn in too close for the pirate to punch or bite him.

Mad Rogue attacked again, this time a thrust, but Peter, changing to a two-handed grip, swung hard at the strike, the pirate's steel blade chipping into Peter's wooden one. But the counter blew opened the pirate's defense and Peter took full advantage. He pivoted and struck, but instead of a direct blow to the man's stomach, he turned his wooden sword and slammed the flat edge against the side of Mad Rogue's other hand, the one that, a moment ago, had been empty, but was now pulling a dagger free from his belt behind him.

Peter recognized the weapon immediately. The silver blade shone mirror-bright in the sunlight. The black leather hilt was capped with a green pommel stone.

Green like Peter's eyes.

Green like William Till's eyes.

Peter's strike sent the weapon flipping end over end, until the blade buried into the deck boards.

Smirking, Peter ducked under an incoming leg strike and came up with his father's blade, once again in-hand. He spared the wooden sword a glance before tossing it behind him.

Mad Rogue disengaged, clearly re-thinking his strategy now that his opponent was armed with something more than a toy.

Peter leveled his head and stared at the man and mirrored the crazed pirate's wild smile. A dangerous glint came to his eyes.

"I see you, Mad Rogue," Peter mocked.

The man snarled at Peter and charged.

Peter feigned an overhead strike as the man approached, but at the last second brought the dagger down, piercing the man's boot.

Mad Rogue howled in pain, and grabbed at his foot, his sword falling to the ground. Peter spun, bringing the hilt of his dagger around as fast as he could and slammed it into the man's temple.

Mad Rogue fell to the deck, still conscious but struggling to rise. Before he could, Peter looped the shackle chain neatly around Mad Rogue's neck, then stepped on the back of his neck, creating a garrote. The pirate flailed, pounding at the deck as he struggled to breathe.

Peter looked Hook in the eyes. The man stared back. Peter pressed harder, and Mad Rogue's flailing became desperate.

Hook rolled his eyes and, looping his hook into the loop of the lantern that was Tinker Belle's prison, held it up. It was a silent threat: kill Mad Rogue, kill Tinker Belle.

Inside the lantern, Tinker Belle pounded on the glass and made stomping motions, urging Peter to finish the pirate and not to spare her.

Hook raised his eyebrows. Peter released his hold on Mad Rogue.

The pirate skittered away, coughing and sucking in air and holding his throat.

Hook placed Tinker Belle's prison atop a crate.

Inside, Tinker Belle stormed back and forth, stomping at the floor and punching the air in silent rage.

"So, the boy doesn't have what it takes to kill?" Hook mused.

"Don't confuse ability with restraint," Peter replied.

"Well," Hook said. "How would you rate that match, Rogue?"

"Peter Pan cheats," the pirate wheezed between coughing fits. Then a pistol appeared in Mad Rogue's hand and Peter heard the snap of a pistol's hammer being cocked.

"So this is it?" Peter asked, his jaw tightening in resignation.

"Cheater," Mad Rogue hissed, then trained his pistol on the lantern and fired.

"No!" Peter screamed.

The lantern exploded in a shower of golden dust.

"Tiiiiink!" Peter screamed, lunging forward.

But the end of his chain yanked him back, nearly dislocating his leg in the process. Peter spun around and nearly impaled himself on Hook's incoming sword thrust.

He threw himself away from the blade, then came up crouching.

"Good," Hook purred. "Let's see how the boy fights blinded by grief."

Peter's lip quivered with rage as he stared past Hook at Mad Rogue. The crazed pirate still stared at where the lantern had been a moment earlier, a look of absolute joy embedded on the man's face.

"Tsk, tsk," Hook chided. "Eyes on the threat, boy. Didn't your instructors teach you anything?"

Hook raised his hook and struck.

But Peter dived out of the way.

"Rogue!" Peter demanded.

The pirate stared at the layer of dust that had settled across the crates the lantern had rested on. The dust soaked into the wood, the golden brilliance fading into nothing.

Then, and only then, did Mad Rogue look away. His gaze slid away from the crates and met Peter's eyes.

"Bye, bye." Mad Rogue waved, still grinning.

"Enough," Peter spat.

Hook struck, but just before his descending hook could connect,

Peter raised his dagger, catching the hook on his blade.

"Ah, there he is," Hook said.

Peter spun out of the blade-lock and attempted to reset his footing. But Hook gave no quarter.

The pirate struck, a quick slash with his hook, but Peter was faster. He flew up, narrowly avoiding the silver barb, then landed on the hook with both feet and propelled himself down, burying it into the decking.

But in one fluid motion, Hook kicked his own wrist, freeing the barb from the ship and struck back, this time with his sword.

The strike was fast and inaccurate, but near enough to land, especially since Peter thought his move had bought him a few seconds.

The tip sliced into Peter's forearm.

He stumbled back, holding the wound with his free hand. It hurt, but thankfully, the wound was shallow.

Hook swung his own sword around him, a dizzying pattern obviously meant to intimidate opponents.

But Peter was unfazed.

With a cry, Peter launched himself at Hook.

Hook struck at Peter, an upward slash with his sword that Peter batted out of the way before ducking under a hook strike aimed at his chest.

He rolled past the man then changed directions, flying to give him more speed. The move caught the man in the leg, tripping him.

Again, Peter reversed direction and charged, slashing towards his left side, intentionally making his strike look sloppy—just as he had done when he had first sparred with Shiiklah.

Hook shifted his weight to parry the attack.

Peter slid to his knees and reversed his strike, letting the momentum of his swing spin him around.

He swung as hard as he could, opting to drive the weapon hilt-first into Hook's side rather than waste valuable time repositioning his dagger. He hoped that the maneuver would work better on the pirate than it had on Shiiklah.

Hook was no mermaid. The hilt smashed into Hook's side; a sickening crunch told Peter his strike had been true.

The man roared in pain, then lashed out at Peter, punching the boy in the face with his sword's handle guard.

Peter stumbled backwards, tripped, and fell hard on his tailbone.

He tried to scurry away, but Hook reached out and snagged Peter's chain, yanking him back within striking range.

Peter raised his weapon to block the strike he knew was coming, then screamed in pain when, instead, Hook stomped on his ankle.

Instinctively, Peter sat up, reaching for the injury, but that's when Hook again punched him in the face with the sword-guard.

The blow sent him slamming into the deck. His entire head erupted in pain. Weakly, he raised his weapon again, but Hook easily batted it aside, knocking it free of his grip.

Then Peter felt himself being dragged by the leg. He tried to resist, but a weak moan was all that remained of his defenses.

Suddenly, Hook had him by the throat and was lifting him into the air. He batted at the man's hand, but it was useless. The next thing he knew, he was being slammed against the mast.

Peter's vision went blurry for a terrible instant before clearing. And all he saw was the silver hook, swinging towards his face.

He tried to move but Hook held him fast. He kicked at the man, but Hook ignored the blow.

Then the hook struck.

But the barbed tip didn't slice his throat like he was expecting.

Instead, it buried into the mast, nicking his skin in the process. The curve of the hook wrapped around his neck, pinning him to the mast, but not obstructing his breathing.

With a yank, Hook's arm pulled free of whatever contraption secured the hook to his arm, leaving Peter pinned to the mast, his feet dangling helplessly above the ground.

"Leave him until morning," Hook ordered. "If he dies in the night, it's more than he deserves."

Hook turned and began limping towards his cabin, holding his side.

"Either way, Peter Pan's story is over," Hook said to anyone in ear shot.

"Are you sure, Captain?" Smee asked as Hook walked past him, stealing a glance at Peter. "After all, he's just a boy."

Hook glared at the man, then slowly raised his arm, the one without the hand, to make his argument without words.

Peter watched him leave, trembling from pain and fear and grief. He had to remain in flight to keep from dropping all of his weight on the hook and strangling himself.

He gripped the hook with both hands, trying to relieve some of the stress on his neck as well has testing to see if he could free himself, but it was buried too deep.

He strained even more, his arms shaking with the exertion. Suddenly, the hook slipped free and fell, bouncing across the deck.

Peter landed hard on the decking, pain exploding in his hip and down his leg. He thought about retrieving the hook and trying to escape.

But Tinker Belle was dead.

And with that thought he felt complete hopelessness wash over him. He could fight it no longer.

So he sat and watched the sun slowly journey across the sky.

Tomorrow couldn't come soon enough.

TWENTY SEVEN

The shot had been close. So close. But she had seen it coming, had watched the glint of excitement in Mad Rogue's eyes as he drew and fired his weapon. And in that moment, Tinker Belle knew she had once chance to make her death look convincing.

As soon as Mad Rogue squeezed the trigger, she expelled as much dust as she dared and then threw herself flat against the bottom of the lantern.

Once, seemingly forever ago, she had showed Peter how fairies could, for lack of a better word, shed dust from their bodies. It was how they kept their reservoir full, it was how they crafted everything. They were made of dust, but release too much dust and there would be nothing left.

Nothing but stone.

And Tinker Belle might have released too much dust.

Her arms and legs felt impossibly stiff. If she strained with all her might, maybe, just maybe, they might be moving, but she couldn't tell.

Everything felt cold and foreign, almost as if she didn't have arms or legs anymore.

Thankfully, when she had fallen from the shattered lantern, she had bounced between the crates her lantern had rested on. Even more thankfully, she had not shattered into a thousand pieces when she hit the decking.

But now what?

She was within a hairsbreadth from death, and a single question occupied her mind: Had she lost too much of herself to be restored?

She knew that the dust inside of her could regenerate, eventually. But was there enough left? And would it be enough to take back the places that had nearly turned to stone?

The ship rocked as it turned. She didn't feel it so much as she saw it. The movement caused her to shift and create a knocking sound as her hard wings tapped against the wooden deck. She tried to breathe, but her chest would not move. All she could manage were shallow breaths, which teased more than actually satisfyied her need to breathe.

She tried to look around, but her eyes itched whenever they moved. The scraping of her hard eyes against their sockets was unbearable. She wanted to cry, but couldn't.

All she could do was sit and stare at whatever was directly in front of her. And across the deck, still chained to the mast, sat Peter.

He was bruised and bloodied, but from the look on his face, his defeat was much more than physical.

"I'm still here, Peter," she managed to whisper hoarsely. "You're not alone."

She managed to close her eyes and, concentrating, willed the dust to spread through her body.

Nothing.

With effort, she forced her eyes open again.

Anger and fury ignited deep within her chest.

Peter needed her. More than ever, he needed her.

She tried to move her arms.

Again, nothing.

"Come on," Tinker Belle rasped, straining with all of her might.

Her arms quivered, brittle little things that threatened to snap under the pressure of her efforts.

She stopped struggling and sat, resigned to just watch Peter, helpless to do anything else.

She licked stone-dry lips and blinked. Tears eventually began to work their way to her eyes, then down her cheeks.

"Silly boy," she whispered. "I'm still here."

After the first night watches had changed, she felt something else. It began as no more than a memory of herself.

Then, as gradual as morning's first light sneaking into the night, she began to feel it. It started in her toes, the slightest tickle of feeling. Then in her fingertips. The feeling, warm like summer, made its way down from deep within her chest, down her arms and legs and to her feet.

Excitement ripped through her. She was being restored! But her excitement quickly turned to horror as the tickling turned to agony. It felt like a thousand knives were stabbing every part of her body.

For a single tortuous moment, she wished she were still made of stone. If this was what she had to go through to feel again, she wasn't sure if it was worth it.

But a single glance at Peter instantly sobered her. She would suffer any pain, any torture to be at his side again.

So she would wait.

She would endure whatever the regenerating dust within her demanded.

She watched the night watch shift change again, then a third time. She watched the pirates routinely checking and re-checking Peter's chains. But mostly she watched Peter.

All through the night, she waited. At times the pain was almost unbearable. It took everything in her to keep from screaming.

Just before daybreak, the pain subsided. In an instant, she went from being in complete agony to feeling no pain at all.

Tinker Belle looked down, realizing that she could bend her neck to look down. Her legs—gray, unfeeling things before—had returned to their familiar color, except now they were covered in a fine, white dust. She held out her hands, slowly opening them. They, too, were coated in the strange white dust. She flexed them experimentally. Their movements were stiff and languid, but they moved nonetheless.

She inhaled and found she could take a deep, full breath. She blew the dust from her hands, exposing ten perfect, pink fingers. She clapped her hands in excitement, sending a cloud of dust into the air around her.

A gasp of surprise escaped her, causing her to inhale a mouthful of dust. Immediate, she regretted her action when a fit of coughs doubled her over.

She laughed, never remembering a time in her life when she was happy to cough. She sat up and wiped tears of joy from her eyes. Deciding to give her legs a test, she slowly rose. Expecting them to be weak and shaky, she took her time, making sure not to overdo it right away. But to her amazement, she found them strong as ever, if not stronger.

She paced back and forth in the shadows between the crates to better test them before she realized her glow, which had been completely extinguished, had begun to return and was now eating away at the darkness.

Immediately, she reigned in her glow, rejoicing again at being able to do something she had taken for granted for so long.

She turned back to Peter. He was awake and still staring blankly. Tinker Belle considered illuminating herself to try and get his attention, but thought better of it.

Hook, Mad Rogue, Smee, and a handful of other pirates were walking towards Peter.

She would fly over, disrupt whatever they were about to do, free Peter, then the two of them would escape.

She waited, watching for an opportunity.

Mad Rogue held a length of rope with a lock tied to one end. He tied the end without the lock around his waist, then secured the locked end to the loop around Peter's ankle. But the heavy chain that was secured to the mast was still secured to his leg.

By the looks of it, they were taking him somewhere, and Mad

Rogue's rope would be the leash to prevent Peter from flying away. Tinker Belle checked her belt, making sure her daggers were still in their sheathes.

They were.

A rope she could easily cut through. A chain, she could not.

She gauged the distance, maybe twenty yards away. She could easily cross the distance in a heartbeat. The rope seemed no thicker than the length of her blades. She could cut them as she passed. The two of them would be gone before anyone even knew what had happened.

She'd flare into full brightness when she'd make her move. Peter would no doubt see her and understand the plan even as his role approached him.

Hook was talking now, but he was too far away and not speaking loudly enough for her to make out what he was saying.

Mad Rogue tested the knot around his waist and double-checked Peter's ankle.

"Yes," Tinker Belle whispered. "Make sure it's locked, you fool."

Then the insane pirate unlocked the chain on Peter's ankle.

Tinker Belle drew her daggers and crouched, ready to launch into the air.

Mad Rogue fumbled with the chain, struggling to free it from Peter's ankle. Then it was free. All that kept Peter captive were a few inches of twisted fiber—her blades were more than enough to handle that.

Tinker Belle scowled, relishing what was about to come, and leapt into the air.

But she fell flat on her face after traveling less than a foot. She scrambled to her hands and knees and retrieved her daggers, which had fallen from her hands when she hit the ground.

Twisting her neck, she reached behind to feel her wings.

Tinker Belle's heart sank when she felt them. Instead of their normal smooth, light filmy texture, they were hard and glass-like. She tried to move them. They moved, but in their current state, they were no use to her.

She sheathed her daggers and watched, helpless, as her best chance to free Peter came and went.

The pirates removed the chain from the mast and wrapped him in it, securing the chain with a lock.

"No, no, no," Tinker Belle whispered, desperately trying to think of a way to save Peter, but without her wings or any other way of flying, she could do nothing but watch.

More pirates were joining the group, bringing more chains until Peter, unable to stand under the weight of the chains, had fallen back down to the ground.

It took three pirates to lift him, and Tinker Belle watched in horror as they carried him to the side of the ship.

Panic sized her. At once, her daggers were in her hands again and she prepared to run after him. But her immediate fears were momentarily relived as Peter was lowered into a long boat rather than thrown overboard.

The rest of the pirates climbed into the boat and disappeared, lowered into the water.

Impatience thundered in her ears. She was a fairy of action, after all.

Unsure what to do next, she sheathed her weapons and knelt.

Then clasping her hands and placing them in her lap, she closed her eyes, and waited for her wings to regenerate.

So she would wait for the instant her wings could hold her. Then she would race to Peter's rescue. And if she were too late, she would unleash a retribution so fierce, it would turn the Jolly Roger into a ghost ship.

TWENTY EIGHT

The boat rocked as Hook leaped from the ship, landing next to Peter in the longboat.

"You know," Hook said, inspecting the silver barb attached to his wrist as the longboat was lowered into the water. "I never thanked you for this. I really should. I was quite the fool. You helped me see that."

Peter tried to ignore him and watched Mad Rogue. The crazed pirate had settled across from Peter and was vacantly staring out across the water, chewing on a piece of orange.

The boat splashed into the water, scraping against the side of the ship as it landed. The boat pitched, momentarily throwing the pirates off-balance.

Mad Rogue reached out an arm to steady himself, inadvertently knocking the orange he held in his hands free and into the sea.

"Rotters," Mad Rogue hissed, glaring up at the men who had lowered the boat into the water, before digging into his satchel and producing another one.

He bit into it, tearing free a piece of peel, then spit it at Peter.

Peter closed his eyes as the peel bounced off his face, saliva and juice flecking his cheeks.

Mad Rogue laughed and began to tear the remaining peel from the fruit, flicking pieces out of the boat.

Hook continued to ramble on about lessons and balancing wrongs done, as Peter watched Mad Rogue.

The man wore several pieces of jewelry. His fingers were caked with rings, and several necklaces were knotted around his neck. But it was one in particular that drew his attention.

It was a white piece of coral, hollowed, with tiny holes drilled in dizzy patterns throughout.

Peter recognized the mer call instantly and something akin to hope leapt inside his chest, surging through him, but he kept it buried inside, far away from his face.

"Rogue," Peter called to the man, still ignoring Hook's pontificating.

The man blinked slowly, then shifted his gaze to Peter.

"Peter Pan," he said.

"That necklace," Peter said, nodding towards the pirate. "The white one. May I have it back?"

Mad Rogue frowned, craning his neck to look down and see the item Peter was talking about.

"My father gave it to me," Peter lied. "It was his favorite whistle. And since I'm going to die soon, I'd like to hold it, to remember him, for a few minutes."

Mad Rogue took the necklace from his neck and inspected it cautiously, as if he expected it to attack him. He sniffed at it.

Peter's heart slammed against his chest as he watched, silently willing the man to blow the mer-call.

The crazed pirate squinted at it, looking for some hidden message in the dots.

"Hmph," he said, replacing the necklace around his neck. "No, it's mine."

Mad Rogue returned to staring out at the horizon, still feeling the call with his fingertips, but showing no signs of doing anything more with it.

Peter was about to speak again when all of a sudden Mad Rogue plucked it up and put one end in his mouth.

Peter held his breath.

Mad Rogue blew his out, into the mer-call.

But nothing happened.

The pirate's face creased in confusion, then he blew again. Frowning, he took the whistle out of his mouth to inspect it. He peered through the hole looking for a blockage, but found none. He blew hard two more times, then, still not hearing anything, took a deep breath and blew as hard as he could. His face grew a deep shade of red and his body shook as he strained to make the tiny whistle sing.

It took every fiber of Peter's strength not to laugh aloud. He bit his cheek until he tasted blood and shook with silent laughter as he watched a winded Mad Rogue summoning his own doom. Peter imagined every mer within a league being drawn to this location.

They had killed Tinker Belle and they were doubtless about to kill him. But he had successfully maneuvered Mad Rogue into securing final judgment for the pirates. Even in his own death, Peter had secured Neverland's safety.

"Give it up, Rogue," a pirate said, chuckling. "The boy's playing you."

"Shut it, Jakes," Mad Rogue snapped.

Immediately, the man, Jakes, stiffened and stopped laughing, paling visibly.

Panting, Mad Rogue returned his gaze to the call. He sniffed it one more time then dropped it, letting it swing back into place around his neck.

"Worst whistle ever," he muttered.

Peter leaned back against the boat, and listened to Hook ramble on about lessons and inevitability.

Hook's story was not all that uncommon. Pirates came to Neverland and one way or another were turned away. Neverland's lure was strong, especially for men like Hook and Teach. But where Edward Teach had known when to cut his losses, Hook's pride had been so wounded that revenge had trumped reason or logic.

Still, the man was not to be underestimated, if the chains wrapped around Peter were any indication.

Over the course of several months, Peter and Hook had exchanged blows and now, soon it seemed, Hook would make his final strike, ending the pair's duel.

With Tinker Belle gone, Peter was fine with dying. He hadn't realized just how much like family Tinker Belle had become. And with the mers hopefully on their way, Neverland would finally be safe. And Peter's promise to protect it would be fulfilled.

The cold chains wrapped around him were uncomfortable, but now it didn't matter. Now it was just a matter of time.

The boat rowed into shallow waters towards a group of rocks, just barely above the water level.

A few of the pirates jumped out of the boat into the knee deep water, pulling the boat the rest of the way.

Hook leapt from the boat, landing in the water and looked around.

"Come on, come, on," Hook said motioning his men to hurry.

The rest of the men piled out of the longboat, two of them hauling Peter out into the water.

The salt water burned his eyes as waves splashed him in the face. The men half carried, half dragged him towards the boulders, managing to bring him to the center of the rock crop.

"This," Hook said, his arms spread wide, clearly immensely pleased with himself. "Is where it all ends. The tide will be coming in soon. And with it, the conclusion."

Peter slumped against the rock. He looked up, searching for any sign of kite or fairy. But there was nothing.

Shifting his gaze to the sea, he looked for any signs of mermaids. Nothing.

And with each passing minute, the waves rose higher and higher.

Being the son of a sailor, Peter had heard countless tales of people drowning at sea. Panic threatened to seize him, but he knew it would only bring more satisfaction to Hook. If this was his time, and it seemed with all certainty that it was, he would die silently, without struggle.

Hook drew Peter's dagger from his belt and inspected it.

"A marvelous weapon," Hook said, turning it over. "A shame you'll have no need of it anymore."

He tossed the blade to Jakes, who caught it.

"Thank you, Captain!" he said, beaming at the weapon. Then he sneered at Peter as he sheathed the weapon in his own belt.

"I have learned much from you, Peter Pan. But now, the lesson is yours," Hook said, exulting in his final victory. "Although, it seems you won't benefit from its knowledge for long."

The waves rolled into Peter. The tide was so high now he was forced to hold his breath as the peaks rolled in, then catch a quick breath as they ebbed.

Hook spread his arms wide and watched Peter struggle to breathe in the water. He timed his breathing wrong and inhaled a mouthful of seawater. He coughed and gagged.

Hook smiled, a sinister grin that snaked across his face.

"Behold," he said, chuckling. "The end of Peter Pan."

Mad Rogue clapped wildly next to Hook.

"You see," Hook said. "You may have drawn the first blood. You may have taken my hand and humiliated me in front of my men. But in the end, you lose, and with your loss comes your final lesson."

Hook indicated the men who stood around him as he watched Peter struggle in the waves.

"My young friend, there are few forces more deadly than pirates," Hook said.

"Or mermaids," Peter choked.

"What?" Hook said.

No sooner had the words left Hook's lips than both Mad Rogue and Jakes disappeared beneath the now waist-deep water.

Peter watched with grim satisfaction as the water behind Hook churned with activity. A thrashing, foaming wave slammed into Hook, hurtling him into the water.

The wave broke and Shiiklah was in front of him. Her long coral blade was in one hand. She grabbed Peter by the chains and lifted him up out of the water with the other hand.

Jakes, who had been released, or had kicked free of the mer who had pulled him under, burst out of the waves, pulling his sword from its scabbard and wiping water and blood from his face.

The pirate advanced on Shiiklah. Peter opened his mouth to yell but she was already responding to the attack. She tossed Peter to one of the other mers as if he weighed no more than a pillow. The mer caught him while a second one set about freeing him.

The second one struggled against the chains, but the lock held fast.

"You need the keys!" Peter yelled over the waves and fighting.

He continued to try and peel the chains off of Peter. But they were wrapped too tightly. Suddenly the mer's shoulder jerked forward, and he grunted in pain as a small hole appeared in it. Peter felt hot, black blood splatter his face. The creature ignored the pain and continued to pull at Peter's chains. A second hole appeared in the mer's body, this one in his chest. This time Peter heard the shot.

"Pirates!" he shouted.

The mer turned and saw what Peter saw, the Jolly Roger cutting through the waves towards the rocky bar.

The pirates on deck were firing at Peter and the two mers. A second longboat, filled with more pirates, was gliding towards the fray.

The wounded mer continued working on freeing Peter when he staggered, losing his balance as Mad Rogue leapt out of the water and onto the mer's back. The mer spun, trying to throw the insane pirate off of him, but Mad Rogue clung to him like a shadow. The mer slashed with his claws over his head, raking Mad Rogue's back, but still the pirate hung on, arms wrapped around the wounded mer in a chokehold that he shouldn't have been able to maintain.

A third shot sounded, this one zipped right past Peter's head, striking the mer who was holding him.

He felt the mer's hold go slack, and both of them slipped under the water's surface. The wounded mer, distracted by Mad Rogue, didn't see him fall and Peter slipped under the waves. He tried to stand, but with his arms and legs chained tightly at his sides, he couldn't turn himself upright.

Finally, he managed to right himself on the sand, where he jumped with all his strength in an attempt to fly through the water. He broke the surface and saw Shiiklah. The mermaid chieftess had just killed Jakes and was turning back to search for Peter. She was twenty yards away. Their eyes met just as Peter slipped back under the waves. A heartbeat later, she was in front of him, hauling him back out of the water. Her black eyes flew over the chains, examining the locks that bound him.

Drawing a thin coral blade, she inserted it into the first lock and turned. The blade snapped in two.

"Heh," Peter laughed, despite the situation, knowing how much pride mers took in their weapons.

Shiiklah bared her sharp, white teeth and hissed in frustration as she drew Peter's own dagger, recovered from Jakes. She repeated the process and this time the lock opened. She opened it and the first layer of chains shed from Peter. Now his arms and legs were free.

More shots began to fire, splashing into the water around them. The pirates from the second longboat were jumping off into the shallows, firing as they disembarked.

Shiiklah thrust the weapon into Peter's palm and advanced on them.

Peter frantically tried to pick the remaining locks. His hands trembled as adrenaline coursed through his body. The remaining locks wouldn't open.

Peter rose out of the water. At least he could fly. But it was difficult and he couldn't move as quickly as he normally did.

He scanned the scene. Shiiklah was moving with terrifying speed towards the incoming of pirates, ten maybe fifteen of them in all.

The Jolly Roger was running along the edge of the rocks, careful not to run aground, but edging as close as she could.

Mad Rogue, now free of his mer, was making a dash for the ship, yelling something Peter couldn't make out to the crew. The mer he had attached himself to was nowhere to be seen.

And Hook.

Captain Hook strode purposefully through the water, oblivious to the madness around him, sword in hand, hook poised to strike. The man moved with a single thought raging through his mind: the thought that had consumed him since the night Peter had cut off his hand. That thought was etched in the sneer Hook wore and Peter could not have read it more clearly if the words had been tattooed on the man's face.

Peter Pan must die.

Once again, the man had thrown off all other considerations outside of that thought.

Peter flew towards him, his speed and movements feeling cumbersome and exaggerated.

The pair came into sword range.

With a rage-filled bellow, Hook attacked: a powerful overhead strike intended to cut Peter down in a single strike. Peter adjusted his angle as he flew, avoiding the strike, the momentum of Hook's strike carrying his own blade into the water, a trail of bubbles frothing behind it as it cut through the water.

Peter continued towards the man and punched Hook with all his might.

The pair crashed into the water, colliding with each other as they fell. Peter came up sputtering and coughing. Hook, on the other hand exploded out of the water, blindly striking as he surfaced. The first strike raked across Peter's stomach but, thanks to the chains that still covered him, did no damage. The second strike, a thrust aimed at his chest, Peter deflected with his dagger. Then Hook spun, his jacket fanning out around him. He leveled his sword at head-height as he moved.

But Peter ducked under the blow and buried his dagger to the hilt into Hook's thigh. Hook roared, a mix of pain and fury. He ignored the dagger buried in his leg and brought his hook down fast, snagging one of the chain links and using his own weight, together with the weight of the chains, to drive Peter back. He pushed harder, forcing Peter under the water.

Peter frantically tried to rise to the surface, but the man had his full weight pressed down on him. He looked around, hoping against all hope to see an approaching mermaid, but all he could see was the sea roiling around him.

He looked back up, his lungs starting to burn from lack of air, and saw a golden brilliant light sparkling just above the water's surface.

Suddenly, the pressure holding him down slackened and he scrambled up in time to see Hook backing away and swatting at a fairy with his hook as he tugged at the dagger still in his leg with his sword hand.

It wasn't just any fairy.

"Tink!" Peter exclaimed, shock, relief and joy tearing through him.

Hook managed to pull the weapon free with a scream and tossed it away from him.

Tinker Belle intercepted the blade, catching it in her arms, then flew straight to Peter.

"Let's finish this," Tinker Belle said, tossing the weapon to Peter.

Peter caught the blade by the hilt, grinning at her as she zipped past, then slid his gaze back to Hook.

Hook started back, his eyes ablaze with hatred and contempt. He raised his sword and pointed it at Peter.

"Die," the man snarled.

"Not today," Peter replied, shaking his head and offering Hook a cool, controlled smile.

Hook advanced, limping as he moved through the knee-deep water towards Peter. Blood poured from the wound, but Hook ignored it.

Tinker Belle shot towards him, but he kept her at bay, his sword tracing a dizzying defensive pattern around him. Peter let him approach. Knowing his speed was hindered by the chains that still bound him, he was content to let Tinker Belle harass Hook.

The pirate raised his hook and struck, a powerful downward slash that Peter redirected into the water.

Hook adjusted his blade, turning the defensive pattern into an offensive one that sent Peter diving out of reach of his sword. But Hook's attention had drifted a little too far away from Tinker Belle to focus on Peter.

And she made him pay for the mistake.

Hook swore as his blade lashed out at where Tinker Belle had been a heartbeat before. The gash in his face she gave him left him swearing and striking at empty air.

He disengaged from Peter, taking several steps back to put more space between Peter and Tinker Belle.

Hook's eyes darted to Tinker Belle then to Peter, then back to Tinker Belle, doubtless trying to read their next moves. But his wounds clearly demanded his attention now.

Peter feigned towards Hook, who flinched towards him in response, only to have Tinker Belle fire towards the man.

Hook raised his sword and pivoted towards the incoming attack, putting all of his weight on his injured leg in the process. But the wounded muscle buckled under the man's full weight, sending him stumbling back into deeper water.

Tinker Belle altered her course, flying under his raised sword, adding a second cut to his side to match the one she had already given him.

Peter shot forward a second after Tinker Belle, his normal speed slowed by the chains, but quick enough to take the wounded Hook off guard.

The man saw him coming, but could not react enough to brace himself from Peter's strike. He threw up his hook to catch Peter's slash, but the force of the blow forced him back several more feet.

Now up to his waist in the rising tide, Hook was left with no choice but to focus all of his energy on defense.

He spun and pivoted, stumbling at times as his wounded leg gave out. Peter and Tinker Belle strafed him, zipping past to inflict either minor wounds or to drive him deeper into the sea.

Tinker Belle flew dizzy circles around Hook, forcing him to focus all of his attention on the fairy. Peter waited until the pirate's back was completely towards him, then flew towards him.

But a loud explosion startled him, and for a moment the water in front of him erupted, sending him flipping head over feet through the air and into the water. Momentarily dazed, Peter tried to get his bearings, but another blast sent him flying again. He leapt out of the water and gained some height, attempting to see what was happening. He looked around and finally saw it. The Jolly Roger in full sail, bearing down on them, her cannons firing, attempting to create a barrier of gunfire between himself and its captain.

Peter clenched his jaw in frustration at having to split his attention between two targets as Hook had needed to moments ago. He readied himself to close the distance between himself and Hook, knowing both the limited number of cannons that were forward mounted on a ship and how inaccurate cannon fire was.

Peter flew towards Hook, then saw the ship, heading straight towards them a moment ago turning, presenting her flank towards the three of them. He looked back towards Hook and saw the pirate spare a glance towards his ship then duck under the water.

"Tink!" Peter cried, knowing what was about to happen, then hurled himself into the water.

Forward-facing cannons did not fire standard-sized cannon balls. They were slightly smaller due to the lack of space the front of ships offered. But with the ship's entire port side facing him and her entire arsenal of cannons aimed at him, Peter knew exactly what would be happening next.

Peter felt the eruption of cannon fire more then heard it. The water offered some degree of sound buffer from the blast, but vibrations reverberated through him, nearly knocking the breath from his lungs. And from his underwater vantage point, he saw thousands of fist-sized metal balls tear angrily through the water.

Two of them struck Peter: one in the stomach, striking the chain. But the chain transferred the force to his gut, expelling the breath in his lungs and reflexively forcing him to inhale a mouthful of seawater.

The second one struck him in the leg, just above the knee. The water had slowed the balls enough so the blows didn't killed him or tear his leg off, but his leg immediately went numb from the strike.

These were grapeshots.

Instead of loading the cannons with the standard twenty-pound solid shots, grapeshots were canvas bags packed with metal balls. Upon being fired, the canvas bag would be obliterated, allowing the metal balls to scatter, flying in the general direction the cannon was pointed.

They were very effective.

Peter surfaced, spewing seawater and coughing madly. He cleared the water from his eyes and saw Tinker Belle, high above the water, safe from the blast and scanning the water for him.

He looked back towards Hook and saw the man still very much alive and swimming towards his ship.

And he could make out Mad Rogue, leaning out over the starboard railing while hurling one end of a rope towards Hook.

"Hook!" Peter shouted.

The rope splashed just outside Hook's reach, who quickly closed the distance then slid the looped end over his head.

"You will burn, Peter Pan," Hook yelled back. "In time, you will all burn."

Peter saw Shiiklah and her remaining mer, having killed all their pirates, turning their attention to Hook.

Tinker Belle and the mers made for Hook. Peter followed suit, flying as fast as his chains would allow.

Hook sneered, knowing he was already well out of their reach. The pirates hauled him over the side and back onto the deck. Limping, and very much wounded, Hook turned towards Peter and stared at him for a long moment before turning and disappearing into his ship.

Peter flew towards the Jolly Roger, but the ship was now free of the island, and the weight of his chains combined with the new wind in her sails meant he had no hope of catching up to them. He came to a stop and Tinker Belle caught up with him and watched as the mers, too, abandoned their chase.

"Next time," Tinker Belle said, watching the ship sail away.

Peter nodded.

"Indeed," he agreed.

TWENTY NINE

Peter and Shiiklah sat on the beach watching the Jolly Roger, now nothing more than a black dot on the horizon.

Tinker Belle stood on Peter's stomach, working at the remaining locks that still bound him. She was braced against the outside of a lock with one hand, while the other was thrust inside the lock, attempting to cycle it with her dagger.

The soft fluttering of wings caught Peter's attention, but he didn't pull his gaze away from the ship.

"He's gone, then?" Adelaide asked, joining them on the shore.

"Yeah," Peter answered without looking. "For now, at least."

"We came as soon as we heard the cannons," Adelaide said. "Are you okay?"

"I'll be fine," Peter said. "The mers suffered losses though."

"One perished," Shiiklah said. "One was injured, but will recover."

"You have our sympathies," Adelaide offered.

"Aha!" Tinker Belle exclaimed, a metallic ring sounding as another set of chains fell from Peter's shoulders. With renewed vigor, Tinker Belle went to work on the last lock.

He felt the weight of the burden leaving him, relieved to feel himself slowly returning to normal.

Peter half turned to Shiiklah, his eyes still on the ship in the distance.

"We could catch them," he offered, squinting as the black spot shrank into nothing, disappearing into the horizon. "He's gone, but I still make his heading."

"Maybe you," Shiiklah replied. "But it is too far for usss. You'd be alone."

"Never again," Peter replied.

The final lock clicked open, the last of his chains falling away.

"Finally!" Peter said, taking a deep breath and laying backwards on the sand.

Shiiklah rose and snaked her way back towards the sea.

"Where are you off to?" Peter asked, propping himself up on his elbows.

"There are ssstill pirates in my waters," she answered. "There is much to do."

Then turning to Adelaide, she said, "Have you finished it?"

Adelaide nodded. "Just this morning."

"Finished what?" Peter asked, looking from Adelaide to Shiiklah. But a wave broke on the shore and then the mermaid was gone.

"It's ready, then?" Tinker Belle asked, hovering next to Peter.

"Is what ready?" Peter demanded.

Adelaide smiled at him.

"Come with us," was all she said.

"I'm exhausted," Peter said, standing up to follow the party despite his own protests. "And look at this bruise," he whined, pointing to his leg where the shot had struck him. "Where are we going? I need to go back to White Falls and sleep."

They led him deeper into the forest. After some time, though, they finally stopped at the base of an enormous oak tree.

"I don't get it," Peter said, looking from fairy to fairy. "Why are we here?"

When his gaze fell on Tinker Belle, she flicked a finger upward then shot straight up.

Peter followed her, weaving through the forest's dense canopy until the branches gave way to the last thing he expected to find in the trees

A house.

Impossibly nestled in the branches of the giant tree sat a house. A tree house.

"What!" Peter gasped, not believing his eyes.

"We thought a real tree might be better than a dead one," Tinker Belle said, smiling.

"I don't know what to say," Peter said, searching for words.

"You've given much to Neverland," Adelaide said. "More than should be asked. And when your home was destroyed, we wanted to make sure you had a place, a safe place, you could call home."

"This is unbelievable," Peter marveled.

"Of course, you're always welcome at White Falls," Adelaide said, then indicated the treehouse with a wave. "But this is yours."

They flew up to the house. It was a simple one-room dwelling, but it was complete with a roof, port-hole styled windows, and a landing in the front.

Peter alighted on the ledge. It was essentially an open air deck—several feet of planks, real wooden planks, that led to the house's exterior walls. A pair of round windows were cut in the walls on either side of the door.

The door, held secure by a simple latch mechanism, easily released and yawned open, exposing the most wonderful thing Peter had ever seen.

Shelves had been cut into the old tree and were filled with preserved food from White Falls.

"You're always welcome to the stores in White Falls," Adelaide explained, landing on the shelves. "But we thought it might be nice to have a store of your own."

Peter nodded. He looked in the corner and did a double take.

"A stove!" he cried.

Sure enough, in the corner of the room sat a small, black stove. It had room enough for a single pot, which rested on top.

"How is that possible?" he asked. "And how did you get it up here?"

"Shiiklah found it among one of the wrecks off the Black Cliffs," she explained. "As for getting it into the tree, well, that took nearly every fairy on the island."

"And a not insignificant number of kites too," Tinker Belle added, patting the top of the stove. She laughed and shook her head.

Peter continued to survey the room. There was a small table and chair, crafted by fairies, if the simple but elegant style was any indication, and an assortment of coral utensils and tools, obviously the mer's contribution to his new home. There was even a chest pushed against one wall.

But there was one thing that caught his eye and excited him more than the chest or the food-laden shelves or even the iron stove in the corner of the room.

Nestled under a window, in the opposite corner of the room, was a bed. A real bed, complete with a pillow and blanket.

"How?" Peter cried, his hands on his head. "How is there a bed in here?"

Tinker Belle laughed and flew over to land on the pillow.

"We made it!" she said, stretching her tiny body out on the top of it. "We built the frame using the branches we had to remove to make room for the house."

She sat up and tugged at the blanket, exposing a mattress underneath.

"The blanket," she said, grunting as she pulled. "Was made by makers, same with the pillows. But they're stuffed with feathers the kites donated."

She jumped over the edge of blanket she had pulled free, leaping into the bed.

"The mattress took more work," she explained. "Filled with more feathers, getting it up here was tricky. But nothing compared to that stove."

"It's incredible," Peter said, looking from Tinker Belle to every feature in his room, then to Adelaide. "It's too much. It's all too much."

"You've given everything to us, Peter," Adelaide said. "This is nothing."

"We saved the best for last, though," Tinker Belle said, jumping to her feet and flying towards the shelves in the tree. She flew next to them and opened a small, fairy-sized door, exposing a tiny apartment inside, complete with fairy-sized windows.

"This one's mine," she said.

Peter shook his head, still dazzled by the awesome gift.

"I will protect Neverland for as long as I live," he said.

"Even when you're old and boring?" Tinker Belle yelled from within her apartment.

"Yes, even then," Peter said, laughing.

"We gladly accept your gift," Adelaide said. "Though I fear you know not the depth of your offer."

Her gaze shifted from Peter to the dust-preserved fruit on the shelf.

"But the day grows late," she said, smiling again. "I will leave you to your home."

Peter pulled his dagger free from his belt and tossed it onto the table before climbing into the bed, stretching his legs out and lying down.

"Oh," Peter sighed, sinking into the plush mattress.

Peace, absolute peace, washed over him as he drifted to sleep. He had fought and pushed and survived for what seemed like forever. But now he could rest.

Hook would return to Neverland. And the pirates still entrenched in mansion cliffs would doubtless continue to cause trouble.

But for now, for tonight, he could rest.

He closed his eyes and let the sounds of summer carry him away.

"So what are we doing tomorrow?" Tinker Belle asked from her room above Peter's bed.

"Tomorrow?" Peter asked, his eyes still closed. "I don't know. We'll let tomorrow worry about that."

EPILOGUE

The ill-maintained door creaked as it opened, heralding the arrival of patrons to the tavern. The tavern keeper, a man at the bar, and some drunk dead to the world with his head down on the table, were its only occupants.

Hook surveyed the room.

The bar was run down but surprisingly clean, atypical for Port Royal, but still, the perfect place to troll for recruits.

He approached the bar, favoring his wounded leg as he walked.

"What'll it be, Captain?" the keeper, a clean-shaven man with green eyes, asked.

Hook raised an eyebrow at the man.

"You carry yourself like a man in charge," the keeper explained with a grin.

"Grog," Hook replied. "Unless you've got wine."

"Grog it is," the keeper said. Placing a glass in front of Hook, he filled it with cloudy amber liquid.

"Refill, Jas?" the keeper asked the other man seated at the bar.

The man nodded, motioning with a wave to his empty glass.

Hook stood and drank, watching the keeper fill the man's glass.

Turning to the patron, Jas, Hook said, "My ship could use a few extra hands. What do you say?"

"Count me out," Jas said without looking up. "I've had enough adventure to haunt a hundred men."

"Fair enough," Hook said, deciding not to press the man. "What about you?" he said, turning to the keeper. "You look like you could handle a sword."

"Daggers are more my thing," the keeper said, smiling. "But these days I stick with this." He held up his towel and winked.

"A shame," Hook said. "I'm bound for an island filled with treasure and creatures you've never dreamed of."

"Creatures?" Jas asked, looking up suddenly and giving Hook a suspicious glare. "What kind of creatures?"

"Oh, you wouldn't believe me if I told you," Hook said, waving his hook away dismissively.

"Try me," Jas said, his eyes narrowing.

"Very well," Hook agreed with a nod.

"Sail with me and you will bear witness to the final wonder in the world," Hook said. "Bright, shining, flying creatures, so frail and majestic. They glow the most intense golden color you've ever seen."

Hook returned his glass to the bar and began waving his arms around.

"Pixies. They're craftsmen," he said. "They can create anything you desire! Their homes are filled with rubies, emeralds, and gold," he raised an eyebrow. "Diamonds, even."

He leaned towards the two men, his voice filling with passion and wonder.

"They have no need of such things since they create them so readily. Neverland is littered with precious gems, waiting for us to collect them."

"Neverland?" the keeper asked, his eyebrows furrowed.

"Aye, Neverland," Hook said, nodding. "Her waters are teeming with beautiful sea creatures. Her skies are filled with hawks—majestic birds with brilliant red plumage."

Hook sighed heavily, as if relishing the memory of Neverland.

"It sounds like quite the place," the keeper said, whistling.

"Except you left out the part where everything on the island is trying to kill you," Jas said. "And the flying boy who leads them."

Hook shifted uncomfortably.

"A flying boy?" the keeper said, shaking his head. "Mate, that's a fantastic story. And if this Neverland were real, I'd be half tempted to see it in person."

"Oh, it's real," Jas snapped. "And it's nothing like he's describing."

He shot Hook a withering scowl.

"I watched those 'pixie craftsmen' tear through a frigate, turning sail and rigging into ribbons, and leaving her crew in a similar state," he said. "And those 'beautiful sea' creatures?" He sobered, his face growing pale.

"I saw them kill twelve men in the time it took me to stand up. And all without making a sound."

Hook looked to his glass, not liking the turn the conversation had taken.

"Birds that lift men out from their ships and throw them overboard," he said. "But that boy..." He shook his head in astonishment before looking up and locking his gaze with the keeper.

"I don't know who taught that boy to fight, or how he came to fly..." Jas said, trailing off, considering his words. "But mark my words. Take away those pixies, the sea creatures, and all those mad birds," he said, shaking his head. "Neverland, with none of those things, but that boy? No. All the gold in the world wouldn't be enough to get me to step foot on that island again."

"Where's your captain?" Hook asked, changing the subject.

"The Americas," he answered before taking a drink from his glass.

"Teach?" Hook asked.

"Aye," he said, wiping his hand on his sleeve.

"Edward Teach?" the keeper asked, perking up at the mention of the name.

"Aye," Jas repeated. "After the licking we took on Neverland, Teach decided to cut his losses and try his luck in more civilized lands."

"So you're a deserter," Hook accused.

The man spun on him.

"The code says nothing about monsters," Jas spat. "It's a miracle any of us made it off that island. And after we made port, I burned my articles. Now I'm just waiting for a ship to take me back to England, back to my family."

"This is Port Royal," Hook scoffed. "You'll be waiting a long time before any ships bound for England arrive."

Hook turned to face the man behind the bar.

"What do you say, keeper?" he asked. "My offer doesn't apply to cowards and deserters, but it's still open to you."

Jas scowled at Hook, but didn't reply to the insult.

"It sounds like quite the adventure," the keeper said, rubbing his chin thoughtfully. "But that may be a bit more excitement then what I'm looking for."

"Suit yourself," Hook said, draining the last of his drink in a single swallow before slamming it down on the bar. "We're here through the week, if you have a change of heart."

"I appreciate the offer," the keeper said. "But you know, I may head north, see what kind of adventure the Americas have to offer."

"Well," Hook said, nodding. "If you see Edward Teach, give him my regards."

For a moment, the whisper of a smile tugged at the corner of the keeper's mouth.

"I'll do that," was all he said.

THE END